KISS

A Paranormal

(Immortal Hearts Series)

Lilah T. Bane

Published by Aero Productions

COPYRIGHT

Copyright 2021 by Lilah T. Bane

All rights reserved. The right of Lilah T. Bane to be identified as the Author of the work has been asserted by her in accordance with the Copyright Designs and Patents Act 1988.
This book is sold subject to the condition it shall not, by way of trade or otherwise, be copied, lent, resold, hired out, or otherwise circulated in print or electronic means without the author's prior consent in any form.

ISBN: 9798781789535

Except where actual historical events and characters are being described, all situations in this book are fictitious and any resemblance to living persons is purely coincidental.

One

Raya punched the orderly as hard as she could and took off down the corridor. She heard shouts behind her and flung a glance over her shoulder. Griggs was coming fast, his face contorted with rage, one eye swollen shut. In his hand was a telescopic baton and she knew he liked to use it.

She was faster than him, but as she rounded the corner she collided with something. A trolley, left carelessly in the corridor. She went flying and suddenly Griggs was on her, grabbing her hair with one hand, raising the stick with the other.

"You fuckin' bitch, you're gonna pay for that," he snarled.

She headbutted him, smacking her forehead into his nose. As he lurched back, she kicked him in the groin. He folded up, dropping the baton, nose bloodied. She pushed him off, knowing it was only a matter of time before others came.

She'd been planning her escape for days. Ever since she realised she was being watched by... by *something*. But she couldn't run until she had a weapon. And they weren't easy to come by.

Finally one of the doctors had left his biro on a desk. She'd swiped it on her way out of therapy. Waited till the orderly had come in for his afternoon check and stabbed him in the eye.

In a way she was glad it was Griggs. He was the cruellest one. But even he was less terrifying than the thing she'd seen watching her.

She ran breathlessly towards the main entrance. The keys she'd swiped had got her through two locked doors already. Now there was just one more between her and the entrance lobby.

She gave a sob, aware for the first time that tears were streaming down her face. She reached the steel door but her hands were shaking so much she dropped the keys. As she stooped to pick them up the quiet was shattered by the scream of the alarm bell.

She grabbed the keys and shoved them one after another into the lock.

"C'mon, c'mon," she muttered under her breath. The third one didn't turn, nor did the fourth.

Through the little square of security glass she could see the main entrance. Wide glass doors leading to the outside. Blue sky just one key-turn away.

A hand grasped the back of her shirt, yanking her backwards so hard she couldn't breathe. She tried to kick out but Griggs was ready for her. He got her in a chokehold, twisting her arm so far up her back she could feel the bones creaking. He pushed his mouth to her ear. She could smell the blood on his nose where it had congealed.

"I swear to you, you will wish you'd escaped, bitch," he spat. "I'm going to make you pay."

She felt his erection pressing against her. Not because he was remotely attracted to her, though that would be gross enough. No, Griggs got off on the power trip.

She stopped struggling, knowing it was useless. It would only excite him more. Her stomach churned queasily. Two more orderlies came sprinting up, one wielding a syringe.

"Hold her steady," he barked.

Raya's vision blurred with tears. She'd been so close.

"You don't understand, you have to let me go." She felt the prick of the needle enter her arm. "They're after me. They're here."

A black veil dropped as the sedative took effect. The last thing she saw as she lost consciousness was the small patch of blue sky through the security glass.

The orderlies took her by the arms and legs and carted her back to her room.

"Bloody schizos," muttered Griggs.

Two

The doctor looked at Raya over his steel rimmed glasses.

"A most unfortunate episode this week, Suraya. You could have blinded Mr Griggs. Why were you trying to escape? I thought you realised how important your treatment was?"

Raya sat opposite him, fiddling with her hair. The weird copper strand that grew on one side was twisted around her index finger. She wound it tighter and tighter.

She'd been kept under close watch for forty-eight hours, as was usual after a security breach. Griggs had delivered her meals to her on a tray, spitting deliberately and noisily into her food before passing it through the hatch.

"Enjoy, bitch," he'd smirked, walking away. His eye still looked bloodshot and his nose was swollen. *Good*, she thought viciously.

She rubbed the top of her ears. They were itching again. Remnants of her childhood eczema, which always flared up when she was stressed.

"Suraya!"

The doctor dragged her back to the present.

"I'm sorry, Dr Meadows. I didn't mean to hurt him." *A lie*. "But I can't stay here anymore. I'm twenty one. I have rights."

"You know the rules. The court says you have to stay here until we're sure you don't pose any harm to anyone."

"But I didn't do anything!"

"So you keep saying. Your stubbornness is impressive, Suraya. But part of your problem is your inability to accept what you did." Dr Meadows flipped through a manila folder. Raya could see the writing on the top page. *Suraya Nilsen. Female. Date of birth, unknown.* "You've been in treatment since you were eleven. You were adopted as a baby, your adoptive parents died in a fire..."

"I didn't start it," she burst out. "I know everyone thinks I did, but I didn't. We were attacked."

The doctor sighed and took off his glasses.

"I know. By a demon with red eyes." He pinched the bridge of his nose wearily. "You were eleven, Raya, a frightened and confused little girl."

"I'm not imagining it. I know what I saw."

"And yet only two bodies were recovered from your home. No sign of this fire-breathing demon. You need to think rationally."

Raya stood up angrily.

"How can I think rationally when there was nothing rational about what happened?"

"Miss Nilsen, calm down." The doctor's voice was sharp and she saw his hand creeping under the desk. The alarm bell. She couldn't blame him. She *had* stabbed a six-foot tall orderly with a pen. She slumped back into the chair.

"Sorry, doctor."

She went back to fiddling with her hair. Dr Meadows studied her for a second.

"Schizophrenia is a serious mental condition but with the right medication, it can be controlled," he said gently. "In my opinion you could live a productive life but you need to stay here for a bit longer. Do you understand?"

Raya struggled to control the panic rising in her chest. The walls seemed balloon in towards her. She ground the nails of one hand into her palm, aware the doctor was watching her closely. She couldn't lose it now. She took a breath and looked up.

"I understand."

"It's good that you're taking your meds now. I see you've stopped hiding them or spitting them out. That's progress, at least."

"Yes, doctor." *Just don't check under my mattress.*

"This is a minimum security ward, Suraya. Please don't force me to move you to the high security wing. You don't belong with psychopaths and murderers."

He looked at her kindly and Raya felt a little stab of guilt. Dr Meadows really did care about her. He just didn't listen.

Mary took her to the shower block. The older woman was one of the nicer orderlies with a ready smile and an easy manner. Raya relaxed in her presence, enjoying her lilting Irish accent.

"You gave everyone a bit of a turn, so you did," she said. Her tone was mild, and she gave Raya a sideways glance. "Heard you kicked Griggs in the knackers?"

"Yeah. Took a bit of aiming. He has tiny balls."

Mary turned away to hide a smile.

"But you know darlin', they won't let you out unless you show them you're getting better. You've been here ten years. Is it not time to be thinking of moving on?"

"That's *all* I think of," Raya assured her. "But lately I feel like something's watching me. Something evil."

"Is that why you bit Nurse Phillips?"

"But it *wasn't* Nurse Philips." Raya looked desperately at Mary, willing at least one person to believe her. "Something else was controlling her. I swear to you, her eyes weren't hers. They were so cold, so… so inhuman."

Mary sighed.

"Come on now love, let's get you into that shower. Nice hot water will do you good. And afterwards you can watch some telly with the others."

Raya pushed through the door into the shower block and stripped off her regulation scrubs. She knew Mary would be watching her because of her recent escape attempt, but she was long past any embarrassment. There was no privacy in a secure unit.

Raya stepped under the showerhead and turned it on. The first flow of water was shockingly cold. She let it play over her face, feeling the icy needles wash her clean. Then the water slowly turned hot, so hot it made her skin turn red.

"Don't forget to shampoo," called out Mary.

Raya grabbed the plain bottle off the ledge. She didn't know what brand it was, just some generic stuff with a vaguely antiseptic smell.

When she was younger, her adopted mother had used one that smelled of apples. For a moment she remembered Caroline's smile. She pushed the thought out of her head. Her adopted mother was dead. No use thinking about her.

She rinsed the suds out of her hair, feeling the long weight of it hanging down her back. It would become wavy when it dried. Wavy and jet black. Except for the single strand of copper that grew in a streak on one side. Everyone thought she dyed it that way, but she didn't.

It was like the rest of her. An anomaly.

She scrubbed the soap over her arms and legs. The olive tint to her skin suggested something exotic in her background. That, and her dark eyes. Maybe Asian or Mediterranean. But who knew? She had no memory of her real parents.

The only thing she knew for sure was that they hadn't wanted her. They'd given her away as a baby. She didn't even know if they were still alive.

She preferred to believe they weren't. Because otherwise, how could they just leave her here? All alone?

She stood motionless, allowing the stream of hot water to calm her. She pretended she was normal. Just an ordinary young woman preparing for the day.

"All right now, sweetheart, let's get you dried and dressed now."

Raya reluctantly reached out and shut off the shower. She squeezed her hair, feeling the excess water splashing around her feet. She turned to ask Mary to pass her a towel and stopped dead.

Mary was still smiling at her but it wasn't her normal open smile. It was a leer, the corners of her lips pulled back grotesquely, further than was humanly possible. Her eyes were cold and unblinking, her features sly.

Raya felt the breath catch in her throat. Not Mary. Please, not Mary. She gave herself a shake, hoping it was a hallucination, some side effect of her meds. But the vision didn't change.

"Who... who are you?" she stammered, trying to cover her nakedness ineffectually with her hands. The Mary-creature gave a giggle.

"Why, you'll know soon enough, so you will," it simpered, mimicking Mary's Irish accent mockingly. Its grin widened. Little cracks appeared at the corners of its lips. Its voice dropped to a low guttural growl, raising the hairs on the back of her neck. "We've been looking for you."

"Stay away!" Raya pressed herself back against the shower wall, the tiles cold beneath her skin.

The Mary-figure took a lurching step forward, as if the thing inside was controlling her legs.

"You can't escape. Not now we know where you are. We're coming."

Raya stumbled, her feet slipping in the wet shower, her hair hanging over her face.

"Get away from me," she screamed.

She tried to stay upright, her hands scrabbling for a weapon, something to throw, anything.

But her legs slid out from under her and she fell backwards, her screams suddenly cut off as she smashed her head against the shower wall.

Three

She woke up in the infirmary, groaning as consciousness came back with a vengeance. Her head was thudding horribly and when she reached back gingerly, she felt a lump the size of a golf ball beneath her hair.

Her other arm wouldn't move. She saw it was secured to the bed with a leather strap, a drip attached at the elbow. Her legs were also fastened. At least she was dressed again. Silver lining, and all that.

The door opened and Dr Meadows came in. He checked her chart.

"Mary says you fell in the shower. Can you tell us what happened?"

"I saw..." Raya started to explain, then realised the futility of it. No-one believed her. They all thought she was nuts. "I saw black spots in front of my eyes, then I don't remember. Did I faint?"

Maybe he'd just think it was a dizzy spell.

"Looks like it. Could be stress. Or it could be that you haven't been eating. Mr Griggs says you've been returning all your meals untouched." *Well, yeah. He spits in my food.* "Are you hungry now?"

She wasn't, but she wanted to keep him sweet. She nodded and the doctor pressed the intercom next to her bed.

"Mary, bring some dinner in, please?"

Raya started to struggle upright, alarm spreading through her.

"It's okay, I'll go to the canteen with the others." But the leather straps held her tight. Dr Meadows pushed her down again.

"Canteen's closed, I'm afraid. It's late. You've been out for several hours. Mary will be here in a minute, she'll help you."

The door behind him opened and Raya started to panic as the orderly walked in with a tray. The doctor turned to go but Raya forestalled him.

"Wait! Don't leave me! I mean... tell me about the fall, do I have concussion?"

The doctor turned back impatiently. He was tired and he wanted to go home to his wife and children. But as he gazed at Raya's imploring eyes, he softened. He sat on the chair next to her.

"You know, nothing's going to change until *you* decide to change them. You have to take control, Suraya. Stop letting circumstances control *you*. Do you understand what I'm saying?"

She nodded. *Control, yeah right. That's a good one, doc.* He undid her arm restraint, gently talking her through the head injury, reassuring her it wasn't serious.

Raya barely listened. She watched Mary set down the tray of food on the table next to the bed. The orderly bent to unfasten Raya's leg bindings, her face as open and warm as it had ever been. Maybe they're right, Raya thought despairingly. Maybe I'm just delusional.

But then she saw something which hadn't been there before.

Tiny cracks at the corner of Mary's mouth.

Her heart started thumping. She hadn't imagined it. Any of it. Not the malevolent faces she kept seeing around her, and not the demon which had attacked her and her adopted parents ten years ago.

We know where you are. We're coming.

Her eyes darted round as she pretended to listen to Dr Meadows. The infirmary was much closer to the main entrance than her ward. Fewer doors to get through. Just one, in fact.

Her gaze alighted on the desk. His keys. Just lying there. With that stupid rabbit's foot which he'd once told her was a lucky charm. Though obviously not for the rabbit.

Mary finished undoing her leg bindings and turned to help her sit up. Without warning, Raya swiped the mug of tea from the tray straight into Dr Meadows' lap. He yelled as hot liquid doused his trousers.

Without missing a beat, Raya picked up the tray and slammed it into Mary's midriff. The woman's eyes bulged and she collapsed to the floor heavily, trying to draw breath. Raya mentally apologised as she slid off the bed. Mary didn't deserve this. But she had no choice.

She grabbed the keys and bolted, taking a few precious seconds to lock the infirmary door behind her. She saw Mary and the doctor shouting at her through the glass. Then she ran.

She made it down to the ground floor before the alarm shattered the calm. Shit. She ran faster, her head still throbbing from the fall. It pounded with every step and sweat poured down her face.

The moon coming in at the barred windows cast eerie shadows in front of her. They seemed to change and flow and become nightmare faces watching her, mocking her. *We're coming for you.*

She rounded the corner and saw the locked door up ahead. The last barrier between her and freedom.

Adrenaline gave her a spurt of energy. She sprinted towards the exit, keys at the ready. She could almost feel the grass under her feet, the fresh air on her face.

She stopped.

Something was wrong.

Through the small square of glass in the door, she should have been able to look into the entrance lobby. But she couldn't see anything. It was just black.

She squinted. Why were the lights out? Was there a power cut? There was nothing on the other side of the door except darkness. Was it smoke? Was there a fire?

No, not smoke. More like shadows.

Shadows which pulsated and squirmed as if they were alive. As if they knew she was there. They surged forward until they came to the locked door, pressing right up against the glass. Raya stared at them, frozen. The shadows seemed to look right back at her.

The metal door bulged.

She stumbled backwards, not knowing where she was going, just that she had to get away. She couldn't let those shadows touch her. The keys slipped from her frozen fingers.

"Where do you think you're going, bitch?"

Someone slammed into her from behind and she was tackled to the floor. Pain jarred through her head as Griggs pinned her with his knees.

"Let me go! I have to get away!"

Raya thrashed beneath him but he was too heavy. Her head was pounding, the egg-shaped bruise sending shards of agonizing pain through her skull. Her vision blurred as she contorted her neck to look at the door. It was shaking. Tendrils of smoky blackness were squeezing out from around the frame and through the keyhole. She remembered the words of the Mary-thing.

We're coming.

"Griggs, let me go. It's here, it's come for me!"

He was oblivious to the shadows behind him. He leaned down to hiss malevolently into her ear.

"You've done it this time, you psycho bitch. They're gonna keep you sedated for the rest of your life. You won't know what fuckin' day of the week it is."

He yanked her to her feet and she managed to sink her teeth into his hand. He swore violently and slapped her. Her head ricocheted sideways at the same time as the steel door blew off its hinges.

The orderly finally looked behind him.

"What the fuck?"

Shadows spilled into the corridor and something followed them. Something huge.

Raya had the terrifying impression of a giant beast made of smoke. A creature with neon blue eyes.

She couldn't speak, couldn't even scream as the monstrous form filled her vision. It was here. It had found her.

The creature looked directly at Griggs. The orderly stumbled backwards, shaking with fear. Dark coils reached towards him and suddenly he was flung through the air as if he was a ragdoll. He hit the far wall and crumpled in a heap.

Raya sank to the floor, limbs weak and trembling. She mustered what was left of her courage.

"What do you want?" she screamed. "Why are you here?"

The beast turned its fearsome gaze on her. When it spoke, its voice vibrated through her very bones.

"I have come to offer you a bargain. If you agree to my terms, I will take you from this wretched place and give you whatever you desire. Or stay. The choice is yours."

A bargain? With this thing? The thought was incomprehensible. Whatever the hell this unnatural behemoth was, it was dangerous. She could feel the power and rage boiling off it.

Yet it hadn't attacked her. It had thrown Griggs off her. And it had given her a choice.

No-one had given her a choice for a very long time.

Dreaming. She must be dreaming. She'd hit her head and was concussed. This was just a nightmare. Or one hell of a hallucination.

She fought to stay awake but her grip on consciousness was fading fast. Black spots tinged her vision and a wave of nausea threatened to engulf her.

"What is your answer?" The voice vibrated through her, a dark throb edged with impatience. *"Will you come? Or stay here?"*

Dimly she saw Dr Meadows and Mary round the corner and stumble to a halt. Their eyes widened as they took in the monster, the shadows filling the corridor, the orderly lying unconscious.

Mary started screaming, and that, combined with the howling alarm, made Raya feel like her head was exploding. Tears streamed down her face.

She couldn't stay here. She couldn't. She'd rather die. And no matter what this creature wanted, it couldn't be any worse than being trapped here for another second.

"What is your answer, Suraya?" The voice seemed to rumble through her soul. It knows my name, she thought hazily.

The last thing she remembered before sliding into darkness was murmuring two words. Words only the beast could hear.

"Take me."

Four

"*Snap!*"

Raya slammed her hand down on the pile and Caroline groaned in defeat. It was her fourth loss in a row.

"You win again, monkey. You're just too fast for me."

Raya beamed at her adopted mother. Card games on a Sunday – along with salted caramel ice cream before bed - were a family tradition.

"Let's try a hand of rummy." Her adopted father, Ross, reached out and pushed the pile of cards towards her. "You deal."

She gathered them up, absently scratching at an itchy patch on her ear.

"Eczema playing up again?" Caroline said sympathetically. "Do you want me to fetch your cream?"

"Nah, it's fine. I'll put some on later."

"Have you thought any more about which school you prefer for next year?" Ross asked. "Westmore or Dartington High?"

Raya frowned in thought. She'd been offered scholarships to each of them, which was a good job as they were both eye-wateringly expensive.

"I like them both. But I'd have to board at Dartington and I want to stay closer to home. I think Westmore."

"Good choice, pickle." Ross nodded approvingly. "They've got great facilities and it's only twenty minutes away. I can come and embarrass you when the lads try to chat you up."

"Dad! Eww!"

Caroline was relieved. She'd been worried Raya would be excited by the prospect of living away from home and she wasn't ready to lose her daughter yet. God knows it would only be a few more years before she went to college. But right now, she was still their little girl, only just learning about make-up and boys and fashion. There was plenty of time for her to grow up.

There was a knock at the door.

"Who could that be?"

Ross frowned. It was rare that anyone came calling on a Sunday night. Unless it was those Jehovah's Witnesses again.

He got up from the kitchen table and disappeared into the hallway towards the front door. Raya started dealing out the cards.

"I'm glad you've chosen Westmore," Caroline said. "I'm so proud of you, getting the academic scholarship. You must have some real brains somewhere in your genes."

Raya didn't say anything. Her adopted parents were both engineers, they had brains in abundance. But of course, their genes weren't hers. For all she knew, she came from a family of blithering idiots. Maybe nurture really did beat nature.

"What on earth is keeping your father?" Caroline put her cards down. "I'd better check he's not being conned by a salesman or something."

She got up from the table, throwing her a smile as she went. Raya went to the sink to pour herself a glass of water. She heard a male voice in the hallway, a quiet chuckle, and thought perhaps a neighbour had come over.

She debated sneaking a spoonful of ice cream before the next round of cards but decided to wait. It was better when they ate it together. Ross would tell his 'dad' jokes, and

Caroline and Raya would roll their eyes pretending not to find them funny.

The voice in the hallway stopped. There was a strange sound, a gasping, breaking sound. Puzzled, Raya looked towards the doorway. Footsteps came her way and she put her glass in the sink, expecting to see her adopted parents.

It wasn't them.

A stranger came through the door. He looked like a man. An ordinary man, in an ordinary suit and tie. But he wasn't. She took one look and knew whatever this was, it wasn't human.

She had seen a documentary a few days ago, about snakes. One, the python, had large golden eyes split by a single black line down the centre. Their reptilian quality had made her shudder. The eyes on this man, however, made her want to scream. They were exactly like the snake's eyes except instead of being golden, they were blood red.

"Who are you?" she stuttered. "Where are my parents?"

"You are not the one I seek." His voice held a strange accent. He sniffed the air and his nostrils flared. "But you smell like her."

"Like who?" Her lips were frozen but she had the insane thought that if she only kept him talking, Caroline and Ross would come in and everything would be okay.

"Where is she? The one I seek?"

He took a step towards her and she instinctively backed away until she was hard against the sink.

"I don't know who you're talking about."

"No matter."

Something closed around her body. A vice, invisible but unbreakable. Her arms were pinned to her sides and she was inexorably pulled towards the snake-eyed man.

Not a man, her mind screamed at her.

A demon.

Her feet slid across the floor until she was standing directly in front of him. Panicked, she opened her mouth to scream. He clenched his fist and she felt something constrict around her throat. A band, tightening, cutting off her air.

Terror welled in her chest. A single tear rolled down her cheek. There was a momentary sensation of the world tilting about her and she thought the demon might have said something.

Then suddenly there were flames everywhere. Licking up the walls. Rolling across the ceiling. Great orange flames devouring the house. Devouring everything.

The demon disappeared in the smoke and the invisible bonds around her body vanished. Able to move at last, she cried out for her parents and ran into the fiery hallway. The front door was wide open and for a moment her heart leapt, thinking they'd escaped.

That's when she saw the blackened figures crumpled on the floor, their familiar features burned beyond recognition.

The damn dream again. Every night, over and over. She struggled to wake up, to claw her way out of unconsciousness. Her head was thumping and wind was streaming through her hair. She half-opened an eye, disorientated. She had an impression of travelling at great speed. How could that be, in the infirmary?

She tried to focus, bleary with pain and exhaustion.

That looked like a… a man's chest?

There was a noise. A rhythmic beating in time to her heart.

She looked up. Shadows swirled and at first she couldn't make anything out. Then for a moment, they cleared.

She saw a face with a burning blue stare. A face that belonged on a Michelangelo sculpture or a Raphael painting. Beautiful, yet stern. Skin the colour of copper. The scent of ash and burnt cinnamon. And high above, wings beating. Glorious wings of dark silver-grey feathers.

She reached up a shaky hand and the beautiful face turned to look down at her. The blue fire of his eyes seemed to penetrate her soul.

"You're an angel."

The words slid out from between her lips and she lay her head against his chest. Warmth enveloped her.

Safe. She was safe.

She slept. And for once, the demon didn't haunt her dreams.

FIVE

The air grew steadily colder as Shadeed flew north. The landscape below changed from green to white, the snow sparkling like a diamante blanket in the last rays of the sun. He didn't feel the cold. Jinn burned hot, as a rule.

He glanced at the girl in his arms and wondered briefly if *she* was cold. She seemed to be wearing some kind of dull grey garb, institutional in appearance. Certainly not flattering. And against the severe cold of the Nordic weather, deeply ineffective. There were goosebumps on her thin arms.

He held her closer to his chest and she curled against him like a cat. He hoped the heat radiating from his body would suffice.

He reached the Gatekeeper's forest just ahead of dusk, alighting in a clearing among the pines. The rich fragrance of the forest filled his nostrils. A reminder that home was but a short step away.

He concentrated for a moment and his wings melted away, becoming as insubstantial as smoke before disappearing entirely.

He lay his passenger carefully on the ground, frowning as he did so. She didn't look like much. All this way, for *that?* She had better be worth it.

Still, she had agreed to go with him. Either she was very, very brave or very, very desperate.

"So this is her. Took you long enough."

A querulous voice broke into his thoughts. He straightened, reining in the sharp retort that hovered on his lips. The Gatekeeper had been at her post for centuries. She was entitled to be rude.

Indeed, she was the *only* being in the universe he would tolerate rudeness from. Anyone else speaking to him that way would have been ripped limb from limb in a heartbeat.

He nodded gruffly at the figure squatting by a small wooden hut. It was hard to identify her as a woman; her face was brown and wrinkled, and she had a habit of wearing a random selection of clothing that gave very mixed messages.

Currently she was sporting a bright red bobble-hat. Shadeed eyed it with disfavour.

"Good to see you too, Magda."

His voice reverberated through the forest. A flock of birds took wing, startled from their roosts. Magda cackled.

"You can dial down the theatrics, your Lordship. She's asleep." The old woman got up and shuffled over to take a closer look. "Pretty. Nothing like her mother though. Are you sure this is her?"

"Tala found her. We're lucky she traced her before Ravij did."

Shadeed toned down his voice so it merely rumbled instead of thundered. Not as a concession to the old woman, he told himself, but because on this side of the Gate it was wise to be discreet.

The old woman prodded gently at the sleeping girl.

"And she was locked up? Makes no sense, someone of her calibre staying locked up."

"Her calibre?" He snorted. "All she has done since I set eyes on her is cry and sleep. She is a snivelling coward. If I did not need her…"

"But you do. So when she wakes up, try not to scare her. And above all, keep your temper on a short leash."

"I make no promises."

The girl murmured and tightened into a ball. Magda frowned.

"She's injured. There's blood in her hair."

Shadeed stiffened.

"It must have happened before I arrived. She was being attacked. She passed out but I assumed she merely fainted."

"What, overwhelmed by your magnificence?" Magda tutted. She had served jinn for millennia and their power was undeniable. But sometimes they needed a reality check. "Let me see."

Carefully, she bent over and examined the girl's head. Her questing fingers found the lump at the back of her skull. She grunted.

"Concussion, most likely. You can't take her through the Gate like that. You'll have to wait till she's better."

Shadeed bristled in irritation.

"Why could she not protect herself? Her assailant was a mere human."

"Why don't you wait till she wakes up and ask her?" Magda suggested cheerily. "I've got some panacea leaf in the hut. That'll sort her out."

She shuffled into the hut, her bright red bobble-hat standing out in the deepening gloom. Shadeed squatted down next to the unconscious female.

So this was who he was to be shackled with. Someone who had let herself be incarcerated. A pathetic existence. Surely that was not what her mother had intended when she fled Nush'aldaam? Why in the name of all the gods had she stayed in that human hell hole?

He cast his mind back to the moment he had revealed himself to her. She had been frightened, terrified. And she had gazed upon him with no recognition.

Was it possible that she did not know what he was? What *she* was?

Impossible. She was the daughter of Aelah. A legacy like that could not be hidden. And yet...

She had called him an angel.

If that proved anything, other than how deluded she was, it was that she was ignorant of his true nature.

He looked at her again. She was unremarkable. Skinny, weak, defenceless. The Gatekeeper had called her pretty, but he couldn't see it. His blue gaze traced her features. Utterly unmemorable. And yet there was something about the line of her jaw, the curve of her lips...

Magda laid a hand on his shoulder.

"Back up there, your Lordship. Give me some room."

He bit back a rude reply and strode to the edge of the clearing while she tended to the girl. He was annoyed at being here in this blasted world in the first place. Now he had to wait while she recovered

He swore to himself that tomorrow, he would drag her through the Gate whether she was ready or not.

"Is she healing?" he asked abruptly.

"The panacea is seeing to the injury. But she's freezing. I'll take her into my hut for tonight. Why don't you cross through the Gate and come back for her tomorrow?"

Shadeed was tempted. His home was rather more comfortable than the forest. And Leona was there. Lovely Leona with her magnificent hips and wicked tongue. He would like nothing more than to lose himself in her delicious curves tonight.

But the girl was too important. He could not risk losing her now.

"I'll stay," he said, irritation making him brusque. "But we leave before first light. I do not wish to be stuck here any longer than necessary. Humans repulse me."

"Oh the human realm isn't so bad." The old woman said cheerfully. "The people in the village drop me food and firewood once a month. I've developed quite a taste for reindeer steaks."

Shadeed was horrified.

"You are immortal! You should not be consorting with lesser beings."

"Lesser beings, huh? Who says? Just because they don't live as long as us doesn't make them worthless."

"You have been on this side of the Gate for too long, Magda. I worry about you."

"Worry about yourself, my Lord. You have quite a battle ahead of you. And you're relying a hell of a lot on a girl you don't know."

"She agreed to help me."

"She agreed to nothing. She has no idea what you intend to ask of her. And if I were you, I'd hide that disdain you carry around for humans. She might be less inclined to help a bigot."

Shadeed's eyes narrowed.

"Have a care, Magda. I allow you to take liberties because I have known you for a long time. But I will not be insulted."

Magda bowed, the bobble on her ridiculous hat almost brushing his knees.

"Sincere apologies, your Lordship. I am just a foolish old woman. Please ignore my ramblings. Now would you carry our guest into the hut before she freezes to death?"

She did look a little blue. He slid his arms under her and lifted her against him. Immediately she pressed herself to his chest, his supernatural warmth registering with her on some unconscious level.

She made a sound, a little sigh that could have been contentment. Her eyelashes fluttered for a moment against the honey of her skin. He tightened his grip, suddenly ashamed he'd left her on the cold forest floor for so long.

He carried her through into the wooden hut, cursing as he smacked his head on the low door frame. He knew the Gatekeeper could fashion any abode she desired and he understood why she'd want something that didn't look out of place from the outside. But he was surprised she'd chosen to keep the illusion going on the inside as well.

A fire crackled merrily in the hearth, and a little table and chair was set with a plate of bread and cheese. On the side was a small glass brimming with what looked suspiciously like alcohol.

He stood for a moment, unsure.

"Where shall I put her?"

"Take her through to the bedroom. Can you keep her warm while I fetch more blankets? Your body heat is working wonders."

"This is a demeaning chore for one of my stature."

"Don't worry, my Lord. I won't tell anyone." Her impertinence made his temper rise. Shadows started to pour off him, as black and twisted as his mood. Magda paid them no attention. "Go on, now. Through that door there."

She shuffled to a large chest and started rooting through it, whistling tunelessly through her teeth. After a moment, Shadeed stalked through to the bedroom. It was tiny and his bulk filled the room. His shins hit the side of the bed.

Muttering a curse that would have made grown men blanch, he deposited Raya among the sheets.

At least she looked healthier. The panacea leaf had reduced the lump on her head and her skin had lost its greyish tinge.

He eyed the bright amber streak of hair that nestled among her dark locks. It looked like a warning sign.

"I hope for your sake you are stronger than you look," he murmured. "Or your people will burn you alive."

Her fingers were white. Hesitantly he took them between his hands and rubbed them gently. He looked round the room, suddenly claustrophobic. By the skies, how did Magda bear living in such a confined space? He yearned for his castle, for his home. The sooner he could return there, the better.

It took him a moment to realise her eyes were open. There was silence as she took in the fact that she was lying on a bed in a strange place with a shirtless man standing over her, grasping her hand.

He saw her come to an unsavoury conclusion and opened his mouth to explain.

And then she snatched her hand away and shrieked at the top of her voice, fear and anger radiating from her in equal measure.

"Get the fuck away from me, you pervert!"

Six

Shadeed folded his arms and glared at her, his face pure granite. Raya had scrambled to the other side of the bed and was wedged against the wall, screaming blue murder. He let her continue for a while, hoping she would peter out. But her stamina was impressive and eventually he gave in.

"Silence!"

His voice rumbled through the cottage, the trees, and through her very bones. It was impossible to disobey. Her scream shut off abruptly and she blinked.

"How did you do that?"

"You will cease that infernal cacophony and listen. You are here because you agreed to accompany me. I have not abducted you. I am not…" his voice sank even further to a timbre that hurt her ears, "…a pervert."

"Then why have you trapped me in a bedroom? Where are your clothes?"

He frowned.

"I was trying to help you. How I dress is irrelevant, surely?"

Raya examined him. His face was classically good-looking, though currently set in a stony expression. His hair curled darkly to his shoulders, a length which could have been effeminate but on *him* was most definitely not.

He was huge – seven feet tall at least. His head touched the ceiling. His shoulders filled the doorway and his physique was impressively muscled. Not that she had much experience of how men should look, given she'd been locked up with the likes of Griggs for the past ten years. But she'd seen movies, and *this* specimen was definitely what she would call hot.

Her eyes trailed over his abs. At least he was wearing trousers. Very tight trousers.

Embarrassed, she jerked her head up to find him watching her.

"Like what you see?" he asked insolently. She flushed.

"I didn't agree to go anywhere with you," she said. "I don't even know who you are."

"We met very briefly at the drab place where you were being manhandled by a human. I offered you a bargain and you agreed to come with me. Have you forgotten already?"

Take me.

Yes, she'd uttered those words. But she'd been dreaming, hadn't she? She'd hit her head and she thought she'd seen a beast made of shadows. A beast with rage and power pouring off it. A beast with piercing blue eyes…

She met his azure stare and swallowed.

"That was you? The shadow… thing?"

His lip curled contemptuously.

"You will address me as Shadeed bin Shamhurish of Nurhan, Lord of the Jinn."

"Lord of the…?" For a wild moment she thought he'd said 'gin'. "What's going on? Why are we here?"

"We are here because you agreed to my bargain."

"What bargain? I don't understand."

"I require a service from you. In return you may ask for anything within my power to give." He paused. "And my power is considerable."

"A service?" Her voice rose. "What kind of service?"

"I need you to accompany me to Nush'aldaam."

"And where the fuck is that?"

"It's home. I think you will like it. At the very least, I can guarantee no human has ever set foot there."

Human. There it was again. That odd use of the word, as if it didn't apply to him.

Raya's eyes darted round the small bedroom. She was clearly in the presence of a madman, and hot or otherwise, she had to get away. She saw the window to her right, secured by a simple latch.

"Sure, um, okay. Would you mind turning around while I get changed for the journey?"

His eyes narrowed, but he turned away from her. Without pausing to think she lifted the latch and pushed the window up, throwing herself head first through the gap. The cold air hit her a nanosecond before she landed in a shallow snow drift beneath the window sill.

Her breath billowed in front of her as she rolled to her feet and ran for the trees, belatedly realizing she had no shoes on and no clue where she was.

And it was dark and freezing.

Dusk had given way to night. A full moon hung overhead, gleaming off the snow, but all around her trees loomed and she found it hard to see more than a step or two in front.

Low branches whipped her face. The back of her throat ached with every breath of cold air. Panic started to build.

It ratcheted into terror when she heard the first howl.

She stopped dead.

The sound rose in a mournful wail, raising the hairs on her neck. A second joined it, then a third. The cadence was eerily beautiful and wholly menacing.

"Wolves," she whispered. How could there be wolves? Where the fuck *was* she?

She started running again, frantic to find somewhere to hide. An empty cabin, a barn, anything that would give shelter from wild animals and the cold.

Maybe she should go back to the hut? But even if she wanted to face the Shirtless Wonder again, she had no clue which direction to go in. She was completely turned around.

The howling stopped and in the sudden silence, she heard the crunch of her bare feet in the snow. It seemed as if she was the only living thing in the world out here. But her instincts told her otherwise.

Something was keeping pace with her. Several somethings. She glimpsed three or four dark shapes gliding alongside her to her left. She made to veer right and saw another two had already flanked her. She caught a flash of yellow eyes through the trees. The wolves were tracking her.

A sob burst from her throat. Her heart was pounding like a jackhammer, both from fear and exertion as she pushed herself on. But the adrenaline wouldn't last forever. Already she could feel the cold seeping into her muscles, slowing her down.

The wolves understood that. They were waiting for her to fall.

They were closer now, narrowing the line she could run. The moon shone through a gap in the trees and she saw their dark fur, their pointed muzzles. They loped on either side, matching her speed, patiently waiting until she surrendered.

She slowed.

What was the point? Where could she go? She didn't even know where she was.

The wolves turned towards her and she caught a flash of fang. She closed her eyes. She hoped it wouldn't hurt too much.

And then arms were curling round her, pulling her into a haze of warmth. Wings beat and her feet left the cold forest floor.

Shadeed soared above the tree line leaving the wolves circling below. The girl had her hands locked about his neck and her face pressed into his shoulder.

"Why in the name of all the gods did you run?" he demanded. "I was explaining about our bargain."

She lifted her head and looked at him, her expression unreadable.

"You're the angel. I thought I'd dreamed you. But how can that be? You're the beast too."

"I am neither angel nor beast. I told you. I am Lord of the Jinn."

This time she heard the word properly. She took in his blue glare. Shadows were swirling around him and she could sense his fury, barely contained. It seemed to be his default position, she thought distantly. Followed by, *am I going nuts? Scratch that. More nuts?*

At least she knew now why he kept talking about 'humans' as if they were another species.

She became aware they were hovering over the trees. The air should have been bitterly cold up here, even more so than on the ground. But she couldn't feel it. All she could feel was his warmth. And the entire length of his body pressed hard against hers.

Confusion flooded through her. In that moment, only one thing was clear. She couldn't survive out here without him.

Angel or beast or jinn, whatever he was, she was stuck with him. What was it Dr Meadows had said to her? *Take control, Suraya. Stop letting circumstances control you.* She took a breath.

"Okay, I'll listen to your bargain. But you have to promise not to hurt me."

He regarded her stonily.

"I have done nothing to harm you, and to my recollection I have saved you twice now."

"I'll take that as a yes, shall I?"

He inclined his head graciously.

"I give you my word. And you will listen to what I have to say without running, screaming or crying?"

She caught the mockery in his voice and bristled.

"Hey, it's been stressful, okay? Yes, I'll listen to you without *crying* if it bothers you so much. But you have to tell me what's going on."

His jaw tightened. Could he trust her? Then again, did he have any choice? Having her people ally with him was the only chance he had of getting what he wanted.

He needed her. A thought that should have left him furious. And yet it was clear that she needed him too. The way she kept running, the despair in her eyes. Something bad had happened to her.

Without a word he started flying back towards the Gatekeeper's hut. She didn't hide her face in his neck this time. She watched him curiously as they glided silently through the night.

"Where were your wings before?" she asked. "In the bedroom?"

"They come and go as I please," he replied shortly.

"And the shadows?"

"A manifestation of my mood."

"Your mood's always dark then?" He scowled and didn't answer. *Anger management issues, much?* "What happens if you're happy? Do you get pink clouds inste…"

"We are here," he said abruptly. They dropped to the ground and she watched, fascinated, as his wings faded and disappeared, leaving just the merest smidge of smoke.

A figure was sitting outside the hut smoking a pipe. It was bundled into so many clothes it looked spherical. A ridiculous red bobble hat was perched on its head. It took Raya a moment to realise it was a little old woman, and only then because it spoke in a sing-song voice.

"I see you're starting to enjoy the flying, then?"

Bright green eyes twinkled up at her. Raya couldn't help smiling back. The wizened face was alive with mischief.

"It's not so bad," she answered cautiously. "It's an amazing sensation."

"Do you mean the flying, or being held by a jinn?"

Raya blushed and the old woman cackled.

"Gatekeeper." Shadeed's voice rumbled impatiently and small heaps of snow were dislodged from the eaves of the hut. "We require sustenance. And then we will talk."

"All right, all right. Keep your shirt on. Oh, too late."

Raya nearly giggled until the thunderous expression fell on her. She ducked her head and saw his feet were bare. Did he not feel the cold at all?

"Don't mind him. I'm Magda. Are you hungry?"

"A bit. I never really ate the food at the hospital."

"Was it no good?" sympathized the gatekeeper as she led the way into the hut. Shadeed remembered to duck this time.

"The orderly spat in it. So I had to choose carefully. Bananas mostly. Yoghurt. Chocolate bars."

"I think we can do better than that. How do you feel about steak?" Raya's stomach rumbled loudly and the Gatekeeper grinned. "Then I'll cook, and you two talk. Just one thing, my dear. Please keep an open mind."

She disappeared into the kitchen. Raya faced Shadeed, suddenly feeling awkward. She scratched an ear, not surprised her eczema had flared up again. If anything could be categorized as 'stressful', this was it.

She drew closer to the fire on the pretext of getting warm. Though in truth, she could still feel the heat emanating off him.

"So? What's this deal you keep talking about?"

He drew himself up imperiously.

"A deal I expect to be honoured. I will give you whatever you want. And in return, you will be my future bride."

In retrospect, he probably shouldn't have led with that.

Seven

Raya stared at him in disbelief. Had she heard right? Had he actually said she was going to be his *bride*?

"Hell, no. No way. I didn't get out of one prison just to get straight into another." Maybe she should have been scared, but it had been a long day. She'd gone through fear and out the other side. "I'm not being your fuck-toy, no matter *what* you give me. Forget it."

His eyes blazed so blue she could barely look at them.

"You have already acquiesced. When you agreed to accompany me."

"I had a head injury, you moron. And I was desperate to get out of there. I did *not* agree to some weird sex thing."

"I assure you, I am not trying to lure you into some tawdry arrangement for sex." His lip curled. "Believe me when I say I have no desire for *you* to fill that particular role."

Raya was stung. Fine, she wasn't particularly glamorous but there was no need to be rude.

"Well if you don't want… *that*, what *do* you want?"

"I need the Vulcani to ally with the jinn."

She blinked.

"Huh?"

"The Vulcani. The fire fae. The most powerful of the elementals. I need them to form an alliance with me so that I can consolidate my claim to the throne in Nush'aldaam. A union with the head of the clan will make the alliance binding."

He was saying words at her and she understood each individual word. But she didn't understand the sentences. Vulcani? Fire fae?

"Look, pretend I don't know anything. Which I don't. First off, you keep talking about Nush… Nush'aldaam, did you say? Well, I watched plenty of National Geographic in the hospital and I've never heard of it."

"It is the name of our realm. A place not of this world, where supernatural beings reside. It can only be reached through the Gate."

"And that's here? In the middle of a pine forest?"

"You sound sceptical."

"Just a bit. An entrance to another world? If you tell me we have to go through a wardrobe, then I'll know you're taking the piss."

Shadeed frowned. He didn't understand her references. For a fleeting moment he considered simply dragging her through the Gate. But he needed her co-operation. With an effort, he reined in his temper.

"There is no wardrobe. The Gate is here, in the place humans call Norway."

She stared in disbelief.

"You flew us all the way to Norway?"

"The wall between our worlds is thin here."

Questions raced through her head.

"You said your world is for supernatural beings. But you also said you wanted *me* to go with you."

"That is correct."

"But I'm not supernatural. I'm just me."

He gazed at her narrowly. Could it be true? She honestly did not know what she was?

"May I ask, who are your parents?"

"Caroline and Ross," she said promptly.

"No. They are not your parents."

"Okay, they're my adoptive parents. But I never knew my real ones."

He stared at her in silence. She tried to read his expression but drew a blank. For once there were no shadows curling round him, so at least he wasn't angry. She hoped.

He hid his consternation. She did not know who she was. She did not know her heritage, her birthright. She thought she was human.

It explained a lot. It would also make things a lot more complicated.

"Your mother," he began haltingly. "Your *birth* mother, that is, came from Nush'aldaam. Her name was Aelah."

The blood drained from Raya's face.

"You knew my mother?"

"I knew *of* her. She was the leader of the fire fae."

That phrase again.

"What are fire fae?"

"There are several fae clans in Nush'aldaam, but your mother led the Vulcani. The fire fae. One of the oldest clans in the empire."

He stopped, warily. She was frowning in confusion.

"I don't understand. You're saying my mother was like you? Not human?"

"Not exactly like me. The jinn and the fae are only loosely related."

"This is ridiculous. You realise how ridiculous this all sounds, right?" Raya twisted a piece of hair round her finger out of habit. "Next you're going to tell me my dad was Father Christmas."

"Your father was human. I believe that is why your mother left Nush'aldaam. Humans are forbidden to set foot in our world. If I had my way, we would *never* mix with humans."

"And yet here you are."

"I am only in this cursed plane to find you," he said impatiently. "You are the child of a fae. And with Aelah gone, you are the only one who can claim leadership of the Vulcani. Even with your biological disadvantage."

"What disadvantage?"

"Your human side."

"God, you're condescending. Do you really expect me to swallow this bullshit?"

"You have accepted I am a supernatural being. Is it so hard to believe that you yourself may be too?"

"Yes. Because for one thing, I've just spent ten years in a mental institution I couldn't break out of. Doesn't sound like something a powerful fae would do."

"Tell me, why were you there?"

He looked at her quizzically and she found herself answering.

"Because my adoptive parents died in a fire which everyone thinks I started."

"You were the only survivor?"

"Yes. I was lucky."

"It was not luck. You survived because fire cannot harm you."

She started to speak, to tell him he was being an idiot, but closed her mouth. In her mind's eye she saw the flames licking up the walls around her. Everything burning. Caroline and Ross. Yet not one hair on her head had been singed.

It was one reason why no-one had believed her story. That, and the forensics analysis which showed the fire was far too hot to be an ordinary accident.

She licked her lips, suddenly nervous.

"The fire was started by something that was there that night." She took a breath. "I think it was a demon."

"What did it want?"

His tone wasn't mocking or patronising. He seemed to accept that demons did, in fact, exist. She felt oddly grateful.

"It said I smelled like someone. A woman."

"Most likely the creature was searching for Aelah."

Raya jerked.

"My mother... she's still alive?"

"We believe so. And while she lives, her line retains power over the clan. That line ends with you. That is why I need you. As head of the clan, you can ally your people to me."

"My *people*?" She gave a hollow laugh, overwhelmed by everything she'd just been told. She ran a shaky hand through her hair. "Look, I need time to process. I have so many questions. I can't even think straight. Where *is* my mother? And what about my father? Why haven't they…"

"I need an answer, Suraya." He interrupted her, his voice hard. "I know this is a lot to take in. But right now, the throne is at stake. There are forces working to conspire against me. My only hope is to build a position of strength."

"But I don't know my *people*, as you call them. How am I supposed to get them to join with you?"

"By posing as my betrothed."

She shook her head in disbelief, sure she'd misheard.

"You want me to pretend we're getting married?"

"Only for a short time. A matter of weeks. But I need an answer quickly."

"Are you kidding me? You've just landed a shit ton of new information on me and you want a decision *now?* I mean, this is nuts. I don't even know what a fucking fae is."

"It doesn't matter. I only need to know if you agree."

She glared at him angrily, stung by his utter lack of compassion.

"I'm not agreeing to anything until I know what the hell is going on."

"You think you have a choice?"

Suddenly he was right up against her. She hadn't seen him move, but he had his hands wrapped round her upper arms and his face was less than two inches away. Shadows boiled off him and she felt his fury. Her mouth went dry.

"Get off me."

She was surprised she could even speak. She tried to wrench free of his grip and tendrils of darkness wrapped themselves around her waist and hips, holding her still. They may have looked insubstantial, but they were as solid as iron.

"Make no mistake. You agreed to the bargain when you asked me to take you. But *how* the deal is implemented is still open for negotiation. Our alliance, our *betrothal*, has to be convincing. A ruse the Vulcani will believe. Either you can *act* the part of my intended. Or…" his eyes glittered. "We could make the union real. Physical. Perhaps you'd like that?"

Without waiting for an answer, he dipped his head and lazily traced the curve of her neck. Raya felt his lips against her skin, maddeningly slow and sensuous. Angrily she tried to push him away but he was immoveable. One hand let go of her arm and stroked down her back to the base of her spine.

He cupped her backside, pulling her against him. She made a small sound as she felt the press of his thighs against hers. Heat pooled low in her belly and she had to fight a sudden inclination to rub against him.

Her head started to spin. This was ridiculous. She was acting like a swooning virgin.

Okay, she *was* a virgin technically, but it wasn't like she hadn't touched herself. Or spent nights imagining what passion could feel like. She just never thought it would make her feel like this.

Alive. Breathless.

His hand moved to cup her breast, his thumb brushing across her nipple. She stifled a moan as she felt it harden.

Christ, what was she doing? She was making out with a guy who'd kidnapped her. A guy who really only wanted her for one thing. And that wasn't her body; it was her bloodline.

Take control, Suraya.

She slapped him. Hard. It probably didn't hurt one bit but the unexpected violence startled him. He let go, and the steel bands around her waist and hips fell away.

She backed away as far as she could, shaking with anger.

"You said I could have whatever I wanted in exchange for the deal," she hissed. "Well this is what I want. I want to find my mother. And I want you to *never* touch me like that again. Our *union* as you put it will be for show only. Understand?"

He regarded her impassively.

"As you wish."

Magda bustled in with a tray full of food. She glanced from Raya to Shadeed, sensing the tension as the pair of them glared at each other.

"So, did you have a nice chat?" she asked brightly.

With a snarl of rage, Shadeed pulled shadows around himself until only the blue of his eyes was visible. Then he disappeared into thin air.

Eight

His wings beat steadily as he flew straight up above the trees, through the clouds, until he broke into the clear night sky. Stars glittered above him, as pure and bright as handfuls of diamonds scattered onto black velvet.

He hovered, fists clenched, shadows streaming off him until they dissipated some hundred metres away. He closed his eyes and let the sting of the frigid Nordic air cool his temper.

She had hit him. An inconceivable act against a Lord of the Jinn, and one punishable by death. Only the knowledge that she was ignorant of her heritage kept him from exacting the toll.

That, and the fact that he needed her.

Though he was beginning to doubt the wisdom of his plan. If she had no idea of her background, how could she hope to unite the Vulcani? How in the seven hells would they accept her leadership?

Aelah, he thought despairingly. *You left such a mess when you chose to forsake your world for the human one. Your people are divided and Nush'aldaam risks falling into the hands of a sadist.*

"I hope it was worth it," he said out loud, his voice bitter. "Deserting the fae for love. The love of a human, no less."

The words left a sour taste in his mouth.

He could never imagine shirking his responsibility because of some inexplicable emotion. What were feelings, after all? Just the product of chemicals and hormones. If he wanted a rush of endorphins, he could find it soaring on the current of a thermal updraft. Or in the arms of a willing partner.

For a fleeting moment he remembered the way Suraya had responded to his brazenness. The way she had pressed for the barest second against him as he explored her neck with his lips. The way her skin had tasted.

He shook his head, irritated with himself. One thing was clear. She had no more knowledge of the Vulcani than she did of Nush'aldaam. Aelah had given up her daughter and she had been raised as a human.

Did she even have any Vulcani traits? Probably not, judging by the fact she'd been incarcerated by her fellow humans. Perhaps that's why Aelah had abandoned her. But if she couldn't prove she was Aelah's daughter, the Vulcani would not unite around her.

He swore viciously under his breath. He couldn't produce her to the Vulcani like this. He was going to have to test her, see if the halfling had any of her mother's power. And he had absolutely no idea how to do that.

Anyone stepping off without a Gate mark on their bodies would end up smushed on the rocks below. To be honest, even *with* a Gate mark it was going to be touch and go.

Magda put a plate in front of Raya. At first the young woman paid no attention. She was taut with anger, her knuckles white as she dug her fingernails into her palms. How dare he? He had assaulted her, touched her without her consent.

And you liked it.

She ignored the treacherous voice and concentrated on stoking her anger instead. It seemed safer.

But as the appetising aroma of braised steak and creamed potatoes reached her nostrils, her stomach rumbled loudly.

"You'd better eat before that noise brings my hut down," said Magda drily.

Raya fell on the food ravenously. For at least five minutes she did nothing but chew and swallow, chew and swallow, her eyes half closed in ecstasy.

"That is soooo good," she said finally. "Thank you. Um, I don't think I introduced myself. I'm Raya."

"Aelah's daughter. I know."

"You knew my mother?" Excitedly, Raya leaned forward. "What was she like?"

"Complete hothead. But tough. And feisty. I see a little of her in you. That strand of red in your hair for example. That's from her."

Self-consciously, Raya ran her fingers through the matted mess. God, she needed a bath.

"I don't suppose I'm much like her at all. Shade says she was the leader of the fire fae."

"Shade?"

"Oh, um…" Raya flushed. "He told me his name. Shadeed bin Sham… something. In my head I just thought 'Shade'. You know, because of all the shadows surrounding him." She trailed off, embarrassed she'd been confused about a name just because it was foreign. But Magda was smiling approvingly.

"Shade. Yes, that suits him. Although it will annoy him immensely."

"It doesn't seem to take much."

"No. His temper is not one of his finer qualities."

They smiled at each other and for the first time since waking up there, Raya felt at ease.

"So can I ask you something? What exactly *is* a fae? Or a jinn, for that matter?"

"They're supernatural beings. You've probably heard of them in one form or another. In myths and legends and fairy tales. The fae are the 'fair folk', which is a misnomer. Many are dark and vicious. And the jinn are an ancient tribal race immortalised as genies. Though to my knowledge, they've never been trapped in old lamps."

"And they all live in Nush…"

"Nush'aldaam. The supernatural realm. And yes, most do. But there are quite a few on this side of the Gate. Me, for instance."

Raya examined the old woman as she calmly extracted her pipe from the depths of a pocket. She leaned so far into the fireplace Raya was amazed she didn't scorch her eyebrows. She puffed on the pipe until she was satisfied it was lit.

"And can I ask, um, if it isn't a rude question, what *are* you?"

"I'm a kobold."

"A…?"

"Kobold. Type of fae. We do domestic chores. In my case, I guard the Gate. This one, anyway. There are a few scattered around the world. I make sure nothing gets through that shouldn't."

"Like what?"

"In the old days it was armies. The Vikings, the Romans, the ancient Egyptians, they were buggers for trying to find their way into the supernatural world. But that was before my time." The old woman sighed regretfully. "These days it's more about keeping the animals out. Humans seem to have lost their curiosity. Still, it's a good job. Steady. I've done it for eight hundred years, give or take."

Raya was startled.

"Wow. You look great. I would have said fifty, sixty tops."

The Gatekeeper laughed out loud.

"Oh, I like you. You've definitely got Aelah's tongue."

"So what happened to her? Why did she abandon me? Do you know?"

Magda's face grew serious. She took one of Raya's hands in hers.

"I can't say why she left Nush'aldaam or why she gave you away. But whatever her reasons, she did it because she loved you, child. Do not doubt that."

"What about my father? Who was he?"

Magda took a deep puff on her pipe.

"Aelah was exploring on this side of the Gate. She always was inquisitive. And she became trapped in a hunter's snare. When the hunter came along and saw what he'd caught, he fell in love with her at once. And Aelah, well, she was a passionate one. Never really cared much for the rules. One thing led to another and next thing you know, *you* were on the way."

"Did she get in trouble for becoming pregnant by a human?"

Magda snorted.

"No. Fae are always dallying with humans. Notorious for it. Anyway, no-one would have dared say anything. The Vulcani are among the most respected fae in Nush'aldaam and Aelah was their leader. Fae have a complicated hierarchy. There are several different clans, some have leaders, some don't. But they all answer to the Fae King. That's Aelfric. And he's the one you want to watch out for because…"

"Magda!"

The roar thundered through the hut, causing pictures to fall off walls and glasses to shatter in the dresser. The fire guttered and blew out. Raya threw her hands over her ears, her bones throbbing with the intensity of his voice.

Shadows boiled into the room and Shadeed appeared among them, his wings flared, so wide they touched the walls on either side.

Even the normally unflappable Gatekeeper went pale.

"My Lord, I humbly apologise." For once there was no sarcasm in her tone. "I overstepped. Forgive me."

His eyes blazed blue.

"Remember your place, Gatekeeper."

"I beg leniency, my Lord. I am deeply sorry."

"Leave her alone." Raya jumped up, bristling with indignation. "She was only answering my questions. There's no need to bully her."

"Do not presume to tell me how to speak to my people." His voice dropped to a snarl. "We have business, you and I. You have laid out your conditions for an alliance. I accept."

Conditions? Raya thought back to their last conversation. Scratch that, their last shouting match. After he'd... she put that bit out of her mind, and recalled what she'd told him. *I want to find my mother.*

"You'll help me find Aelah?"

"Not so fast. There is the small matter of whether the Vulcani will accept you as one of theirs. And right now, there is not one shred of evidence that you share your mother's power."

"Of course there isn't. I've told you, I don't *have* any power."

"That remains to be seen. But I cannot take you through the Gate until we ascertain what exactly you can do. We must test you."

The gleam in his eyes made her nervous.

"I promise you I have absolutely no special qualities at all. Unless you count being *really* good at stabbing people with biros."

Magda held up a hand.

"My Lord," she said respectfully. "Are you saying you're going to try to make her powers manifest? Because that can be quite risky and I wouldn't recommend it."

Shadeed rounded on her.

"What else do you advise? What other choice do I have? Either I unite the Vulcani behind me, or I lose the throne. Tell me, Gatekeeper, what great plan do you have? Do enlighten me. Because I assure you, I would love nothing more than to leave the pair of you here and damn well go home."

There was a long silence. Then Magda sighed.

"You've made your point. Put your wings away. Let's figure out the safest way to do this."

"You will assist me?" he said warily.

"Of course. I know I'm just a simple people-loving kobold, but I'm always on your side, my Lord."

For a fraction of a nanosecond, Raya thought she caught a totally alien expression flash across the jinn's features. But no, she must have been mistaken. That surely wasn't gratitude, was it? Whatever it was, it was gone. Hidden behind the now familiar granite expression.

"Then it is agreed. We will stay until the halfling finds her powers."

Or she dies trying.

NINE

They stood in the clearing, facing each other. The sky was impossibly blue and the sun glinted off the snow. Its warmth felt good on Raya's face.

She hadn't slept much. She'd had to keep looking out of the window to make sure she wasn't back at the institution, about to be rudely awakened by Griggs.

At least she'd managed to have a bath that morning. The Gatekeeper had insisted.

"You smell of feet, girl."

Not that she'd needed much persuading. Sinking into hot, soapy water was one of the deepest pleasures she'd enjoyed in, well, forever. And best of all, no-one had been watching her.

She'd forgotten how much privacy meant to her.

After she'd dried off, Magda led her to a wardrobe full of warm clothes in different sizes and varying degrees of hideousness. All donated from villagers, she explained helpfully, who thought she was a harmless eccentric.

Raya had grabbed the first things that came to hand; a pair of elasticated fleecy trousers and baggy thermal sweater, topped off with a sheepskin jacket two sizes too big.

She examined herself in the mirror. Holy crap. She looked like a charity shop had thrown up all over her.

Shadeed, on the other hand, appeared relaxed and rested. She didn't know where he'd spent the night but it certainly wasn't in Magda's tiny hut. And he'd found a shirt from somewhere. A tight-fitting tunic that left his arms bare and did almost nothing to disguise the delineation of his muscular torso.

She glared at him resentfully. Did he never look like shit? Or feel the cold, for that matter?

He folded his arms as he regarded her narrowly.

"Fae and jinn are distant cousins," he began. "But in both species, abilities usually manifest during adolescence. If they do not, there are other ways to bring them forth. Emotional triggers. Fear. Anger. Passion. Desperation."

"Okay," she said uncertainly. "Well, I don't think fear is the trigger. I've had tons of that, thanks. Not even a *sniff* of a superpower."

"Perhaps." He started towards her. "But let us make sure, shall we?"

Raya backed away, hands held out in front of her.

"Whoa there, Shade. What are you planning?"

He stopped.

"Shade?"

"Oh. Sorry. It's kind of my nickname for you. Because of all the shadows."

"Nickname? What is that? Is it an insult?"

"No, the opposite," she said hastily. "It's what you call someone when you get to know them a little bit. It's a good thing, I promise."

"Shade." He rolled the word around his mouth as if tasting it. "I like it."

She sagged, relieved.

"Good. For a minute, I thought…" Her words morphed into a shriek as he scooped her up and leapt into the air, his wings appearing from nowhere and continuing his trajectory. They cleared the trees and kept climbing.

"What the fuck are you doing?" She peered down. The ground was now just a patchwork of green and white below them. Shade flashed her an unsettling smile.

"Testing whether fear is your trigger."

And he dropped her.

She fell silently, her throat closed tight in a paroxysm of terror. His winged form hovered above her, getting smaller as she plummeted. The breath was torn from her lungs as her velocity increased. Tears squeezed from the corners of her eyes.

She hoped it wouldn't hurt when she hit the trees.

He caught her after only a few seconds, but it felt like an aeon. And honestly, she hadn't been convinced he *would* catch her. Her fear had been genuine, turning her bones to jelly. She was just grateful she hadn't peed herself.

"You absolute fucking *bastard*," she screamed when she recovered her breath. He held her loosely, lips twitching in mirth. "You think that's funny?"

"It had a certain comedic element," he told her, trying to keep his face straight.

"I'm done with you throwing me around like a sack of potatoes. This is the last time you pick me up, you hear me?"

"Very well. The experiment has served its purpose. You were right, fear is not your trigger. I should have known anyway."

"What do you mean?"

He shrugged.

"You said your adopted parents died in a fire, yes?"

"Yes. Started by the demon. I told you."

"I do not think that fire was started by the demon. I think *you* started it, because you were frightened. And you were so traumatised by the consequences, you have buried it ever since. It is a subconscious thing. You have made sure fear can never trigger it again. We will have to find another way."

Shade spoke matter-of-factly, and it took him a moment to notice the stricken look on Raya's face. He ran back over his words in his head, wondering what the problem was.

Ah. He had basically told her the fire *was* her fault after all, just as she had been accused all these years.

He swore under his breath. Human emotions were a minefield.

"Suraya, I did not mean…"

"Put me down."

Her voice was small but he complied immediately, landing softly on the snow and wondering even as he did so why he was pandering to her. She was half fae. She needed to be less sentimental about her past.

"I apologise for my insensitivity. I am sorry your carers died. But you cannot blame yourself for their deaths."

"I want to be alone."

"I do not think that is a good idea, Suraya."

"Stop calling me Suraya. Only people who want to control me call me that. And you're not going to control me any more. Leave me alone. Deal's off."

She turned away, her heart numb. He was right. Of course he was right. Hadn't she known it all along?

She had killed them. Ross. Caroline. She had been so overwhelmed by fear that she had caused an inferno and incinerated them. Burned them alive.

She started shaking.

Did they suffer? Did they feel their flesh charring from their bones? Did they know it was her?

Even the demon had perished in the blaze. She understood that now. But her childhood mind had altered the facts to make *him* the killer. Because that was more palatable than the truth.

Shade grabbed her arm and swung her round violently.

"You think you are the only one who has suffered loss?" His blue eyes blazed as he towered over her. "I am trying to preserve an empire from falling into the hands of darkness. I have lost friends and allies, and I do not intend to lose any more. I cannot afford to have you crumble with your weak human heart. I am holding you to your promise. The deal is most definitely on."

Anger spilled into Raya. It flooded through her body and into her 'weak human heart', making it pound against her ribs.

"You'd better hope I don't find my powers when you're anywhere near me," she said quietly. "Because the first thing I'm going to do is burn your eyeballs out."

He lowered his head towards hers, his eyes flints of ice.

"Are you threatening me?"

"Oh, very definitely. If there's one thing I've learned in the ten years I was locked up, it's that bullies don't respond to anything else."

He stared into her furious black eyes and for the merest instant he thought he saw an amber flicker in their depths.

"It is right to grieve for those you lost," he said quietly. "But do not mistake me for the enemy, Raya. The one who deserves your anger is the one who sent that demon. And I believe we have a common foe."

"What if I can't forgive myself for what I did?"

"Then use it. Use that guilt and anger to make a difference. Like I am trying to do."

His sincerity jolted her. She wanted to ask what had happened to leave him with so much guilt and anger, but his face closed up again and the moment was gone.

Then Magda came running towards them, her short legs carrying her at an impressive speed. She'd ditched the red bobble hat for an equally ridiculous furry trapper's hat, the ear-flaps bouncing up and down as she ran.

"My Lord, I do not know how… this has never happened. I've failed at my post, I humbly beg forgiveness…"

Raya was astounded to see the old woman's face wreathed in fear.

"What is it, Magda? What's happened?"

"It must have been sometime in the early hours." Magda's voice dropped to a whisper as she twisted her hands unhappily. "I was so distracted by everything, I was late strengthening the warding spells around the Gate. Only by a matter of minutes but something... something came through."

Shade stiffened.

"What is it? Which beast?"

Beast? Raya looked from one to the other. The old woman looked as if she was about to burst into tears.

"Eight hundred years of guarding the Gate, and this is the first time..."

"Gatekeeper!" Shade roared impatiently and Magda cowered, hands over her ears.

"A jotnar, Lord Shadeed. A jotnar came through and it's headed for the mountains. I found its footprints."

"The mountains?" Shade relaxed. The mountains were empty. A jotnar wouldn't cause much trouble up there.

"But if it smells the village..."

"Sorry, what's a jotnar?" asked Raya, mystified.

"Round here, they'd call it a Norse Giant," said Magda. "Big and brutish. If it gets into the village, it'll destroy it."

"What?" Raya's eyebrows shot up. "Then you have to stop it! Send it back through the Gate!"

Shade shook his head.

"If it goes into the mountains, it will freeze to death. Jotnars look fearsome but they have the intelligence of flymould. A type of fungus," he explained as he saw Raya's perplexed expression. "It will lie down somewhere and literally freeze to death. Then the wolves will dispose of it."

"So you're not going to go after it?"

Shade shrugged dismissively.

"It is not a problem. We have more pressing matters."

"But your Lordship... the people... what if it decides to change direction and go towards the village?" Magda looked imploringly at him. His eyes narrowed.

"You really have a soft spot for humans, don't you, Gatekeeper?"

"Never mind her." Raya prodded one of his biceps. "*I* have a soft spot for humans. So if you want my help, you'd better figure out how to get that giant back through the Gate."

"Have a care," he growled.

Black wisps began to gather round him, swirling at his feet and rising towards his chest. Raya swallowed, but she held her ground.

"You keep telling me how powerful you are. What a great leader you'd be. Well, prove it. Show me what you can do."

By all the gods, since when did he need to prove himself? This was insufferable.

But then a thought occurred to him. Maybe he could kill two birds with one stone. Maybe a confrontation would unlock her power. With an effort he yanked the shadows back into himself.

"Very well," he said stiffly. "I will deal with the jotnar. There is just one thing."

"What?"

"You are coming with me."

T EN

"Here, take this." Magda offered up her trapper's hat, and Raya bent forward to let her place it on her head. She supposed it made her look even more ridiculous, but what the hell. At least it was warm. "And these."

The Gatekeeper hung a pouch round her neck and handed her a small tub of ointment.

"What are they?"

"The pouch carries sleeping dust. Strong enough to knock the giant out. The ointment I hope you won't need. It's a healing cream. Jotnar claws are filthy, like Komodo dragons. If it draws blood, make sure to cover the wound in that cream or it will become infected."

Raya gulped.

"Draws blood?"

"You'll be fine, girl. Just stick close to the jinn. You'd better hurry."

Raya looked round and found Shade had already set off. She trotted after him, hustling to keep up as he strode towards the mountains.

The snow made walking hard and the air grew colder as they ascended. She was glad of her thick coat, but made sure to keep close to him to feel some of the heat he continuously radiated.

She glanced at his face. His features were set and he made no attempt at conversation. She cleared her throat.

"So what's the plan?"

"I will incapacitate the creature and throw it back through the Gate."

"So why do you need me, then? I would have thought I'd just get in the way. Weak human, and all that."

"Jotnars are protective towards females of any species. You will distract it sufficiently for me to render it helpless."

"Hang on. You mean I'm…"

"Bait. Yes."

Raya waited, but he didn't offer up any more information.

They trudged onwards. Every now and then Raya saw the outline of a giant footprint in the snow. Maybe a metre long. Four toes.

"How far ahead do you think it is?" She tried to keep the nerves out of her voice.

"Hard to say. It depends on how long a head start it had. But it will be disorientated. It will not know where it is. The Gatekeeper has been effective at keeping them out. Until now."

"Don't blame Magda," Raya said hotly. "She was worried about me. It's not her fault she took her eye off the ball."

"You are right," he said shortly. "It is yours. If you had not run off, she would not have been distracted."

He lengthened his stride, leaving Raya in his wake. Gods, she was adept at getting under his skin. The sooner their alliance served its purpose, the better.

They walked for the best part of three hours. She tried not to think about the appalling revelation Shade had forced on her. She knew if she dwelt too long on what she'd done, the guilt and grief would break her apart.

Instead she thought about her mother. Her birth mother. Aelah was still alive. Surely she would have been told that Ross and Caroline had passed away? Which meant… she bit her lip. Her mother had left her to fend for herself.

And as for the discovery that she wasn't even human, she could barely process it. If it wasn't for the bitter memory of the fatal fire, she wouldn't have believed a word.

Another hour passed. Raya's stomach rumbled and she regretted not bringing any food. She desperately wanted a break but she was damned if she was going to be the one to suggest it.

Shade was some way ahead of her. As usual, he wasn't wearing shoes and she saw the snow was visibly melting under his bare soles. Must be nice not to need thermal socks.

She put her head down and jammed her hands into her pockets, concentrating on putting one foot in front of the other. So when he stopped suddenly, she nearly ran straight into the back of him.

"What are you…?"

"Hush." He held his hand up and Raya bit back her irritation. Like she was a dog or something. Then she saw it.

A shape huddled on the ground. It was lying on its side, curled up with its huge muscular back to them. Its head was bald and it was naked to the waist, its lower half covered in some kind of wrap-around garment.

Raya tried to estimate its height standing up and decided it must be at least three times her size. A huge cudgel studded with nails was propped against a nearby rock.

It was snoring.

"See? Stupid as mould. It has not even had the sense to find shelter." Shade's lip curled contemptuously. "We should leave it here to perish."

"Why does it have to die? It hasn't done anything wrong."

"You have clearly never met a jotnar before."

Black shadows spilled along Shade's arm and metamorphosed into a black blade. It darkened until it was as substantial as steel, its edge diamond sharp. He unfurled his wings. For a moment he hovered just above ground and Raya shielded her eyes. The sun behind him seemed to shine like a halo around his head.

Then he dived towards the sleeping giant, sword raised. His plan was to bring the hilt down on the back of its skull, turning its doze into unconsciousness. But the creature chose that moment to shift to a more comfortable position. Instead of hitting its head, Shade's blow glanced off its shoulder. He swore loudly.

Bewildered, the jotnar opened its eyes. The speed with which it went from sound asleep to fully awake was impressive. As it lumbered to its feet, Raya saw its face for the first time. She gasped.

Tusks curled up from either side of its mouth, reminding her of a warthog. The rest of its features had a porcine quality too. The giant's nose was squashed against its face and its brow was heavy and wrinkled. Two small black pebble-like eyes glowered from the folds.

It smelled rank, like it hadn't washed for a very long time. It reached out to grab its club and Raya saw each wrist sprouted a wickedly-sharp curved claw, like the spur on a cockerel's foot.

Shade tried for the creature's head again, using his wings to raise him higher, but the jotnar was ready. It ducked, moving faster than Raya thought possible for such a lumbering creature. With a roar it brought the cudgel round, barely missing Shade's ribs.

Its next blow met the sword. Shade grunted as his blade took the full force of the club in mid-air. The jotnar forced him down until his feet were back on the ground. It raised the club again, intending to smash it down on Shade's head. The jinn rolled clear at the last minute.

He was up in the air in an instant, wings spread wide. He swept his blade down on the jotnar's arm, and the club fell to the ground. The giant screamed, cradling his wrist.

Shade soared high then came down fast, both hands above his head gripping the hilt. The giant swiped one massive paw through the air and caught him, flinging him to one side.

Raya watched in horror as Shade hit the ground hard. Shadows coiled around him but he looked dazed. The giant raised a foot and tried to slam it down on the jinn's head but the shadows looped around it, holding it away.

"Shade!"

The jinn heard Raya's voice and got to his knees. He spread his wings, preparing to leap up. He was too late. The giant reached down and grabbed a wing, hoisting him off the ground. The other wing beat uselessly.

Shade dissolved his shadow feathers and let himself drop. The jotnar made a grab for him and struck a lucky blow. Its wrist-spur raked across Shade's abdomen.

Blood spurted.

The jinn landed heavily, wings and sword gone. A deep gash was open below his ribs. His face was pale. The jotnar reached out and grabbed its fallen cudgel, raising it high and taking aim.

"No!" Without thinking, Raya ran towards them. "Wait! Hey you! Over here!"

The jotnar turned and Raya caught a gust of its body odour. Sweat, dirt and blood mixed together. She tried not to gag. The giant lowered its club.

"Unhh?"

It made a high-pitched quizzical sound as she slowed to a stop several feet away. She kept her eyes on it, trying to draw its attention away from Shade. She glimpsed him in her peripheral vision. He wasn't moving.

"Hey, big guy." She hoped her voice wasn't trembling.

The jotnar came closer, towering above her. Fuck. It was like the hulk on steroids. It frowned, the folds on its porcine face deepening so much she could barely make out its eyes.

What had Shade said? Jotnars were protective towards females. She hoped he was right.

It occurred to her the giant might not be able to tell she *was* a female. She hardly looked feminine right now. She reached up and pulled the furry hat off, tugging her hair out of the messy ponytail she'd scraped it into that morning.

It fell over her shoulder in a dark wave, the single strand of copper standing out brightly. The jotnar blinked as the sun sent shards of gold through its length. It made a curious crooning sound.

"I really hope that's not some kind of mating call," she said nervously. It took another step towards her. "I mean, I'm not a prude or anything, but I think we need to get to know each other first, you know?"

It dropped the club and squatted down, peering at her closely. From here she had a clear view up its loin cloth. If she didn't know it already, the proof that this giant was very definitely male was staring her in the face. She averted her eyes.

"So, hey, I'm a Libra. You?"

Like a snake, its hand whipped out and grasped her round the waist. She shrieked as the giant lifted her off the ground. She tugged at its fingers, fear rippling down her spine.

It brought her to its face and for a panic-stricken moment, she thought it was going to pop her into its mouth and swallow her whole.

Instead it studied her, turning her slowly this way and that. She realised it was examining her hair.

At least she had its attention. She glanced down at Shade and saw he was sprawled unconscious. The wounds across his abdomen looked red and ugly, and his caramel skin was tinged with grey.

The giant shook her gently, trying to make her hair swing. She fanned it out, hoping to distract it a while longer until she figured out what to do. She felt something bump against her chest and looked down.

The pouch Magda had hung around her neck. Excitement bubbled through her. Sleeping dust.

She had no idea how much she needed or whether the giant needed to eat it, touch it or inhale it. But it was the only thing she'd got.

She opened the bag and shook a small heap of powder onto her hand. It looked as innocuous as cornflour. The giant peered at her curiously.

"Can you come a little closer?" she asked. She lifted a strand of hair with her free hand and held it towards him. "You can stroke it if you like."

The giant didn't draw her towards its face as she'd hoped. Instead, it extended a careful finger and lightly touched the top of her head.

She tried not to cower. The thing didn't seem to want to hurt her, but that didn't mean it couldn't accidentally do some damage.

"Do you want to smell it?" she asked. She held her hair to her nose and mimed an enthusiastic sniff.

Actually, it did smell good. Magda's shampoo was lavender and it had left her hair softly scented. Way better than the antiseptic crap she'd had to use on the psychiatric ward.

The jotnar seemed to agree. It pushed its snout towards her, the tusks on either side of its mouth coming perilously close as it inhaled noisily.

Raya blew the sleeping dust straight into its nostrils.

The jotnar's eyes opened wide. Then they rolled back into its head and with a grunt, it toppled forward. It hit the ground hard, jarring her teeth and knocking the wind from her. The giant hand opened and she rolled across the snow, coming to stop in an untidy heap.

For a moment she lay on her back and stared up at the flawless azure sky.

"Any minute now, I'm going to wake up in a strait jacket," she muttered to herself. "Any minute now."

The silence stretched.

Then she struggled to her feet and went to check on Shade.

Eleven

She moved him so she could see his injuries, trying to be gentle. The bleeding had slowed, thankfully, but the jagged edges of the wound were inflamed and through the raw tissue she caught a glimpse of white. The tear was down to the rib.

"Shade, can you hear me?"

His eyes were closed and he didn't answer. There were beads of sweat on his brow but his skin felt cool. He wasn't radiating any of the heat Raya had become used to.

Maybe the wound was infected. And maybe jinn didn't get fevers like normal people did. Maybe their body temperature fell.

She dug in her pocket for the little tub Magda had given her. She didn't know if it would work on a supernatural being like Shade, but right now it was all she had.

She scooped out a big dollop of ointment. Steeling herself against all the blood, she slathered it across his open wound. He groaned faintly but she forced herself to continue until the thick cream coated the shredded flesh.

Okay. Now what?

She could leave him here and head back down to Magda's hut, but it would probably be dark by the time she got there and she wasn't sure she'd be able to lead the Gatekeeper back to this spot. Besides, she didn't want to leave Shade alone at the mercy of the mountain.

Though obviously it would serve him right if he got eaten by wolves.

She twisted her hair as she thought. They'd passed a hunting lodge a kilometre or so back. A tiny ramshackle thing, but it was shelter. Maybe she could drag him there?

She eyed his prone figure. Shade was more than a foot taller than her and twice her width. She knew she was stronger than she looked; she had a wiry strength that few, including Griggs, had suspected until she unleashed it on them. Nevertheless, dragging Shade was going to be a bitch of a job.

She checked on the jotnar, blowing more sleeping dust onto its face as insurance. It showed no sign of movement and she hoped it would stay unconscious for the next few hours.

Then she got behind Shade and pulled him into a sitting position. She slid her arms around him and laced her fingers together over his chest. Straightening up, she pulled him backwards.

It was slow. He was a dead weight, and she couldn't see where she was going. She had to keep craning over her shoulder to see the way down the rapidly darkening mountainside.

His head lolled against her chest, bumping and jerking over every uneven bit of ground. She glared at it viciously. More than once she entertained the idea of simply dumping him and heading to the hunter's lodge herself.

But she didn't. He thought she was weak. The desire to prove him wrong drove her onwards.

After the first hour, the strain in her arms was almost unbearable and the muscles in her back were screaming. She'd forgotten to retrieve her fur hat and the cold was making her ears itch like crazy. Her gloveless hands locked around Shade's chest were blue. The fact that she couldn't feel them was worrying. The jinn wasn't putting out his normal radiator-like warmth.

She stumbled over a loose stone and fell backwards, landing under his crushing weight. She lay for a moment, lacking the strength to move. Despair tugged at her.

I can't do this. I'm exhausted..

"Get up," she muttered out loud. "Get up and move."

I'm not strong enough. I'm too cold.

She screamed in frustration, her voice bouncing off the trees and disappearing into the void. And suddenly heat flared in her hands.

For a moment she thought the warmth was coming from Shade, that he was regaining his strength. But her cheek was against his face and it was still cold.

She unlocked her hands from around his chest and held them up, trying to see round his head. She caught her breath, unsure whether she was hallucinating.

Orange flames were licking along her fingers. She stared, entranced, turning her hands slowly one way then the other. Her hands weren't burning. There was no pain, no scorching. But her fingers were definitely on fire.

Unless, of course, she was as nuts as Dr Meadows thought she was and this was all in her head.

Instinctively she shook her wrists, trying to extinguish the flames. They went out, leaving her fingers pink and tingling with warmth. In fact, her whole body felt as if there was a current running through it.

With a sudden spurt of energy, she hauled herself up and resumed dragging Shade down the mountain. It seemed a little easier now, as if she'd found a reserve of strength from somewhere.

It didn't last long. It was late in the afternoon before the hut finally came into view and by then her legs were shaking with fatigue. She sobbed in relief when she found the door unlocked.

She shouldered her way in, dragging Shade to the middle of the floor. She laid him down, her spine cracking as she straightened up. She stuck her hands under her armpits, stifling a groan as the blood crept painfully back into her fingers.

The lodge consisted of a single room with a dresser, a log-burner, and a narrow truckle bed along one wall. It wasn't designed to be lived in. It was just somewhere for a trapper to grab a rest or wait out a storm during hunting season.

She wanted nothing more than to lie down and close her eyes for five minutes but she knew if she did, she'd never get up.

She checked on Shade's injury. It seemed to her the wound looked less red but it was hard to tell. Blood had congealed around it. She smeared on the last of the ointment, hoping it was enough.

As dusk fell she searched the room, hoping to find a torch or a lamp. She discovered candles and a box of matches tucked in a drawer.

"Better than nothing," she muttered as she struck a match.

In the glow of candlelight, she checked the small pot-bellied stove in the corner. She almost cried when she saw it had already been prepared with a pile of logs.

She prepared to strike another match, then hesitated. Checking that Shade was still out cold, she tentatively held her fingers over the logs and tried to conjure up some fire. She wasn't the faintest bit surprised when nothing happened.

Chiding herself for her stupidity, she struck a match and touched it to the kindling. The logs roared into flame and she spent a few precious minutes basking in their warmth.

She dragged Shade closer to the stove. There was a bare mattress on the bed but she simply didn't have the strength to lift him onto it. She laid a hand gingerly on his brow. His skin felt less clammy than before.

"I guess it's my turn to keep *you* warm. I'm bloody glad you're asleep for this."

Raya shrugged off her coat and put it over him, then lay down next to him. She hoped the combination of the fire and her body heat would restore him.

The logs crackled in the stove, and the sound of Shade's breathing was reassuringly even. Her eyelids drooped as tiredness overcame her.

She raised her forearm and it was wreathed in flame.

"I don't want to hurt you," she whispered. Shade stood behind her and closed his hand over hers, fire pouring through his fingers like molten lava.

"You could never hurt me," he replied. He kissed the back of her neck and it seemed to her as if heat was rushing through her whole body. "Your fire makes me whole."

He pulled her hard against him so she could feel his arousal pressing against the small of her back. He reached round to cup her breast and she arched into it. He stroked her stiffening nipple, pulling on it gently until she moaned in helpless pleasure.

He left her breast and caressed her waist, her stomach, moving lower with aching slowness until his hand slipped between her legs. He inhaled sharply as he discovered how wet she was.

She parted her thighs for him, wordlessly urging him on. He circled a finger around her sensitive little nub and she ground her hips, desperate for his touch.

Liquid warmth pooled in her stomach.

She was close. So close.

She surfaced from her dream, panting. There was a moment's disorientation, a blurring of lines between fantasy and reality. Then she felt Shade pressed up against her back.

His arm was slung over her hip and his hand was beneath the waistband of her trousers. He was stroking her with an expertise that made her want to cry out in pleasure.

"Shade…"

She should stop him, she thought wildly. But she was so wet, so aroused. No-one had ever touched her like this. No-one had ever made her feel like this.

Heat coursed up and down her body. It was as though tiny flames were flickering beneath her skin, waiting to explode out. She could scarcely bear it. And she wanted it to go on forever.

He nuzzled her neck and groaned into her hair.

"Leona."

Her eyes flew open. In an instant she had thrown his arm off her and rolled away. Furious tears pricked at her eyelids as she got to her feet adjusting her clothes.

"Bastard," she hissed, trying to cover her humiliation. "You had no right!"

Shade woke fully. The puzzled expression on his face changed to thoughtfulness as he took in her flushed cheeks and his own state of arousal.

"Don't take it personally," he drawled. "I was half-asleep. And my body tends to take over when it finds a woman in bed next to it."

"Your body wouldn't fucking *be* here if I hadn't dragged it down a fucking mountain," Raya yelled, so angry she wanted to punch him. "If it wasn't for me you'd be dead!"

"Well, I definitely feel alive now." Shade rubbed his fingers together and Raya was mortified to see they still held traces of her. "As do you. Come here."

"I will not!"

"You cannot mean to leave me like this?" He raised an eyebrow. "I thought you were enjoying it?"

"I... that's... mind your own business. Who the fuck is Leona, anyway?"

"She is a friend."

"Then go fuck *her*. You said our alliance was purely for show. Or are you not a man of your word?"

His brows drew down. He got to his feet, and she had time to see the wound from the jotnar's claw had almost completely scabbed over before he caught her round the waist. Shadows coiled around him and she felt the smoky warmth of a tendril brushing her cheek.

"You are lucky I *am* a man of my word. Or I would bend you over right now and finish what we started." His eyes blazed blue neon. "And you would beg me not to stop."

She forced herself to hold his stare.

"I will never beg you for anything. *Anything*."

The shadows grew until they brushed the ceiling of the hut and expanded outwards. She heard the glass pane in the window crack as pressure was exerted against it.

He let her go, putting distance between them.

"What happened to the jotnar?" he asked abruptly. Shakily, she tucked her hair behind one ear.

"Asleep, about a kilometre up the mountain."

Shade left the hut. It was barely dawn and the heat of his body formed wreaths of steam in the cold morning air. His wings unfurled and without a word he took off, gliding gracefully uphill.

"Hey! What about me?" Raya watched him disappear. "Bastard."

She pulled on her coat and closed the door to the lodge. Then she set off towards the Gatekeeper's hut, cursing Shade every step of the way.

Twelve

"And then he just left me there!"

Raya spluttered indignantly, though it was hard to keep talking when she was stuffing her face with Magda's delicious fresh bread and salted cheese.

She hadn't told her everything, of course. She'd left out the bit about the flames appearing on her hands. She still wasn't sure if that had happened, or if she'd been hallucinating.

And wild horses wouldn't make her tell about the almost-sex.

"Ah. Well, it explains why Lord Shadeed has disappeared off."

"Disappeared? What do you mean?"

"He flew the jotnar back to the Gate and chucked him over to the other side. Then he went through himself. I don't think we'll see him for a while."

"Why not?" Raya was mystified and Magda looked at her narrowly.

"I know you don't know much about arrogant jinn, girl. But surely you know about men?"

Raya shrugged.

"I was locked up all through puberty. My experience of men is limited to patients with schizophrenia, arsehole orderlies, or doctors with saviour complexes. Oh, and Baywatch. We watched a lot of Baywatch, for some reason."

"How very strange. Well, let me explain. Shade set off to heroically capture a ferocious giant. Instead, not only does he get knocked out, but a skinny female, a human at that, saves his life and incapacitates the beast. I expect he's furious and embarrassed, and like most men he doesn't know how to handle it."

"He could just say thank you," Raya grumbled. "My back is killing me. He weighed a ton."

"One day you'll have to tell me how you did it."

"So what shall we do in the meantime?"

"What would you like to do?"

"Well…" Raya pulled her knees to her chest and wrapped her arms around them. "Would you tell me more about Nush'aldaam? While Shade isn't around?"

"What has he told you already?"

"Nothing. Not much, anyway. He said he was trying to take over the throne and he needed the fire fae on his side. But I don't really know why. Does he have a *right* to the throne?"

"Yes, he does." Magda nodded. "He's not a usurper or anything like that. But the old emperor died and didn't leave an heir. Shade is a possible successor. His father is descended from one of the Seven Kings of the Realm. But unfortunately he has a rival, Salaq bin Amar, who hails from *another* of the ancient Kings."

"Ah. So it comes down to who has most support?"

"Exactly. Salaq is readying his forces for war but if he realises his side isn't strong enough to win, he will stand down. Shade wants to avoid war at all costs. He doesn't want to see his people suffer. He isn't like Salaq at all. He is by far the cooler head of the two. Which is ironic given he's an Ifrit."

"An…?"

"Ifrit. All smoke and heat and shadows, as I'm sure you've noticed. Salaq is a Marid. Exact opposite, his power is rooted in water. That's why Shade thinks he can win the support of the fire fae. They can relate to him. But Salaq is sneaky. He's promised more power to Aelfric, the Fae King, if he pledges allegiance." Magda shuddered. "And Aelfric is a dark one. He's… he's not right. There are stories about him…"

"But you're fae too, aren't you? Isn't he your boss?"

"Technically. But I prefer to stay as far away from him as possible."

"He's the one you tried to warn me about, isn't he?"

Magda hesitated, then spoke in a rush.

"Shade doesn't want me telling you this in case it scares you off. But Aelfric had a thing for your mother. He tried to woo her and she was flattered. But in the end she rejected him. He was the reason she left when she found out she was pregnant by a human. She was convinced he'd find a way to harm you."

Raya rocked backwards as she tried to take it all in.

"But he's still there. What if he's holding a grudge"

"I'm sure he is. But it's one thing threatening an unborn child. It's quite another to threaten the daughter of the head of a respected clan. Especially if she has her mother's powers."

"But I don't, do I?" Raya hunched her shoulders. "I bet my mother can throw fireballs or shoot heat-rays from her eyes, or something. I can't do anything like that."

"Not sure about heat-rays. Fireballs, yes. She was notorious for them. But power is relative. Shade doesn't need you to take down an army. He just needs you to bring the Vulcani to his side."

"And how the hell am I supposed to do that?" Raya dragged a hand through her hair and started twisting the end of it. "They're not going to believe I'm Aelah's daughter. *I* can barely believe I'm her daughter."

"Then maybe you'd better look at these," Magda said quietly.

She got up and went to a chest in the corner of the room. Delving into the dark recesses, she pulled out a battered photo album and placed it in Raya's hands.

"Your mother sent me these after you were born. Just before she gave you up for adoption. Shade doesn't know I have them and I'd really rather you didn't tell him. I'm not sure my ear drums can withstand that roar of his."

With shaking hands, Raya opened the thick pages. And for the first time in her life, she laid eyes on her mother.

She had tried to picture her mother so many times. Sometimes she was tall and regal, other times she was short and cheerful. But always she had long black hair and dark eyes, like her own. The truth was rather different.

Aelah stared into the camera with the ferocity of a she-wolf. Her hair was a deep copper red, short and spiky, barely covering the tips of her ears which Raya saw with a shock were gracefully pointed. Her skin was coffee and cream, warm and silky. And her eyes were a deep marmalade, the colour of a banked ember ready to leap into flame.

Raya stared at the picture and felt no connection at all.

"She doesn't look like me," she said in a small voice.

"She doesn't need to. Look at how she's holding you." Magda gently turned the pages so Raya could see. "Look at how she cradles you as if you are the most precious thing in the world. Look at her face. She would fight to the death to protect you. You're hers. Her blood is your blood. She even gave you that strand of hair colour in amongst your own. Trust me, child. She loved you."

"So why did she leave me? Where is she now?"

"I cannot say. Somewhere Aelfric can't reach."

Raya swallowed down the lump in her throat. She leafed through the rest of the pictures, committing them to memory.

"Are there any of my father?" she asked. Magda shook her head.

"Aelah had to protect him as well. If Aelfric knew who he was, he'd send a shaitun to kill him."

"Shaitun?"

"Type of demon. Sneaky buggers. They can slip into people's heads for a while. Know what they know. See what they see. It's hard to hide from a shaitun once they start tracking you."

Raya bit her lip. In her mind's eye, she saw the sly faces peering out from behind the eyes of staff at the hospital. The Mary-thing. And before that, the thing that had watched her from inside Nurse Phillips.

In a way, it was a relief. She wasn't mad. She had been right.

"Can I keep this?" she asked, pointing to a photo of Aelah.

Without waiting for a reply, she peeled it carefully from the album and tucked it into her back pocket. It was the first picture she'd ever had of her mother, and she wanted to keep it close.

Thirteen

Shade turned over in bed, the silken sheets rustling down to his navel. Moonlight streamed in through the floor-to-ceiling doors. He rarely closed them. They opened straight onto a cliff-edge drop. Sometimes, when the mood took him, he would simply step through them and take flight.

There was nothing like the feeling of gliding silently through the night sky of Nush'aldaam. Aside from birds and insects, flight was a power held only by the very old or the very powerful. He could count on one hand the number of beings in the realm who possessed it.

The fae weren't one of them. Not any more. Not even Aelfric, thank the gods. If he thought he'd ever meet that lunatic in mid-air, he'd stay grounded forever.

Not even the Vetali possessed the ability, which was ironic given that in the human world, legend associated them with bats.

He shifted restlessly, trying not to disturb Leona. She was sleeping beside him, white-blonde hair fanned across the pillow behind her.

He studied her face and felt the prick of a guilty conscience. He had been selfish, seeking his own release and using her to bury his frustration and anger. She had let him take his pleasure without question or complaint. She had just held him until he was spent.

She had been thinking only of him. And he hadn't been thinking of her at all.

He touched the remains of the wound on his torso. The jotnar had left a scar, but nothing else. He had been lucky.

No. Not luck. Raya.

Raya had applied healing balm on his wound. And she had beaten the jotnar. She had succeeded where he had failed. A part-human girl. A halfling. How the hell had she done it?

Not a girl. Woman.

His breathing quickened as he remembered his dreamlike awakening next to her in that strange hut. The heat pouring off her body. The feel of her against his hand. He felt a stirring in his loins and for a moment he considered rousing Leona again, but then his mind leapt to another question.

How had they got there?

He frowned as their angry conversation replayed itself in his head. Her shouted words. Something about pulling him down a mountain?

Realisation tumbled over him. She had dragged him, unconscious, for a kilometre or more. She could have left him. By the gods, she probably wanted to. But she hadn't.

And he'd repaid her by groping her.

He shut his eyes as a hot wave of shame engulfed him. No wonder she hated him. He had been boorish, chauvinistic and aggressive. He sat up, unable to lie still for a moment longer.

"What's wrong, my Lord?" Leona's soft voice cut through his self-recrimination. "Are you feeling all right?"

"I am sorry if I woke you. Go back to sleep."

"If something is bothering you, you know you can talk to me about it." Leona leaned on one elbow and put a hand on his shoulder. "I'm a good listener."

"I know you are. But there's something I need to put right."

"Now? Can't it wait till morning?"

"No. I have to apologise to her. And you know how much I hate apologising."

Leona paused a beat.

"Her?" she asked neutrally.

"Raya. The one I told you about. The one who will help me win the throne."

Leona lay back among the pillows.

"You seem to be spending a lot of time with her."

"Believe me, it is a hardship. And one I could do without."

"Why don't you just tell me what she looks like? I can take her form and we can win the Vulcani over that way. Is she dark?" Leona shifted. Suddenly she was a Nubian queen, skin like polished ebony. "Or a redhead?" Hair the colour of autumn leaves spilled over the bed and emerald eyes sparkled with mischief. "Maybe a blonde with attitude?" Pale dreadlocks framed cheeks tattooed with warrior markings.

Shade shook his head ruefully.

"I wish it were that simple."

"You know I can be whatever you want me to be, my Lord."

"In that case, I like the redhead."

One of the benefits of a si'lat companion, Shade mused, was that she could be many different women. Or men, if your tastes ran that way. Leona shifted back to the redhead and held out her arms.

"Come here, my Lord. Let me help you relax."

But she could already see by the set of his shoulders he didn't intend to stay. He got out of bed and allowed the shadows to form his clothing. His feet, as usual, were bare. He strode to the open doors.

"Stay as long as you like," he said over his shoulder.

Then he stepped off the edge, falling fifty feet before unfurling his wings and soaring on the currents towards the Gate.

Fourteen

Raya watched the lights undulating overhead. She hadn't slept much and when she woke it was still dark. But she'd seen the strange illuminations from her window and gone outside for a closer look.

Against the night sky they were green and yellowish, sometimes tinged with violet. She'd never seen the aurora borealis before. She was transfixed.

She didn't hear Shade land behind her but she knew he was there. The air moved under the beat of his wings and she smelled his scent of burnt cinnamon. She deliberately didn't turn to greet him.

"Raya."

His voice was soft but she kept her eyes fixed on the northern lights. There was nothing he could say that would stop her being angry.

"I came to apologise. I am sorry."

Her jaw dropped.

"Say that again?"

"I am deeply sorry for losing my temper. And grateful for… for what you did."

"What I did?" She swung round at last, her eyes glittering dangerously. "Just remind me. What did I do?"

"You knocked out the jotnar."

"And?"

"You treated my wounds."

"Uhuh. And?"

Shade folded his arms.

"You are really going to make me say it?"

"Oh yes. Damn right I am."

"Very well. You dragged me down a… I think you called it a *fucking* mountain."

"I saved you."

"I wouldn't go so far as to say…"

"I fucking *saved* your arse. That jotnar was going to smash your stupid head in."

"Okay. Fine. You saved me. I am grateful for that too. Happy?"

They glared at each other.

It wasn't exactly a thank you. But she knew it had taken a lot to admit he owed his life to her. With a conscious effort, she unclenched her fists.

"That was a rubbish apology but I'll take it. What did you do with the jotnar?"

"I flew the beast through the Gate. It was still asleep."

"Bet that was fun. It absolutely reeked."

A smile tugged at Shade's mouth.

"It did. Exceedingly."

There was a long pause. Then they both spoke at once.

"About what happened …"

"When we woke up…"

They stopped, awkwardly. Raya was glad it was dark and he couldn't see her blushing. He cleared his throat.

"The fault was mine. I was dreaming and I may have… I *did* overstep the mark. I apologise."

Two apologies in one conversation. That had to be a record.

"Fine. Let's just forget it."

"Good."

"Good."

They stood in silence for a while and watched the lights.

"So what now?" she asked.

"I do not know. I thought the confrontation with the beast might awaken your power, but so far neither fear nor anger seems to have worked."

Raya hesitated, then spoke in a rush.

"Something happened when I was dragging you. I'm not sure if I was imagining it but…" she trailed off as his eyes suddenly blazed down at her.

"What? What happened?"

"My hands. I think they were on fire. I was cold and desperate and suddenly there were flames. I'm not sure though. I was so tired I might have been hallucinating."

Shade looked at her thoughtfully.

She said she had been desperate. It was certainly possible that desperation had kickstarted her fae powers, but why would that work when other triggers hadn't?

What was different?

He closed his eyes as realisation hit. He was an idiot. A blind idiot.

"Of course. How could I have been so stupid?"

"What?"

"I thought I could force your powers to manifest on this side of the Gate. But I was wrong. You needed to be exposed to supernatural energy."

"How do you mean?"

"First you faced the jotnar. Then you spent, what, an hour? Two hours? However long it was, dragging me in your arms. That contact, plus your state of mind, must have activated your powers. Only for a second. But it was there."

"So you think I have to mix with others like you? Does that mean we have to go to Neverland?"

He was bemused.

"Neverland?"

"Nush'aldaam. Are we going?" She felt a spark of excitement, followed by a rush of fear. "But what about Aelfric? Magda said…"

She stopped, biting her lip. Shade looked at her narrowly.

"Magda has been talking about Aelfric?"

"Only because I asked her. Don't go and roar at her, it was all me."

He bit back a smile.

"I have no doubt. I won't roar, as you put it. And don't worry about Aelfric. He will not dare venture into my territory." His voice was low and steady. "I will keep you safe."

He held her gaze and unexpectedly, her stomach did a slow flip. *He's keeping you safe because you're a political pawn. Nothing more.*

She hid her confusion by pretending to fasten her coat against the night air.

"So when do we leave?"

"How about now?"

"Now? Just like that?"

"No time like the present. Magda will have to brand you so you can get through the warding spells."

He started in the direction of Magda's hut and Raya scrambled to follow.

"Hey, what do you mean, brand me? Will it hurt?"

He shrugged.

"I do not know. My pain tolerance is exceptional."

Great.

It did hurt, but only for a second. Magda pressed her fingers to Raya's forearm and muttered a few strange words. Her skin suddenly felt as if it had been pricked by a thousand red hot needles, and for an instant she saw the outline of a circular symbol blazing vividly just above her wrist. Then it faded, leaving just a faint pinkish marking.

"There you go. This is like a front door key to Nush'aldaam. If you don't have one of these, you can't get in or out. Unless a silly old kobold forgets to renew the warding spells," she added hastily, as Shade raised a sardonic eyebrow.

"Thanks Magda. Though I'm not sure how much coming and going I'll be doing if I can't even see the Gate," Raya said doubtfully.

"But you can. Now that you're marked, it will be clear to you. Take a look."

Raya dashed outside and gaped.

Where there had been a simple clearing among a forest of pine trees, now there were two glittering pillars rising straight up into the sky. They were so high, Raya couldn't see where they ended. Their tops were lost in the heavenly display of colours that were the aurora borealis.

The pillars stood some ten metres apart. And beyond them, Raya glimpsed soft grass waving in a warm breeze that played across her face. The sweet scent of jasmine and lily drifted to her nostrils, and in the dark velvet of an alien sky she glimpsed strange constellations and a giant silver moon starting to dip below the horizon.

"It's beautiful," she breathed. "I can't believe the Gate is always here. Don't people ever sense it?"

"Did you?" asked Magda.

"No. But it looks so solid. Like, if I walked into one of the pillars, I'd feel it."

"You would. Now that you're marked, your senses can detect what's there. Ordinary humans don't have a clue."

"This Gate opens directly into my territory," said Shade. "My home is not far."

"*This* Gate? There are more?"

"There are several. Some are used more than others. This is the southern-most entrance. It is my misfortune that it opens into the coldest part of the human realm."

"Coldest?" Raya laughed. "You're kidding. This is nothing. There are *way* colder places than this. You're lucky the Gate doesn't open into the North Pole. You'd definitely be wearing a shirt then."

"Doubtful," muttered Magda under her breath. Shade looked aghast.

"Colder than this? How do you humans bear it?"

"Plus, it's totally dark for six months of the year." Raya caught Magda looking at her quizzically. "What? They had National Geographic magazines at the hospital."

"The sooner I get home, the better." Shade turned to Magda. "As ever, Gatekeeper, it was a pleasure to see you."

The kobold bowed from her waist.

"Thank you, my Lord. Look after our guest. And Raya, it was an honour to meet you."

Suddenly, Raya didn't want to leave.

"I need to know more about my mother," she said. The kobold patted her hand.

"If you don't find the answers you're looking for in Nush'aldaam, you can come back and find me. I'm always here."

Impulsively, Raya reached down and gave the Gatekeeper a hug.

"Thank you," she whispered fiercely. "For looking after me." She straightened and looked Shade in the eye. "I'm ready."

He walked through the Gate, his feet melting the snow, until he stepped through the pillars into Nush'aldaam. He waited while Raya hovered at the threshold for a brief second. Then she, too, left the human world behind.

Fifteen

The warm night air caressed her skin like a cashmere blanket. Raya slipped off her coat, then her sweater. She stood in her vest top letting the scents and sounds of this new world wash over her.

It's just a grassy meadow, she thought. *Yet it feels so different. And I feel different.*

Butterflies danced in her stomach. Her skin tingled and her heart was light with an emotion she had never felt before. It took her a moment to identify it.

It was joy.

She spread her arms and closed her eyes. Shade watched, amused.

"Would you like to roll around in the grass?" he suggested. She stuck her tongue out.

"How can you be so foul-tempered when you breathe *this* in all day?"

"I have exacting standards. People disappoint me."

"Yeah, well, if I lived here I'd be like Mother Theresa."

"She is a saint?"

"According to some people. Wow, is it dawn already?"

A sliver of sun was peeking over the horizon. A chorus of birdsong started up as the sky began to lighten.

Raya glanced behind her towards the Gate. It was still night on the other side. Time obviously worked differently here.

"This is my favourite time of day," said Shade. And though she could never imagine him looking outright cheerful, his face did seem more relaxed. She smiled at him shyly.

"Nush'aldaam seems very beautiful," she offered. He gazed at her for a long moment and the butterflies in her stomach started their jig again.

"May I show you my land from the air?"

"Um…"

Being in his arms didn't feel like a smart move to Raya. She took an involuntary step backwards, cursing herself as his expression hardened.

"You have no need to worry. I will not touch you any more than is strictly necessary."

He let his shadows form around them and dark tendrils snaked round her waist. They held her snugly but didn't squeeze. When he beat his wings and lifted from the ground, she rose too, separated from him by several feet of thin air.

"Woah!" She clutched the dusky band around her, not feeling secure in the least.

"Be calm. I will not let you fall."

"Easy for you to say."

Suddenly, she regretted not being in his arms. It seemed way safer than being held by mere smoke.

"Look down, halfling."

She did so, and gasped. Shade had flown them so high, Nush'aldaam was laid out below them like a map. Light crept across the landscape, chasing the dark away as dawn fully broke.

"If you look to the west, do you see the faint glow?" Shade pointed. "That is the reflection from the Gilded Palace in the heart of Nush'aldaam. It is empty now. But for a thousand years it was inhabited by Emperor Mazhab, the Golden One. His territory was large and he delegated rule over key parts of it to trusted lieutenants. My father was one of them. He settled the land to the south. It is called Nurhan, green and fertile, full of valleys and meadows."

Raya shaded her eyes, following the line of green all the way to the horizon.

"It's beautiful. Is that the sea over there?"

"The Ocean of Whispers. The coastal territory belongs to my rival Salaq. He is Lord of the Marid, as was his father before him. He is very powerful. But control of the coast isn't enough for him. When Mazhab died, he made it clear he wanted the throne for himself. He wants all of Nush'aldaam."

"How come there's no proper heir?"

"There was. Kamran, the son of Mazhab. We were friends, we practically grew up together. But he died."

Shade stopped. His face held no expression but in the light of dawn, Raya could sense his sadness. She tried to distract him.

"So you hold the south. Salaq has the coast. Where does Aelfric hang out?"

Shade pointed.

"He controls Feyir in the east of the empire."

Raya squinted.

"It looks like one big forest."

"It is extremely beautiful, mostly woodland with grass plains and several rivers. Feyir used to be home to both jinn and fae. As cousins we have co-existed for many centuries. But time passed and the population became predominantly fae. They wanted autonomy, so Mazhab gave them Feyir on condition they would remain loyal to the empire." Shade's face darkened. "But now Aelfric is overstepping. Kamran never did trust him."

"You think maybe Aelfric had something to do with his death?" Raya was genuinely curious but Shade didn't answer her question. Instead he gave her a stern look.

"You must never go into Feyir alone. Fae can be cold and cruel."

"Magda's fae. And she's lovely," Raya said indignantly.

"Not all fae are like Magda." Shade hesitated, then ploughed on. "There used to be a type of fae called a faerie. A tiny creature. I believe they are quite popular in human mythology?"

"Fairies!" Raya's eyes shone. "Yes, there are whole stories about them. They're real?"

"Not any more. Faeries could fly, you see. They had wings. And one day Aelfric became jealous. He decided if *he* could not fly, no fae would. He ordered all the faeries to be rounded up and imprisoned in glass jars."

Raya stared.

"That's fucking horrible. What happened?"

"He forgot about them. They say his Court is littered with jars containing faerie bones."

And people said *she* was nuts.

"He sounds psychotic."

"That is as good a description as any. His mind is twisted. So you understand why I do not wish him to form an alliance with Salaq? If we go to war, I would not just be fighting Salaq's forces. I would be fighting Aelfric's too. And if Salaq wins, if he becomes emperor, Aelfric will be his right-hand man. He will expand his influence beyond Feyir. I cannot allow that."

Raya swallowed. She was beginning to understand the stakes. The butterflies in her stomach had turned into rats and were gnawing at her with self-doubt. Was Shade really depending on *her* to help him win the throne?

"Anything else I should know?" she said faintly. "Like, who lives over there?" She gestured to the mountains in the north. They were a long way off, hundreds of miles. But she could see white at the top of the darkly brooding peaks.

"That is Palissandra. The realm of the Vetali. Separate to Nush'aldaam. You need not concern yourselves with them."

"Why? Who are they?"

"They are neither fae nor jinn and maintain strict neutrality in our affairs. We do not interfere with them, and they do not interfere with us."

"Couldn't you ask them to support you against Salaq?"

"They do not support anyone but themselves. Not even Salaq would be fool enough to request an alliance with them. The Vetali are even more dangerous than the fae."

"But what if…"

"Enough!" His voice roared through her and she practically felt her ear drums vibrating. "While you are here, you will cease questioning everything I say."

Her teeth were chattering so much she could barely get her words out.

"F… fuck… y… you."

His shadows tightened around her waist and yanked her close enough to see dark flecks in the depths of his furious azure gaze.

"If we are to maintain the illusion of a betrothal between us, then you must act the part. No woman of mine would continually second guess me."

"No woman would put up with your temper tantrums."

"Nevertheless, in public we must present a united front."

"Okay, okay. I get it. But when we're alone, you have to stop shouting at me."

"By the gods, are all humans as argumentative as you?"

"What's wrong with arguing? This isn't some weird backwards world where women aren't allowed to speak, is it? Because if it is, I'm out of here. I've already spent ten years being told what to do."

"Women can live as they please. But astonishing as it might seem, the women in my life try *not* to anger me."

"Clearly you haven't met the right woman yet."

"On that, halfling, we are agreed. For now, we will settle for a crash course in protocol. And..." his eyes flickered over her clothing, "...some more appropriate attire."

Raya's cheeks reddened. She knew she looked like shit, but he didn't have to make it so obvious.

"Fine. Where are we going?"

His wings flared as he turned his face to the south.

"Home."

Sixteen

'Home' was a massive stone castle perched at the top of a hill. One side was built right to the edge of a sheer drop. Hundreds of metres below, a river thundered through a valley like a rafter's white water dream.

There was a platform jutting out over the abyss and this was where Shade alighted. He set Raya down, the shadow bonds melting from her immediately. She peeked over the side nervously. There were no guard-rails. One wrong step and it was instant death.

She scooted after Shade as he strode into the room beyond. A bedroom, she saw. Strike that. *His* bedroom. At least, she assumed it was his bedroom because there was a half-naked woman lying languidly on the bed among tangled silken sheets.

Shade stopped.

"Leona. What are you doing here?"

"My Lord, you said I could stay as long as I wanted." The red-haired beauty ran her eyes over Raya. "I did not realise you would be bringing company back."

She slid out of bed, not bothering to cover herself. She wore nothing but a sheer chemise through which her body was clearly visible.

So this was Leona. No wonder Shade dreamed about her.

Raya tried to look anywhere but at the woman's breasts. They were magnificent. Shade didn't seem to notice. He was obviously used to half-naked women wandering about his bedroom.

"Leona, this is Raya. The one I told you about."

"Nice to meet you, Raya."

Leona's bright green eyes examined her with frank curiosity and Raya was embarrassed at how she must look.

"Hi. Um, sorry to disturb you."

"Not at all. I'll leave you both together. No doubt you have things to discuss."

"Actually I could use your help, Leona." Shade gestured at Raya. "With this. Clothes and such."

"It may take some work, my Lord." Leona's tone was doubtful.

"I need her to *look* like a Vulcani, even if she can't *act* like one. Yet."

"Hey, I'm standing right here!"

Shade ignored her.

"Give her a bath. And do something with her hair. I will be back shortly."

Shade turned and dived full length through the entrance, his wings unfurling to carry him out over the chasm and up into the air.

There was a short silence as Leona and Raya sized each other up.

"Well. I have my orders." There was a trace of bitterness in Leona's voice. Raya didn't blame her.

"Look, I can bathe myself, thanks. Just point the way."

Leona waved her hand.

"Through there. There's plenty of soap and cleansing lotions." She looked Raya up and down. "Use it all. Twice."

Cheeky bitch. She wasn't wrong though. Raya went through to the bathroom and the first thing she saw was her reflection in a floor-to-ceiling mirror. She stared at herself. Dear God.

Her hair was matted and there were dark hollows under her eyes. She was still wearing the same baggy clothes from the fight with the jotnar, and somehow she'd managed to tear a big hole in the trousers which she hadn't even noticed till now.

No wonder Shade had used his shadows to carry her. Compared to Leona, she was about as enticing as week-old cat food.

And that's how I want it. Right?

Shaking off the thought, she inspected the bath. It wasn't so much a bath as a small swimming pool set into the floor with steps down into it. There was seating round the edge but she could see immediately if she filled it to the brim, the water would almost cover her head.

And how on earth *did* you fill it? There was an array of buttons and knobs around the side.

Throwing caution to the winds, she pushed and twisted all of them. Hot water gushed into the bath at impressive speed. By dint of trial and error, she managed to get it half full in a short space of time.

She upended every bottle she could find until the bubbles reached a preposterous height and the room was filled with exotic aromas.

She took the photo of her mother and put it next to the sink. Then she dropped her clothes on the floor and stepped into the bath.

"Oh. My. God." She groaned with pleasure as she sank into the scented bubbles, the silken water caressing her skin.

Closing her eyes, she slid below the surface. *I wish I could just stay here forever,* she thought, as she floated languorously and held her breath for as long as she could.

When she surfaced, Leona was sitting on the edge of the bath.

"You look like you're enjoying yourself," she commented. Raya folded her arms around her breasts, even though Leona would have needed X-ray vision to see through the bubbles.

"I prefer to bathe by myself," she said stiffly, hoping she didn't sound like a prude.

"Really? I always prefer to bathe with someone else." Leona dipped a hand into the water. "I enjoy having someone wash my back."

"Is that what Shade does for you?" Raya hadn't meant to ask such a personal question, but she was curious. Shade acting like a boyfriend seemed such an unlikely prospect.

"Shade? Is that what you call him? How sweet. Yes, he washes my back. He also enjoys washing my front. Especially my…"

"Yeah, I get the picture. So you and him, you're an item?"

"An 'item'?"

"You're together. A couple."

Leona shrugged.

"He likes my company and I like his. We've been together for a while. But a creature as volatile as Shadeed… it's not wise to think you could ever tame him." Her gaze sharpened. "He is the kind of man who would drop someone without a second thought as soon as he's done with them."

Raya had the distinct impression she wasn't talking about herself.

"Well, don't worry about me. This is purely a business relationship. He wants the Vulcani to support him."

Leona tilted her head to one side.

"He came to my people with the same proposal. My father leads the si'lat, and his first instinct was to support Salaq. If I hadn't petitioned him to change his mind, Shadeed would have lost a valuable faction."

"So you formed an alliance with Shade?"

"One we cement most nights."

Raya blushed.

"Okay, I get it. You don't need to spell it out. I promise you, our partnership is for show only. Nothing like *your* alliance. You keep cementing it all you want. Now can I wash my hair in peace?"

Leona held her gaze for a moment longer, the challenge unmistakeable. As far as she was concerned, Shade was *her* territory. Then she rose to her feet gracefully.

"I will see you outside when you are ready."

Raya didn't bother replying. She closed her eyes and sank beneath the surface again. Leona had it wrong. She had no interest in a stupid turf war over an arrogant son-of-a-bitch like Shade.

When she finally got out of the bath, her skin was pink and her fingers wrinkled. Her hair had been washed three times and hung down to the small of her back in a damp curtain.

Her clothes had gone. Raya sincerely hoped Leona had burned them. She wrapped a big fluffy towel around herself and sighed happily. It was like being cosied up in a soft cloud.

Leona had laid a selection of clothes on the bed. All of them were long flowing dresses and mentally Raya discarded three of them straight off the bat.

"No way am I wearing anything see-through," she said firmly. "And while we're on the subject, can you put something on? Something else, I mean?"

Leona looked at her in surprise.

"One's body is a beautiful and natural thing. Are you so averse to showing it?"

"To complete strangers, yes."

"Is such prudery a human trait?"

"Mostly, yes. I like to keep my boobs covered."

"Boobs?"

"Look, what about this one? The orange. That looks all right." Raya picked up a garment in a shade of apricot and held it up to herself. It fell to the floor in soft folds. Leona nodded approvingly.

"A good choice. You have unusual colouring. The dress will bring out the warmth of your complexion. Try it on."

Leona waited expectantly and Raya rolled her eyes.

"Can you at least turn around?"

She glared until the other woman faced away, then let the towel drop. It was only when she pulled on the dress that she realised Leona had a clear line of sight from the mirror in the bathroom.

Dammit. A world away from the psychiatric ward and she was still fighting for privacy. One day, she vowed, she was going to have her own place with her own door that she could lock whenever she liked. From the inside. She pretended not to notice Leona's smirk.

"What do you think?"

The si'lat walked round her slowly. The sun-toned dress accentuated Raya's curves, hugging her bustline and leaving her arms bare before falling delicately from the waist to the floor. She nodded approvingly.

"You're starting to look the part. But you will need a lot of work to resemble a Vulcani."

"Why? Are they like supermodels or something?"

"I don't know half the words you use. But if you mean, are they very beautiful, then yes. They are extraordinary-looking." Leona regarded Raya and shook her head. "Shadeed must expect me to perform miracles."

Raya bit back a rude retort.

The next hour was one of the most miserable of her life. Her hair was pulled, primped, and curled to within an inch of its life. She swore repeatedly as her head was yanked back and forth by a succession of torturous styling implements.

Then Leona got out the make-up and Raya's heart sank even further. She fidgeted as the si'lat applied kohl and powder, finishing with a little rouge on her lips.

"Are you nearly done yet?" she complained.

"Anyone would think you've never used cosmetics before," Leona said tartly.

Raya stayed silent.

When Leona finally proclaimed she was finished, she bolted from her chair and went out through the doors to get some fresh air. Shutting her eyes against the bright sunshine, she filled her lungs and rolled her shoulders to ease the tension.

"Fuck, *nothing's* worth this."

But she was wrong.

When she opened her eyes, she saw Shade had glided down from nowhere and landed silently on the edge of the platform.

For a moment, neither of them moved. The breath caught in Raya's throat as Shade took in her appearance. His eyes deepened to a shade of sapphire she'd never seen before. It seemed as if he tried to speak, but words failed him.

And in that moment, she knew the suffering had *totally* been worth it.

Seventeen

Shade broke the spell by striding past her. She turned and called out.

"So what do you think? How do I look?"

"You look fine," he answered gruffly.

Fine?

She hurried after him as he reached his bedroom.

"Is it the make-up? It's too much, isn't it? I mean, I don't normally…" she skidded to a halt as she caught sight of herself in the mirror.

She blinked.

Her hair was plaited all about her head but left to fall in long luxurious curls down her back. Tiny diamond-tipped pins were worked into the braids, giving off sparkles every time she moved.

The darkness of her lashes was accentuated with kohl, making her eyes seem huge and exotic. And her lips were dark red, setting off the gold tint of her skin which seemed to glow against the apricot hue of her dress.

She stared at herself wordlessly.

"As I said, you look fine." The dismissiveness in Shade's voice jerked her back to reality.

"Yeah, it's… it's not bad."

"Are you pleased, my Lord?" Leona glided between them and Raya was relieved to see she had changed into a long green dress which covered all her important bits. "It took quite some time."

"She will suffice. I am grateful to you, Leona. You may return to your own quarters now if you wish."

If Leona was put out at being dismissed this way, she didn't show it.

"Of course. And the halfling is to stay here?"

"For now. I will find her some rooms later. Come, Raya. We must go."

"Go where?"

She ignored the high-heeled sandals Leona had picked out and pulled on a pair of soft-soled shoes. She'd never worn heels before and the last thing she wanted was to fall flat on her face.

"We are meeting with the Vulcani council. They have agreed to discuss whether you can act as your mother's proxy until her return."

He strode back towards the platform and she jogged to keep up with him. Why did he always have to walk so fast? He halted suddenly.

"Raya..." he sounded uncharacteristically uncertain. "May I be permitted to carry you? Or would you prefer I used my shadows again?"

"Oh. Um. I guess carrying is okay. If you don't mind, that is."

"I do not mind."

He stepped close to her, his bare chest level with her face. A slow blush warmed her cheeks and he hesitated.

"Perhaps I should..."

Shadows swirled around him, and suddenly he was wearing a black tunic. It strained over his muscles but at least he was covered. Raya cleared her throat.

"Thank you."

He scooped her up, one arm under her legs and the other supporting her back. She was reminded of the first time he'd carried her like this, when she'd barely been conscious and thought she was hallucinating.

He leapt out over the chasm. There was a moment of weightlessness when gravity seemed to have ignored them.

And then they dropped, the wind streaming through her hair as they plunged in freefall.

Strangely, she wasn't scared. Not the way she had been when he'd dropped her from the sky in Norway. Instead of bone-freezing terror, her heart pounded in a glorious mix of adrenaline and exhilaration.

When Shade finally unfurled his wings and soared upward, she caught him smiling. It only lasted a second but the flash of uncomplicated joy on his face did something to her insides. She looked away.

"So where are we meeting the Vulcani?" she asked when she had her breath back.

"At the border with Feyir. When I told them I had found Aelah's daughter, they agreed immediately. But Raya, it is imperative you let me do the talking." His face was deadly serious. "They will want a demonstration of your Vulcani power and we must not give in to their pressure. Not until you're ready."

"Okay. I'll just keep quiet and look pretty."

Shade didn't answer. He flew east in silence, and Raya saw the lines of tension around his mouth. This meeting was really important, she realised. She vowed not to fuck it up.

They landed at the edge of the forest. The line of trees was so thick, it was almost like a barrier. She could hear birdsong and buzzing insects, but it was hard to see into the dark interior.

No-one was there to meet them.

"Where are…"

"Quiet."

Shade waited motionlessly and Raya forced herself to do the same. The silence stretched.

Suddenly she caught movement from the corner of her eye. She turned, squinting, trying to make out what was happening. A gasp escaped her lips as the scene in front of her changed. Or maybe she was simply seeing what had been there all along.

The innocuous pattern of leaves shifted imperceptibly. A random wall of foliage morphed into figures and faces. A curve of branch transformed into a set of shoulders. A peculiar looking bush unfolded and stood up. It was like a giant optical illusion coming to life in front of them.

A dozen figures stepped out of the trees. Shade nodded at them.

"Council members. Thank you for meeting with us."

Raya looked at them curiously. There were males and females, all as attractive as each other with long, golden limbs and perfect glossy hair. They were willowy and tall, though not as tall as Shade. Their ears were delicately pointed and they seemed insubstantial, as if a good puff of wind would blow them away. But she sensed that wasn't the case.

They all stared intently at her with their strange marmalade-coloured eyes. There was something steely about them. A ferocity she'd seen in the photo of her mother. And she knew instinctively they weren't to be trifled with. The Vulcani were dangerous.

Anxiety gnawed at her stomach.

"Lord Shadeed," greeted one of the males. He looked fractionally more mature than the others, though it was hard to tell their ages. For all she knew, he was a thousand years old.

So much you don't know, her inner voice said derisively. *And you think you're going to pretend to be one of them?*

"Loris, this is Aelah's daughter. Raya, this is the head of the Vulcani council. Loris was your mother's right-hand man."

Plastering a smile on her face, Raya held out her hand. The fae looked at it in silence, and she dropped it.

"Pleased to meet you," she said instead. Loris examined her. She felt the sharpness of his stare and tried not to look away.

"You have something of Aelah about you, I suppose. Around the nose and brow. Not your eyes or ears though. I suppose it was too much to hope you would escape your father's features."

He seemed to be expecting a response.

"Um, yes. Sorry about that."

"What do you know of your mother, child?"

"Nothing, really. She gave me up when I was born."

"You have Vulcani abilities?"

Shade intervened.

"She has inherited Aelah's talent, I assure you. She is more Vulcani than human. And as Aelah's progeny, she wishes to take her mother's place as clan leader until she returns."

The Vulcani's expression hardened and his glance raked Raya from head to toe.

"You dare to presume you can lead us? A half-human?"

"It is her birthright..." Shade began, but the fae held up his hand.

"I am talking to her. Answer me, child. What makes you think you can take Aelah's place?"

"I..." Raya had no idea what to say. She knew so little about her mother. But she did know one thing: Aelah was a fighter and no way would she let herself by intimidated by this skinny dude. "I want to honour my mother's legacy. She gave up everything to save me. I want to prove I'm worthy of her sacrifice."

Was it her imagination, or did the fae's expression soften slightly? Shade intervened.

"And, of course, under fae lore it is her right."

Loris snapped his gaze to the jinn.

"And why do you care so much about Vulcani affairs, Lord Shadeed? Is it to do with the battle over the throne, perhaps? Do you think by bringing us someone purporting to be Aelah's daughter you can win our favour? Convince us to rebel against Aelfric and support *your* claim instead?"

"No, not at all." Shade paused, weighing his words carefully. "But as Aelah's proxy, Raya would be entitled to pledge Vulcani allegiance to whomever she likes. And she has formed an alliance with me."

"An alliance?"

"She is my betrothed."

Shadeed spoke matter-of-factly, as if he'd said something as banal as 'she likes chocolate,' but hearing the words made Raya jump.

Loris fell back a step, his face a mask of outrage.

"This is a bold move, Lord Shadeed. Forcing a schism among the fae. Aelah would not countenance division."

"Aelah would never have supported Aelfric, you know that as well as I do, Loris. If she were here, she would be pledging for me. Do you really think it wise to give Aelfric more power? Because I assure you, if Salaq wins the throne, Aelfric will run unchecked over Nush'aldaam like a disease."

"But to force a betrothal to plead your cause…!"

"I assure you, no-one has been forced to do anything," Shade growled.

A woman with skin the colour of honey stepped forward.

"Perhaps on this point we should hear from Raya?" she suggested. "Hello, Raya. I'm Kaemari. Tell us, are you betrothed to Lord Shadeed of your own free will?"

"Of course," Raya said firmly. "He asked me and I said yes."

"And may I enquire why?"

"*Why* I said yes?"

"Yes. Why are you with Lord Shadeed?"

"Um…" Raya's mind was whirling. Shade had told her to let *him* do the talking, She hadn't prepared for twenty questions. She was conscious that all eyes were on her. What the fuck was she supposed to say?

"In your own time," prompted Kaemari. Raya took a breath.

"I'm with him because he's a good person. Brave and honourable, though he does his best to hide it. I've never met anyone like him." *Well, that was true.* "He found me when I had lost all hope. And he rescued me when I needed rescuing most. I don't know much about your problems or politics, but I *do* know that Shade would be an excellent emperor."

Shade concealed his surprise, taken aback by the conviction of her words. But Loris still wasn't satisfied.

"This is all well and good, but it is entirely academic. The girl has not yet convinced us she is Aelah's daughter." The Vulcani pinned Raya with his amber gaze. "Show us what you can do, child."

"She has only just arrived in this realm, she is acclimatizing," Shade interrupted. "Once she is rested she will demonstrate her abilities."

"When will that be?"

"Perhaps in about…"

"Again, I am not addressing you, Lord Shadeed." Loris narrowed his eyes. "I want to know from her own mouth. Tell me, girl. When can you show us you are a true Vulcani?"

Raya hesitated, and Shade willed her to name a date far in advance. Allow them some time to prepare. A month, at least. His heart sank as she answered.

"Maybe next week?"

Loris nodded.

"One week. So be it."

"And I would be honoured if you would mark the occasion by attending a feast at my castle," Shade said smoothly, hiding his dismay. "All Vulcani dignitaries are welcome. They can meet Aelah's daughter for themselves."

"If she *is* Aelah's daughter." Loris looked entirely unconvinced. "But we accept your invitation. I will send someone with you to make the necessary arrangements. Torven!"

A figure melted from the trees. Raya could have sworn he hadn't been there a moment ago. Another fae, she guessed, but he didn't look like the Vulcani. He was blond for a start, and broad of shoulder. His ears were more oval than pointed, his features boyish, open and honest. When he caught her gaze, he grinned straight at her, his hazel eyes twinkling. It was the first time anyone in Nush'aldaam had looked happy to see her. She found herself smiling back.

"Torven will accompany you back to your castle if that meets with your approval," Loris told Shade. "He will oversee food preparation and security arrangements."

"I'm sure we can make those arrangements without assistance," Shade said tersely.

"Nevertheless. We wish Torven to go on ahead."

"Very well." He hid his irritation. "We will see you there in seven days."

"Seven days. We look forward to confirming the girl's heritage. But Lord Shadeed, if this waif turns out *not* to be Aelah's daughter, there will be repercussions. For both of you."

Shade narrowed his eyes at the implied threat and Raya held her breath. She didn't know what would happen if he lost his temper, but it probably wouldn't be anything good. He answered calmly.

"I understand."

The Vulcani melted back into the forest, disturbing not one leaf or twig as far as Raya could see. One minute they were there, the next they weren't.

As soon as they vanished, Shade turned on Raya.

"A week? A *week?* Are you insane?"

"I didn't know what to say! He put me on the spot!"

"Why did you not use your brain? We will need more than a week to..." Shade abruptly realised they still had company. "Let us continue this conversation at the castle. Mr Torven, can you find your own way there?"

"Aye, don't mind me," said the young man cheerfully. His accent was gently lilting, pleasant to the ear. "I have my horse. It'll take a few hours but I'll be there by sundown."

"Horse?" Raya's eyes widened. "You have a horse?"

"I have several. Do you ride, my Lady?"

"I used to."

For a moment, Raya was wistful. She'd had riding lessons when she was young. She'd become quite good, too. She'd hoped one day she could have a horse of her own. Before her dreams were all ripped away.

"You never forget, no matter how long it's been since you sat on a horse. Would you like to try, my Lady?"

"Raya." Shade's voice was cold. "We do not have time for this. Let us go."

Raya lifted her chin. A wave of resentment swept through her. Everything she'd done since she'd left the damned hospital was for him, and he hadn't even said thank you.

"Actually, I'll go with Torven, if that's okay with you?" She looked hopefully at the fae and he nodded.

"You can ride Martha, she's a good mare."

"Out of the question," Shade snapped. "She will come with me."

Want to bet? Raya treated him to a sweet, innocent smile.

"But *darling,* I would like to see more of Nush'aldaam."

His lips tightened with the effort of not roaring in anger.

"I only wish to keep you safe, *beloved.*"

"I'm sure I'll be perfectly safe, *sweetheart.*" Raya was suddenly enjoying herself. "Torven will look after me. Won't you, Torven?"

"I will indeed, Lord Shadeed," Torven said quickly. "And after all, your Lady is Vulcani. There is not much out here that could alarm a fire fae."

Shade raised an eyebrow meaningfully at Raya but she ignored him.

"How long will it take to get back, Torven?"

"It's an easy ride. Four hours at most. If we are not back by then, Lord Shadeed, you may have my head."

Shade glowered at the shorter man.

"You can count on it."

His shadows unfurled, deliberately engulfing both men in a cloud of darkness. By the time it cleared, Shade was already a dot in the sky. Raya was impressed that Torven seemed unruffled by the display of power.

"This way, my Lady," he said casually. He walked into the trees.

Raya hesitated, remembering Shade's warning. But he'd told her not to go into the forest on her own and she *wasn't* on her own, was she? She followed.

Eighteen

Strangely, what had seemed an impenetrable wall of foliage was less so when she was standing inside it. A path ran through the trees, dappled with sunlight. Birds swooped and trilled, and the whole thing felt magical.

She caught up with Torven.

"Shade – I mean, Lord Shadeed – told me the forest was dangerous. It doesn't feel dangerous."

Torven cast her a glance.

"It isn't dangerous to fae. Especially one with the power of the Vulcani."

"I guess." Raya shifted uncomfortably. "He said fae were cruel. But you don't seem unkind."

"He was probably speaking of the elven, my Lady. Some are very capricious."

"Elven?"

"The fair folk. The highborn. Glamorous but volatile. Our king is an elven."

"Aelfric? I heard he was unstable."

"Aye. He's unpredictable."

"Is it true? About the fairy bones?"

"That, and more. It isn't helped by the fact that he's surrounded by fawners who egg him on."

"What about you? Are you elven?"

He laughed out loud.

"No, my Lady. And if you ever see elven folk, you'll realise what a daft question that was. Here we are."

He led them into a clearing where a cottage stood. Smoke came from the chimney and flowers curled around the windows. It looked like a fairy tale – until she saw what was lying outside the door.

A wolf.

A large silver-grey wolf with yellow eyes. It rose to all fours when it saw them and Raya froze. The thing was huge.

"What should we do?" she quavered.

"Stand still, or it may eat us."

"Eat us?"

"Aye. Bones and all. That's a dyrewolf. One of the fastest, strongest creatures in Nush'aldaam."

Heart pounding, Raya tried not to breathe. The wolf prowled towards them, eyes locked on hers. Its shoulder came to above her waist. If it were to stand on its hind legs, it would tower over her.

It sniffed at her hand and she tensed, sure it was going to bite her. Then it turned to Torven. A low growl issued from its throat. It sank onto its haunches, readying itself to pounce.

"Torven! Watch out!"

In the next second the wolf had launched itself at Torven and he went tumbling backwards. Man and wolf rolled in the grass as Raya watched in horror.

It took her a moment to realise Torven was laughing.

"Get off me you soppy old thing." He rubbed the dyrewolf behind its ears and the beast tried to lick him.

"Hang on. Is he some kind of pet?" said Raya disbelievingly.

"No, not a pet. Just a friend."

"You said he was going to eat us!"

"Sorry. Couldn't resist." Torven smiled up at her, his lap full of wolf. "Come and be introduced. Raya, this is Gray. Gray, Raya. She's a friend." The wolf glanced at her and it seemed to Raya he had the most knowing eyes she'd ever seen on an animal.

Cautiously, she knelt next to them in the grass.

"Can I stroke him?"

"Aye. He knows you can be trusted."

She rubbed her hand across Gray's coat. The fur was soft and thick, and her fingers sank into it. The wolf's jaw dropped open as its tongue lolled out contentedly. Raya couldn't help noticing the teeth.

"He seems very nice."

"Don't let his goofy face fool you, my Lady. Dyrewolves are dangerous, and fiendishly intelligent. If you have one hunting you, you may as well kill yourself there and then because it won't give up until it's caught you."

"So how come *this* one's tame?"

"He's not tame. I told you, he's a friend. But he's still a wild animal. Don't worry, you're safe as long as you're with me."

"Why does he listen to you?"

"I'm Sylvan, my Lady. I have empathy with living creatures. I see their auras so I know how they're feeling. Whether they're scared or in pain. I can also tweak their feelings a little. Make them less aggressive. Encourage them to trust me."

"That is seriously impressive. You're a regular Doctor Doolittle."

"I don't think I've heard of him. Is he another Sylvan?"

"Definitely. Wait, does that mean you can see *my* aura?"

"I would never invade a lady's privacy like that." He gave a cheerful grin. "Not without an invitation. I only see auras when I'm specifically looking for them."

He gave the wolf a final pat.

"Time to go, you big softy. I won't be around for a few days so keep an eye on my cottage, will you?"

The wolf barked, a throaty sound that made Raya jump.

"Does he understand you?" she asked curiously.

"Only when it suits him."

The wolf got to his feet. He trotted into the woods and was quickly swallowed up by the trees.

"This way, my Lady. Come and meet Martha."

The stables were round the back of the cottage A small, sleepy looking mare was thoughtfully munching hay, while a large bay tossed its head next to her.

"I'll ride Strider. Let's saddle up. Time's wasting. Your jinn will have my guts for garters if we're late."

Raya felt a momentary panic. She hadn't ridden for ten years, what was she thinking? But as Torven tacked up the horses, she saw how quietly Martha stood. She also noticed how the young man whispered to them both, running his strong fingers deftly along their necks.

He waited patiently as she took hold of a stirrup, dithering over how best to boost herself into the saddle.

In the end, Torven solved the problem for her. He grasped her by the hips and lifted her off the ground.

"Excuse me, my Lady," he said as he settled her easily into the saddle. Flustered, she picked up the reins and was pleased she remembered how to hold them correctly.

"I'm not really dressed for riding," she said, as her dress rucked up. Thankfully it had enough folds to cover most of her legs.

"Martha will do the work. Just sit comfortably. Let's go."

He vaulted onto the bay and they headed out of the woods and into the sunshine.

Out on the plains, with the sun's warmth on her face and the rhythmic gait of the horse swaying beneath her, Raya felt an unexpected spark of contentment.

For the first time since Shade had rescued her, she finally felt as if her brain was knitting back together.

Nineteen

Raya was grateful that Torven felt no urge to make small talk. They rode in companionable silence for a long while before she spoke.

"It's Raya," she said.

"I beg pardon, my Lady?"

"My name. Not 'my Lady'. Just Raya."

"In that case, I'm Tor. Only my mother and the Vulcani council leader call me Torven. I'm not sure which of them is scarier."

She giggled.

"Loris did seem terrifying. I can't believe he took orders from my mother." A thought struck her. "Did you know her? Aelah?"

"No. I was a bairn when she left Nush'aldaam. But I heard all the stories." He glanced over at her. "She was known for her outspokenness. She hated injustice and she always took the side of the weak. Of course, she was a thorn in Aelfric's side."

"I thought Aelfric liked her? Magda, the Gatekeeper, said he had a thing for her."

"Maybe at first. And maybe she thought she could redeem him. Change him into someone different. But she gave up in the end. It's almost impossible to turn someone into something they're not."

Raya fell silent.

Wasn't that what *she* was trying to do? Become someone she wasn't? What would happen in seven days when she tried and failed to summon her powers in front of the Vulcani council?

Tor broke into her thoughts.

"May I ask *you* something my La... I mean, Raya?"
"Sure."
"What is the human world like?"
"Completely unlike this. Normal."
"Normal?"
"You know. Ordinary. Anyway, I'm the wrong person to ask. I spent most of my time there locked up."

Tor was shocked.

"You were a prisoner?"

"Sort of. Something bad happened and everyone thought I'd done it." A wave of guilt and shame washed over her. "I spent ten years arguing I was innocent but I found out recently they were right. I *did* do it. And I won't ever forgive myself."

There was a long silence. Then Tor spoke quietly.

"What did Lord Shadeed mean when he said a week wasn't enough time?"

Raya stared straight ahead, not knowing how to answer.

"He just wants me to rest properly, I think."

"Are you having trouble controlling your power?"

She felt a flutter of panic. Tor seemed nice but he still worked for the Vulcani.

"Of course not. Everything's fine."

"Only, sometimes when our minds are tired and confused, our bodies don't do as they're told. I imagine it's overwhelming, being brought into a world you know nothing about." He shrugged casually. "If you want, I could take a look at your aura and maybe smooth out any rough edges."

Raya glanced at Tor but he kept his gaze steadfastly on the road ahead. She felt a rush of gratitude. He was giving her a reasonable excuse for why her powers were dormant and offering to fix it.

Shade wouldn't like it. But Shade didn't need to know.

"That… that would be great."

"No problem. Perhaps tomorrow? After I've made a list of requisitions for the kitchen?"

"Thank you. I mean it, thank you so much. Honestly, I could kiss you."

Tor ducked his head, a little pink about the ears, and Raya realised he was blushing.

"How about a gallop?" he asked abruptly, changing the subject. Without waiting for an answer, he spurred the bay forward and Martha followed.

Raya gathered the reins and leaned forward as she'd been taught to do all those years ago. She held tight, terrified she'd fall off.

But the mare's stride was smooth and balanced, and Raya found galloping was no effort at all. By the time she'd caught up with Tor, she was grinning from ear to ear. Any awkwardness was forgotten.

"That was brilliant." She laughed, breathless, and patted Martha's neck. "I'd forgotten how amazing it is to ride. I wonder if Shade has any horses?"

"Lord Shadeed? I think he prefers flying."

"I suppose. And flying is amazing too. But there's something about being on a horse."

"Aye, there is." He paused, then asked casually, "So you're betrothed to Lord Shadeed? That's quite a coup."

"What do you mean?"

"Many ladies have tried. Many have won his affection, but not for long. And never long enough to take his name. He must think a lot of you."

Many? She frowned. How many, exactly?

Tor mistook her silence for offense.

"Apologies, Raya. I didn't mean to speak flippantly about your intended. I just meant, you must be very special to him."

Yeah, right.

"Tell me more about Nush'aldaam. It seems like a fairy tale. Everyone has such amazing abilities."

"Does magic not exist in your world, then?"

"No. I mean, people *say* they can do magic but it's mostly just tricks. Illusions. But here, people can fly. Or make fire with just a thought. Or communicate with animals." She shook her head. "In a normal world, that's superhero stuff."

"To us, they're natural abilities. But some are stronger than others. Your mother, for example, was extremely powerful but many Vulcani can only conjure a single weak flame. Lord Shade, as you call him, is the only Ifrit powerful enough to fly. Is it not the same in the human world?"

"Yes, it is. Some people are stronger or smarter than others. I never thought of it like that."

"And then, of course, there are those that envy the gifts of others and wish to control them. Like Aelfric."

He stopped suddenly, and Raya looked at him curiously. "What?"

Tor turned to face her, his expression serious.

"Please do not repeat the things I say in public, Raya. Out here, in the open, we are safe but in other places there are ears always listening for signs of dissent. Aelfric will not tolerate subversion. Other fae who have criticised him have disappeared. I don't want that to happen to you." He gave a crooked smile. "Or me."

"You don't like the boss. I get it. Your secret's safe with me. But if he's such a bad guy, how come he's in charge?"

Tor shrugged.

"Elven are powerful fae. They bend reality around them. Make you feel one thing, or see another. It's called a glamour. All elven can do it, to some extent. But Aelfric's glamours are the strongest and darkest. He can create things so real you can touch them. Instil any emotion in you. Reduce you to helplessness. And if he wants you to think you're dying, you'll die."

"But Vulcani throw fire, you can control animals…"

"No defence at all against someone who can get inside your head."

Raya shuddered.

"How could my mother have been attracted to that?"

"Don't judge her too harshly. The elven aren't called 'the beautiful folk' for nothing."

"I hope I never run into them."

"Don't worry. You're not likely to. They tend to stay close to Feyir. Now, Raya of the Normal World, tell me about some of the marvels where you come from."

They spent the rest of the journey talking and laughing. Tor was pleasant company and Raya relaxed with him. The fact that he was easy on the eye didn't hurt. And when she spied the castle in the distance, she was almost disappointed the ride was coming to an end.

"Nearly there," Tor said cheerfully. "And well before sundown. Looks like I'll get to keep my head after all."

The road to the castle became more populated. In the outlying villages they passed carts and donkeys laden with bags, and people carrying baskets on their heads. Children smiled and waved from huts where women were cooking over open fires. Goats and sheep seemed to wander at random, and dogs barked as they passed.

As they drew closer to the castle, the villages gave way to the suburbs and finally the main town. Houses became larger and more ornate, interspersed with shops and cafes. Groups of people were gathering after a day's work, smoking pipes or sitting at tables outside the taverns with a well-earned ale.

When they reached the town square, Raya saw bunting had been strung between the buildings. Every door had a banner or streamers hung from it, and children chased each other with brightly coloured balloons and flags.

"Is something going on?" she asked. "It looks like a celebration."

"Aye, they're getting ready for the Melae. It happens every year to welcome in the spring. There's feasting and merry-making across Nush'aldaam. You should go. It's quite a party."

"I'd have to check with Shade."

"Bring him too."

Shade? Letting his hair down? She suppressed a grin.

"Maybe."

The road turned sharply upwards and they left the townsfolk behind. From this angle the castle looked forbidding. Its turrets and towers stabbed unyieldingly into the sky, more fortress-like than it had appeared from the air.

They trotted the last few hundred yards to the front entrance, a massive gate guarded by a dozen soldiers. Raya looked at them curiously. Some were Ifrit, judging by the shadows that curled off them. Others she wasn't sure about.

She expected them to challenge her and Tor, but they stood aside, nodding respectfully. They'd obviously been primed for their arrival.

In the courtyard, Tor helped her dismount. She put her hands on his shoulders as he lifted her down, effortlessly setting her on her feet. He smelled of fresh-cut grass and she wondered if that was true of all Sylvan, or just him.

"Thank you," she said, her voice a touch husky.

"It was my pleasure, my Lady," he said.

"I told you, call me…"

He leaned forward quickly and whispered into her ear.

"I think in public it's best if I observe protocol." He grinned at her conspiratorially and she grinned back.

I've made a friend. The unexpected thought made her warm.

"Raya."

She jerked as she heard Shade's disapproving voice. His tone wasn't quite raw enough to send vibrations through her skull, but it wasn't far off.

"Lord Shadeed," said Tor respectfully. "Delivered safe and sound, as promised."

Shade looked from one to the other, his eyes narrowed. Raya quailed inwardly. He looked calm but she was starting to know how to read him. He wasn't happy. At least he sounded civil enough.

"I will have someone take care of your horses and show you to your quarters, Mr Torven. I trust you will be comfortable in the servants' wing?"

"He's not a servant, he's an advisor," Raya said indignantly. "He should stay in proper guest quarters."

"No, no, Lord Shadeed is right," Tor interjected. "And in any case I will need to liaise with the staff for next week's banquet. It's quite all right, my Lady."

One of the soldiers took hold of the horses' reins and nodded at Tor to follow. Raya hesitated for a moment, then ran after him, acutely aware Shade was glaring at her. Fuck him. She made a show of stroking Martha, giving the mare a farewell pat.

"You haven't forgotten about your promise? To help me with my power?" She kept her voice low, praying superhearing wasn't one of Shade's many abilities.

"Tomorrow. Come find me." Tor glanced back at Shade. "If you're sure your betrothed will not object?"

"It's fine. He'll understand."

"Very well then. Tomorrow."

She watched him go regretfully, knowing she was going to have to face Shade whether she wanted to or not. He wasn't going to let her forget she'd defied him by travelling with Tor.

She straightened her shoulders.

Okay. Let's get this over with.

Twenty

She walked slowly, hoping he might have cooled down in the hours it had taken her to arrive at the castle. But as she got closer she could see shadows curling around him, flicking back and forth like the tail of an irritated panther.

The courtyard, which had been filled with servants and soldiers, quietened as everyone suddenly discovered they needed to be somewhere else.

So they all knew about his temper, then.

She raised her chin defiantly and met his stare.

"What? I'm here, aren't I?"

"You deliberately disobeyed me."

"Disobeyed?" She gave a bark of laughter. "I don't do well with orders. You know that."

"You put yourself at risk. It would have been safer to fly with me."

"I was perfectly safe, thank you. As you can see."

He ground his teeth in frustration. Why did she not understand?

"It is not just that." His hand closed over her arm and he jerked her closer, keeping his voice low. "Half the castle just saw you ride in with another man. Alone."

"So?" His closeness was unsettling and she pulled against his grip. It was unyielding.

"You are meant to be betrothed to me. If anyone suspects it is a ruse…"

"The only one making this look like a ruse is you," Raya hissed angrily. "Always glaring at me, yelling at me, pulling me around. At least Tor treats me with respect. He's probably wondering why the fuck I'm betrothed to *you*."

Shade's gaze darkened to the blue of the deepest ocean. He dropped her arm abruptly.

"You think I care what that *boy* thinks?"

"He's not a boy, he's a man."

"A man?" Shade's lip curled in contempt. "He's barely old enough to grow hair on his face. Do you think him sweet? Kind? Are those the things you require in a lover? That Sylvan peasant could never satisfy you."

"How the fuck would you know?"

His eyes flared.

"I have seen you aroused. I know how passionate you can be."

"You're a bastard."

"Your appetites aside, we have a more pressing problem. Mr Torven's presence means we have to be on our guard. He will undoubtedly be reporting back to the Vulcani."

"Tor's not a spy."

"He works for the council."

"So what? All he'll tell them is that the Lord of Nurhan is an arrogant jerk."

His jaw tightened, and the shadows around his face darkened.

"I am more concerned with the fact that he will be expecting the Lord of Nurhan and his beloved to share the same chambers."

Raya narrowed her eyes.

"No way. I'm not sharing a room with you. We can say we're waiting till we're married or something."

"They will not believe that of me," he said dismissively. "I am Ifrit. Abstinence is not my way."

"And sharing a room with you isn't mine. Forget it. Anyway, I bet Leona wouldn't like it."

"On the contrary. She is very open-minded. There is more than enough room for all three of us."

Raya spluttered.

"I hope that's a joke."

His eyes gleamed.

"You may relax. Leona has her own rooms and my private chambers are big enough for both of us to keep our distance. Now come."

He strode towards a stone archway and she hurried to keep up.

"Where are we going?"

"To eat. You must be hungry. But you will change first. You have a certain odour of horse about you."

Great.

"Well, I certainly wouldn't want to embarrass you."

"On that, we are in agreement. You should be prepared for a certain amount of scrutiny."

"Scrutiny? You mean, like people staring at me?"

"They will be curious." He shrugged. "I have never been betrothed before."

"Well, that's not unusual, is it? You're what, in your twenties? Early thirties? Lots of people don't get engaged till they're…"

"I am four hundred years old."

She may have squeaked, she wasn't sure. *Four hundred?*

"So there's a bit of an age gap, then?" she said faintly.

"Do not worry. You are half fae, your own longevity will also be expanded. Fae can live for centuries."

She was still processing that revelation as he led her to a set of huge wooden doors flanked by soldiers. A smaller door was set into one of the bigger ones and a guard hurriedly pulled it open as they approached.

Raya stepped through, wondering why Shade hadn't simply flown them up to his chambers as he had done before. Then she realised. He wanted her to see his home.

And it was impressive. The forbidding exterior hid a warm and vibrant centre. A vaulted ceiling soared above them, the surface painted a deep cerulean blue with constellations picked out in glittering gems. The flagstones were made of polished creamy marble. A fire blazed in an enormous fireplace. Doors led in every direction, and people were constantly bustling through them.

"Are these all your servants?" Raya wondered.

"Some. Others are administrators, advisors, visitors, bureaucrats. There is also a few of the local aristocracy who stay here at the castle when they have business to attend to."

"Any of them just plain old friends?"

He frowned, but was prevented from answering by a tall skinny man in a long black robe who approached them. Raya eyed him cautiously. He had 'butler' written all over him.

"Lord Shadeed, we do not normally see you in the public part of the castle."

"I am showing my intended around. Raya, this is Pasha, my chief steward. Pasha, this is Lady Raya of the Vulcani. You may let it be known that we are betrothed."

Pasha bent his head respectfully, but not before Raya caught the flash of surprise in his eyes.

"Lady Raya, welcome to Castle Elumina. We are honoured to have you."

"Castle Elumina? That's its name? It's lovely."

"Inform the kitchen we will dine within the hour," said Shade. "Nothing too rich. We'll take it in the night-garden."

"Of course, my Lord. I'll see to it."

There was a sweeping staircase to each side and Shade led her up the one to the right. People nodded respectfully as they passed. Raya was conscious of furtive glances being cast in her direction, and wondered if people assumed she was another of Shade's casual flings.

Or maybe she just looked a mess after riding for four hours. She sniffed furtively at her wrist. Shade was right. She smelled of horse.

They went through what felt like a maze of corridors. The walls were covered in rich panelling inlaid with gold filigree. Glass lamps placed at intervals gave out a warm light. Not powered by electricity, she saw, but a strange undulating glow that seemed more magical than technological.

Another set of stairs took them to the top of the castle. Here, skylights flooded the hallways with late afternoon sunlight and made her feel as if she was walking on air. Finally, they reached Shade's chambers.

He didn't have just one room, she realised. He had a whole suite of them. His quarters consisted of a dozen living areas, full of rich tapestries and jewel-coloured rugs. Floor cushions and sofas were scattered about. Large dishes full of fruit and candy were dotted everywhere.

Candy? Shade didn't look like he had a sweet tooth. Belatedly, she realised the treats were most likely for his visitors, not for him. His *female* visitors. She picked a perfumed scarf off the floor and raised an eyebrow at him.

"I probably should have had the place tidied," he acknowledged without a hint of embarrassment.

"Do you want to give this back to Leona?"

"It is not hers. The lady it belongs to left last week."

"Just how many girlfriends do you have?"

He gave her a sardonic look.

"Now that I am betrothed, none, of course."

"Yeah, right."

"Do not worry. I will keep my liaisons discreet."

He led her past his bedchamber, the one she'd already seen. The door was open and she stiffened at the sight of the large bed, but he didn't pause. He continued on to the next room.

It was a second bedroom, nearly as sumptuous as his, decorated in turquoise and silver with a circular bed taking up most of the middle of the floor. She eyed it cynically.

"Is this where you make your booty calls?"

"Excuse me?"

"Adjoining rooms. Is this where you keep your floozies? I mean, I'm surprised you don't just have a harem."

The corner of his lip tugged upwards.

"Harems were popular in my father's day. However, I prefer not to keep my women as sex slaves. It seems archaic. And unnecessary."

"How progressive of you."

"Do you not like these chambers?"

"They're not bad, I guess."

An understatement. They were a massive step up from the *last* room she'd called her own. One wall was taken up by a set of large wooden doors. Curiously, she pulled them open. Beyond was a space almost as big as the bedroom, crammed with clothes. Rail upon rail of dresses, tops, and skirts; shelves full of scarves, shoes and sandals; drawers stuffed full of jewellery. Raya's mouth dropped open.

"Oh. My. God."

"You may use anything in here. It is yours. I believe there are cosmetics and other female necessities in the bathroom."

"There's a bathroom as well?"

She ran back into the bedroom and spotted the door. Flinging it open, she stopped dead.

It was beautifully tiled in silver and aquamarine marble, with a sunken bath big enough to float in. But that wasn't what she was staring at.

The end wall was open to the elements, just like the one in Shade's bedchamber. But it was covered in bars.

Ornate, gold-coloured bars shaped into roses and birds which formed an elegant trellis over the opening, but bars nonetheless.

Her heart started to pound and she felt short of breath.

"Raya. Raya, what's wrong?" Shade was at her side in an instant. He frowned at her, perplexed.

"Bars. There are bars on the window." Her mouth felt slow and stupid.

"Of course. To keep my guests safe. I do not want anyone to fall."

Raya licked her lips, trying to moisten them. *It's not the same as the hospital. I'm not a prisoner.* But her heart didn't seem to hear what her head was telling her.

"There were bars at the hospital," she said faintly. He leaned forward to hear her. "Over the windows. The doors. There was a man. An orderly. His name was Griggs. He liked… he liked to push my face into the bars while he… while he touched himself."

The memory made her shudder.

Shade's hands closed into fists as he tried to control his anger. Too late.

Shadows started to boil from him, writhing into the room, growing with every breath. They were as dark as ebony, as dense as granite.

They smashed into the trellis, grasping the metal with smoky coils. Raya jumped as it groaned and bent under the immense pressure. With a thought, Shade wrenched the whole thing from the window and threw it out of the opening.

There was a moment's silence. Raya cast a look at Shade. His eyes were blazing bright blue and his lips were thin with fury.

"No more bars. Not ever," he told her.

And he stalked out, his shadows gathering around him like armour.

Twenty One

"So, four hundred years old?" Raya ventured. Shade seemed calm but smoke was still curling from him. She wanted to thank him for his empathy, for his outrage on her behalf, but she couldn't find the words.

"It is still young, for a jinn." Shade gestured around them. "What do you think of the garden?"

"I think it's beautiful. Why's it called the night-garden?"

"You will see after dusk," he replied enigmatically.

They were sitting in a pagoda in a green and luscious oasis bursting with flowers. The air was heavy with the scent of rose and jasmine. An ornamental pond at one side was filled with golden carp, a fountain at the other cascaded with water that changed colour constantly.

"My mother… my adopted mother, I mean, Caroline, she would have loved this. She was obsessed with plants and flowers."

"When she died, was she… I do not know what human customs are. Were her remains placed somewhere?"

"Her ashes are under a rose bush in a cemetery. Ross's too. I've never been there. I doubt they'd want me there after… after what I did."

She shied away from the memory, deliberately focusing on the beauty in front of her. Peacocks roamed the grounds, their haughty cries answered by exotic songbirds in the trees. Branches hung low with the weight of fruit; apple, pear, fig. And though it was evening, golden sunshine still dappled the lawn, catching the wings of the butterflies which flitted from bloom to bloom.

This is what Eden must have looked like. Raya took another piece of cheese from the plate in front of her, savouring the tangy flavour. She was glad she'd changed into a free-flowing kaftan. Her stomach was so full it was close to bursting.

"I am sorry," Shade said abruptly.

"For what?"

"For your suffering. For the indignities inflicted on you in the human world. I am sorry I did not find you sooner."

"It wasn't your fault."

"The man you spoke of. Griggs. Did he force you to..."

"No, no, not that," she said quickly. "He just got off on seeing me helpless. He was a creep. Anyway, he's probably traumatised for life after seeing you. Maybe he's locked up somewhere in a strait-jacket. Now, *that* would be perfect."

"We have to find your power. Then no-one would be able to terrorise you again."

She put down the grape she'd been about to eat.

"Have you thought about the fact that I may *never* find my powers?"

"No," he said dismissively. "Your fae side cannot be suppressed."

"I'm not sure that's how genes work."

"Try."

"I don't know how."

"Stand up," he said impatiently. She got to her feet and he moved round to stand behind her. "When I summon my shadows, it starts here, in my head." She felt his fingers press lightly against her temples. "But I feel it here, in my stomach."

His other hand pressed flat against her belly. She inhaled sharply.

"I can't…"

"Do not think about it. Simply envisage what you want. Your flames live inside you. You just need to let them out."

He was so close she could feel the heat from his body. If she just leaned back a little, she would be touching him. His hand on her stomach was spreading tendrils of warmth that reached downwards.

She flashed on the memory of waking up after the jotnar hunt. How he'd touched her.

"I think I need to do this on my own," she said quickly, pulling herself out of his grasp. "No distractions. I'll spend all day tomorrow practicing. Promise."

He looked as if he was about to say something, then stopped. He narrowed his eyes, staring intently into the garden. She followed his gaze, but couldn't see anything.

"What...?" she began, but he gestured her to silence. He stood taut, his body tense, shadows beginning to form a blade in his hand. Then abruptly he relaxed.

"I know you are there, Tala. Come out."

Puzzled, Raya peered around the garden. It looked empty. Then she blinked and in that moment a figure appeared.

She was the most beautiful woman Raya had ever seen. Honey blonde hair fell in a silk curtain to her waist. She was dressed in black and moved with a feline grace that immediately left Raya feeling like an ungainly giant.

She could have been a princess straight from a fairy tale, except for the coldness of her ice-blue eyes. And the fact that she was armed to the teeth. Curved daggers gleamed at each hip.

"My Lord."

She bowed her head. Shade regarded her stonily.

"Enough with the fake formality. You should not sneak up on me, Tala. One day I might mistake you for the enemy."

"It's good practice for me, boss. If I can sneak up on an Ifrit as powerful as you, then I can sneak up on anybody."

"Fair point. Raya, this is Tala. She occasionally does some work for me. Tala, this is Lady Raya of the Vulcani."

The cold eyes flitted to Raya.

"We have met."

Raya jolted in surprise.

"No, I don't think so."

"In the human world."

The woman never blinked, never took her gaze off Raya, and a memory started to claw its way from her subconscious.

Those eyes. She'd seen them before. A wave of dread washed over her.

"You… you were in Nurse Phillips. You were watching me."

Tala nodded.

"I'm a tracker. It took me a while to find you."

"But… how…?"

"Tala is a shaitun," said Shade. "A kind of demon. She can temporarily see what others see. Hear what they hear. It makes her an extraordinary spy. But rest assured, she does no harm to the host."

"No harm?" Anger made Raya clench her fists. "She made Mary tear the skin around her mouth. She used her like a puppet."

"That wasn't me," Tala said dismissively. "That was Ravij. One of Salaq's. He's an evil bastard."

"Are you saying some demons *aren't* evil?"

"I'm *saying* we don't all harm innocents."

"Really? Because a shaitun attacked me when I was just a child."

Tala paused, taken by surprise.

"I'm sorry." Her voice was unexpectedly sympathetic. "How did you escape?"

"I killed it. With fire."

"Ah." Tala cocked her head to one side. "Did the demon by any chance have red snake eyes?"

"Yes. Creepy as fuck."

"That was Sughal. He worked for Aelfric. I wondered where he'd got to." Tala mentally reappraised the woman in front of her. "And you were just a child? I'm impressed. But just so we're clear, Sughal was a sadist. I'm nothing like him."

"Oh, because you're a *nice* shaitun?"

Tala gave a bark of laughter.

"Not even a little bit."

"What are you doing here, Tala?" Shade interrupted. "The last I heard, you were freelancing in the mortal world."

"Yes, I was. Tracking some crime lord who'd ripped off the wrong person. In his lame attempt to buy me off, he let slip some interesting information."

Shade raised a cynical eyebrow.

"'Let slip'?"

"You know me, boss. I can be very persuasive."

"What did you learn?"

"That there's a kill order out for Lemar."

"Someone wants him dead? Who?"

"Well, that's the interesting thing. Apparently, it's you."

Shade rocked back on his heels. Raya looked from one to the other.

"Who's Lemar?" she asked curiously.

Shade didn't answer, so Tala obliged.

"Count Darian Lemar the Third, the son of Prince Vassago Lemar of Palissandra. He left the kingdom ages ago. Lives somewhere in the human world now. What's he done to piss you off, Shadeed?"

"I barely know him, and I certainly do not want him dead. What would that gain me, except the hatred of the entire Vetali clan?"

"Bingo."

Raya felt she was losing the thread of the conversation. "Sorry, can someone explain what's going on?"

Shade turned a troubled face towards her.

"Somebody is trying to turn the Vetali against me. I assume it is Salaq. I underestimated him. I never thought he'd seek their support."

"I thought the Vetali didn't get involved with what the fae and jinn do?"

"They would if they thought their heir was being targeted."

"You need to nip this in the bud, boss," Tala said. "I stopped off at a hunter's bar in London on the way here. Half the mercs in the place were talking about the hit. It's worth a fortune."

Shade swore under his breath.

"I cannot leave here. Not now. We have to win over the Vulcani."

"But the Vulcani won't matter if the Vetali side against you," argued Raya. "They're just one small fraction of the fae. The Vetali are an entire realm of people."

"Well," muttered Tala," I wouldn't call them *people*."

Shade looked at her.

"Will you go?"

Tala folded her arms.

"No way. I hate those bloodsuckers. They're all psychopaths."

Bloodsuckers?

"Tala, you are the only one who can save him."

"He's somewhere in the mortal world. That's seven billion people, give or take."

"So track him. You always claim to be the best tracker in the empire. Prove it."

Tala snorted.

"You can't appeal to my vanity, boss."

"Then let me appeal to your sense of preservation. Do you really want to see Salaq on the throne?"

"You're a bastard."

"Please, Tala. I have to stay here with Raya. A lot is depending on her."

The cold eyes took her in once more.

"Hard to believe the future of the empire is riding on you."

Raya lifted her chin.

"Well, apparently, some of it's riding on you too. That is, if you can be bothered to save someone's life."

A reluctant grin spread across Tala's face.

"Ouch. I like her, boss."

"So you will do it?"

Tala chewed her lip for a moment.

"I want triple rate if I'm bringing that bastard back here alive."

"Double. But only if there isn't a mark on him."

Tala gave a wolfish grin, and Raya suddenly felt a bit sorry for this Lemar, whoever he was.

"I promise not to harm a single hair on his evil vampire head."

Raya's mouth dropped open.

"Wait a minute. Vampire? The Vetali are *vampires*?"

"There's a lot you still have to learn about this place, Lady Raya of the Vulcani." The shaitun studied her. "It's a grand title. I hope you live up to it."

She gave a nod to Shade and turned to go. Dusk was finally approaching and the garden had emptied of butterflies and peacocks. Tala strode across the lawn as sinuous and silent as a cat. Raya watched her go, envious of her grace.

"She seems…" she blinked. The shaitun had vanished. One minute she was there, the next she wasn't. "…nice," she finished weakly. "Do you think she'll find Lemar before the others?"

It was getting dark and Shade's face was shadowed as he answered.

"Tala is extremely talented. I just hope she remembers I need him in one piece. She thoroughly dislikes vampires."

"But, I mean, vampires? Aren't they dangerous?"

"Undoubtedly. But so is Tala."

"Did you hear what she said? Another demon found me at the hospital. One belonging to Salaq. What does that mean?"

"Nothing good. It means Salaq and Aelfric both know about you."

"Do you think they know I'm here?"

"Do not worry, Raya. You are protected here."

"But what if…" Raya stopped dead and gazed around her, her train of thought entirely derailed by the scene in front of her.

The garden had suddenly lit up in a blaze of colour. It was as if someone had flipped a switch. Ethereal multi-coloured lights gleamed and glittered as far as her eye could see. The luminescence sparkled all around her, both on the ground and in the trees. The effect was wondrous and Raya caught her breath.

"Where's the light coming from?"

"Let me show you."

Shade led her to the nearest crop of lights, a dazzling radiance of violet that sent bright shards of blue and purple across the garden. Raya bent to look closer and inhaled the glorious scent of lilac.

"Flowers," she breathed. "Flowers are making the light. But how?"

"They are night-garden blooms. Common only in this part of Nush'aldaam. They are the reason the castle got its name."

The whole garden was lit up in a rainbow of colour.

"It's the most beautiful thing I've ever seen."

Her face was suffused in joy and Shade was startled to find he was pleased he'd made her happy. He gave himself a mental shake. Her happiness was not his concern. He only needed her to fulfil her end of the bargain.

"I have things to do," he said gruffly. "Stay in the garden as long as you like. But tomorrow, you will do whatever it takes to find your power."

He strode back towards the castle and Raya saluted at his back.

"Yes sir, Mr Jinn sir. Whatever you say, sir."

She spent a long time exploring the night-garden. She wished Caroline could have seen it.

"It's not quite Westmore, mum," she whispered. "But you'd have loved it."

Twenty Two

She spent the next morning trying to set her hands on fire. Closing her eyes, she attempted to summon up the power she'd felt coursing through her body the day she'd dragged Shade down the mountain. She imagined flames bursting from the tips of her fingers, heat exploding from her cells.

Nothing. She didn't even break a sweat.

At midday she gave up. She searched through the wardrobe, looking for something to wear that didn't belong in the boudoir. It was tough. Most of the clothes were either too short, too tight or too see-through.

Eventually she found a pair of loose trousers and a black top. She had to keep pulling the top down over her midriff but at least it covered her cleavage.

Her best find was a pair of suede boots, as soft as butter, which she privately vowed to keep forever. She twisted her hair into a knot and surveyed herself in the mirror.

"Rocking the street urchin look." She stuck her tongue out at herself and went in search of Tor.

She found him in the kitchens, more by luck than anything else. He was speaking animatedly to the cook, who, judging by the expression on her face, hadn't been this close to a handsome young man for quite a while.

Tor spotted Raya and his face broke into a wide grin.

"You're here. Perfect timing."

"This place is a maze," she told him. "I got lost three times."

Tor handed a list to the cook and she went off, looking rather dazed.

"The council are picky eaters. One doesn't eat meat, another will eat dairy as long as it follows a protein course, and one only eats lentils and beans. She says it cleanses her system."

"I bet she's fun to be stuck in a lift with."

"My Lady?"

"Stop with the Lady business. Call me Raya. No-one's listening."

"Aye, why is that?" Tor looked around. No-one was paying any attention to them. "Don't they know who you are?"

"I just arrived yesterday. Shade hasn't had time to introduce me around. I've only met the butler so far."

"Your human words are confusing. But your anonymity is a bonus. Enjoy it while it lasts."

"So have you got time to help me with my power?" she asked eagerly. He nodded.

"Let's find somewhere a bit more private."

Tor led her out of the castle towards the stables. They checked in on Martha and Strider. Both horses were contentedly munching hay in their stalls.

"Here?" asked Raya. Tor looked at her as if she was mad.

"A barn full of straw? Somewhere less flammable, I think."

"Oh yeah. Good point."

They wandered to the back of the barns and Tor pointed to a low stone-built building.

"There. I was hoping the castle would have one."

It was a forge. A large hearth dominated the centre of the room, heaped with wood and charcoal. A table next to it held various implements; bellows, hammers, an anvil. And all around the walls were piles of finished ironmongery. Raya cast her eyes over a beautiful sword and a quiver of steel arrows. In one corner was a heap of discarded horse-shoes, in another a set of farming tools.

"Where is everyone?" Raya asked. "Why is no-one here?"

"Everything slows down in the run-up to the Melae. Blacksmith's probably knocked off early. But it's fireproof, so its perfect."

Raya took a breath.

"Okay. So how does this work?"

"With your permission, I'll take a look at your aura. I also may need to touch you. Just your face, maybe your hands. Do I have your permission?"

"Yes," she said. Her throat was dry. If this didn't work, she didn't know what else to do. Shade wouldn't help her find her mother if she was no use to him.

"There are no guarantees, Raya," Tor warned. "I may not be able to help. If the reason you're having trouble is physical, rather than in your head…"

"Just try, Tor. Please."

"All right then. Hold still."

He stared intently at her. No, not exactly *at* her. Into her. Through her. Beyond her. She couldn't explain it.

His hazel eyes deepened, changed colour. Fascinated, she watched as his irises became green, the same green as the forest. The hairs on her arm rose, as if there was static electricity in the air. He held out a hand, tracing an outline around her face, her shoulders. He didn't touch her, but she felt something ripple lightly across her skin.

"Interesting," he murmured.

"What? What do you see?"

"Two distinct auras. That's normal for a halfling. But your human aura and your fae aura should be blended. Instead, yours are separated by… I'm not sure how to describe it." Tor frowned and traced an invisible shape with his forefinger. "It looks like bruising. It's dark and jagged. It's keeping the two sides of you apart."

"What do you think it is?"

"Some sort of damage. Guilt, maybe? It's burned itself into your psyche. I think it's stopping you from accessing your fae power." He looked down at her, and his voice was gentle. "What are you holding onto, Raya? What are you guilty about?"

Ice gripped her heart, squeezing until she thought she couldn't breathe. Of course she was guilty. She had done something terrible. Something she could never put right. Now she was paying the price.

She was damaged, all right. She was broken. And she deserved to be.

"Raya?"

Tears spilled down her cheeks.

"I found something out recently. When I was a child, I started a fire. It was an accident but I… I killed two people I loved very much."

Wordlessly, Tor folded her into his arms. She leaned against him, taking comfort in the steady beating of his heart, the quiet strength of his arms.

Eventually, when she'd thoroughly soaked his shirt in tears, she straightened up with a sniff. He handed her a clean hanky.

"I can't take your guilt away. It's a burden we all have to endure and it can't be erased. But I can perhaps help you come to terms with it."

"Will that help me control my power?"

"Maybe. Right now your guilt is a solid barrier. If I can help you accept it, perhaps you'll be able to access your fae side. And more importantly, maybe you'll be able to forgive yourself."

Never. I'll never forgive myself.

She gave a wobbly smile.

"What do I need to do?"

"It won't be easy. Like I said. No guarantees. And it will mean reliving the memory of…"

"No!" Raya was horrified. "I can't go through that again."

"You can only make peace with it if you fully embrace what happened. I know it's hard, but it's the only way. Are you brave enough, Lady Raya of the Vulcani?"

No. I don't think I am. She wasn't Vulcani, not really. She was a halfling abandoned at birth, scared of her memories.

Then Magda's voice swam into her head.

Your mother was a strong fae. Absolutely fearless. She would fight to the death to protect you.

Aelah hadn't hesitated. She'd run from Nush'aldaam to protect her unborn child. She'd taken the hard path because it was the right thing to do.

Didn't she owe it to her mother to do the same?

She straightened her shoulders.

"Do it."

"Remember, I'll be right here next to you."

Tor's gaze deepened to the jade of a rainforest. He held his hands on either side of her face, not quite touching her, yet she felt warmth radiating from his fingers. Time seemed to slow. The dust motes dancing in the air spiralled lazily, and the shards of sunlight penetrating the roof faded to sepia.

Tor moved his fingers gently around her face, stroking something only he could see. A curious sensation tugged at her brain. The room around her changed.

She was back in her childhood home playing cards with Caroline and Ross. And a demon with blood red eyes was knocking on the door.

She wanted to stop Ross when he got up to answer, wanted to beg him to stay. But she was helpless to stop it playing out. She couldn't change anything. How could she? The tragedy had already happened.

She watched Caroline get up from the table. The last time she'd ever seen her.

"Why are you making me do this?" she screamed.

"Just watch. Witness. Accept."

Tor's voice sounded in her head. The snake-eyed man appeared and she tried to turn away.

"No. You cannot block it out. You must make this part of you. It's the only way."

She forced herself to focus.

Again, she sensed the invisible restraints around her body. Felt her feet slide across the kitchen floor as she was dragged towards the demon. Tried to call out and was prevented from doing so.

And then the flames, everywhere.

This time she saw the demon's face. Saw its confusion and shock as her flames hit it, and then it was melted out of existence.

She jerked. That detail was new. Her powers must have unconsciously targeted the demon first.

And now she had to face the part she dreaded most. She quailed but Tor encouraged her.

"Keep going, Raya. You have to do this."

She was powerless to stop her memory. The dash into the hallway. The brief moment of relief, quickly replaced by horror. The despair and pain with the realisation that she had lost the people she loved most.

"Tor, I can't. I can't do this."

"You need to accept what happened. You can't move forward until you do."

She steeled herself to look. To relive the terrible scene that haunted her dreams. And this time she saw, really *saw* what was there.

Caroline and Ross crumpled on the floor, engulfed in the flames she'd created. They were burning, yes, and that was dreadful enough. But now through adult eyes, she saw what she hadn't seen as a child.

Their limbs twisted into strange angles. Their necks bent unnaturally.

The torturous position of their bodies gave away the truth. They were dead before the fire reached them.

The demon must have killed them while she sat waiting in the kitchen. That strange sound she'd heard, that choking sound. That had been Caroline dying.

Grief and anger rushed through her like twin tidal waves. Nothing had changed. And yet *everything* had changed.

Her adopted parents were still dead. But not at her hands.

The truth wouldn't bring them back. Her grief was still raw, still piercing. But now at least she knew she wasn't responsible for their deaths.

She watched the flames roll through the house and was finally able to let go of her bone-crushing guilt.

She was dimly aware of Tor crying out. With an effort, she remembered this wasn't real. She wasn't a child anymore.

The scene evaporated and she was back in the forge. It took a moment to orient herself, to find herself in the now.

Tor was sprawled on his back looking up at her. Her lashes were wet with tears. Her body prickled with a strange energy that felt both alien yet familiar.

And her hands were alight with fire.

Twenty Three

She held them up, wonderingly. The flames were a delicate shade of pink and orange, almost pretty. She couldn't feel any heat from them. But evidently there *was* heat, because Tor stood up rubbing his arm gingerly.

"You nearly took my eyebrows off," he said. "Are you all right?"

"Better than all right. Look at this. I did it!"

"Aye, you did. You've found your balance. Your aura is a beautiful orange now and the bruising has gone. Almost gone," he amended, peering closely. "There's still a tinge of guilt there."

"It's because I'm not completely blameless for what happened to Caroline and Ross," she said slowly. "If I hadn't been with them, the demon would never have killed them. But to know I didn't directly cause their deaths…" she took a deep breath and exhaled. "I didn't realise how much it had affected me."

"Their deaths will always be a part of you. But you can use it. That memory is what triggered your power. Can you control the flames? Direct them?"

She concentrated on her hands. For a moment, the flames burned blue. Then they returned to their normal pinky-orange shade.

"It's harder than it looks."

"Try to create a ball," Tor suggested. "Apparently your ma was deadly with the fireballs."

She put her palms together, imagining a fireball shaping between them. But when she pulled her hands apart, there was just the tiniest dot hanging in mid air. It span like an orange marble.

"Well, *that's* completely unterrifying," she said, disappointed.

"Didn't anyone ever tell you size isn't everything?"

"Only really short people."

"It's what you do with it that counts."

"Yes, maybe I can singe someone's ear."

"Just throw it at something. Maybe it's more powerful than it looks."

"Throw it? How do I do that?"

Tor frowned doubtfully.

"I'm not sure. The Vulcani sort of flick their hands, but I think it's more mental than physical."

"Ooooookay..."

She looked for a suitable target. There were some finished shields hanging on the wall, ready to be collected. She looked at her pathetic little spot of fire, still spinning between her hands, and thought about where she wanted it to go. Then she flicked it towards the shields.

They both watched as it wobbled uncertainly across the intervening space, splatted against a shield, gave a low hiss and vanished.

The shield didn't have a mark on it.

"At least you managed to direct it properly," Tor said brightly.

"Yes. Maybe I could get a job as a hands-free candle lighter."

Her earlier excitement at finally finding her power was quickly fading. The Vulcani would never accept her as their leader. She may as well wave a torch around at them. Angrily, she shook her hands and the flames went out.

"It wasn't that bad," Tor said soothingly. "You just need practice. You've got a week."

"Six days."

"You've proven you're Vulcani. That's the main thing."

"But they'll only accept me as leader if I'm as powerful as Aelah."

"You think Aelah could shoot fireballs overnight? She had to learn how to shape her power, same as you do."

"I guess." She glanced at Tor from under her lashes. "Thank you, by the way. I couldn't have done it without you."

"No thanks necessary. It was my pleasure. Though I'm glad I kept my eyebrows." He waggled them at her comically and she couldn't help laughing. On impulse, she stood on her tiptoes and kissed his cheek.

He turned bright red and she immediately regretted her action. Flustered, she strove for a nonchalant tone.

"Just my way of saying thank you," she said airily.

"That's how they say 'thank you' in the human world?"

"Only to the best people. I hope I didn't offend you."

"No, it was just… unexpected. Um…" He broke off and strode towards the door. "I have to go. Things to do."

Raya ran after him.

"Wait. We haven't finished practicing yet."

"You don't need me for that. You've found your power, now you have to hone it."

He left the forge, and Raya stood at the door watching him walk away. She cursed herself for kissing him. It was only his cheek, but for all she knew that was foreplay here in Nush'aldaam.

Then she remembered she was supposed to be engaged to Shade. She groaned inwardly. If Shade was right, and Tor was a Vulcani spy, then she'd just undermined the whole betrothal charade.

She became aware she was being watched. Turning, she caught a flash of red hair and an impressive cleavage.

"Leona. How long have you been there?"

The si'lat smiled.

"Long enough. He's a handsome one, isn't he?" She glanced in the direction Tor had gone. "Does Shadeed know you're spending time with him?"

"It's not like that," Raya said irritably. "He was helping me with something."

"Your uptightness? I hear Sylvans are very good with their hands."

"Not everything's about sex, you know."

"I know, it's disappointing, isn't it?" Leona looked the other woman up and down. "What in the skies are you wearing?"

"Normal clothes. You should try it sometime. Why are you here?"

"Lord Shadeed asked me to fetch you." Was it her imagination, or was there a spark of jealousy in those impossibly green eyes?

"I'm not a dog," Raya said irritably. "Anyway, I'm in the middle of something. I'll come when I'm ready."

"He doesn't like to be kept waiting."

"He doesn't like anything, as far as I can tell."

"I could tell you ten things right now that he likes."

"Are we back to sex again?

"He's more sensitive than you give him credit for."

Raya snorted.

"He's the worst-tempered person I've ever met. And I spent half my life in a loony bin."

"You should be more understanding. He's under a lot of pressure."

"Just as well he's got you to relieve it then."

Leona's eyes flashed.

"Not anymore. He says we must end our liaisons to make your betrothal more believable."

Raya was taken aback.

"Oh. I'm sorry. I didn't expect him to do that."

Leona shrugged dismissively.

"It's only temporary. You are just a means to an end. He'll be back with me as soon as he wins the throne."

Raya rolled her eyes.

"Yeah. I've no doubt. Tell him I'm busy."

She walked back into the forge.

Twenty Four

She spent the next few hours lighting and extinguishing her flames. It didn't always happen straight away. It was like trying to wiggle your nose or move each toe separately. But by the end of the hour, she could at least produce fire on command.

Fire*balls*, however, were another matter.

The largest projectile she could manage was still woefully small. Barely bigger than a golf ball. And no matter how hard she threw it, it moved with all the urgency of a half-dead sloth.

"I mean, seriously, I can *walk* faster than this," she complained as she overtook her latest creation. It bobbed haphazardly towards the far wall and dispersed even before it hit anything. "For fuck's sake."

She gave up.

The sun was low by the time she made her way back to the castle. She climbed the stairs to her chambers, feeling inexplicably exhausted. She steeled herself for Shade's wrath, knowing he would be furious she hadn't come running when he'd called.

But when she knocked on his door, he didn't answer. Breathing a sigh of relief, she made her way to her own rooms.

The first thing she did was head to the bathroom and turn on all the taps. Hot water gushed into the bath and steam drifted out through the gaping hole in the wall.

She looked out as the bath filled, making sure she wasn't too close to the edge. The view was breath-taking. The sky was impossibly blue and she could just about see the tip of the mountains where the Vetali lived.

She glanced at the sheer drop below her. She knew there was a river at the bottom of the gorge, but it was too far down to see.

She undressed and stepped into the bath with a sigh of contentment. Grabbing one bottle after another, she poured ointments and lotions into the water until bubbles filled the entire surface and a dozen different perfumes permeated the air.

She sank below the surface, washing the grime from her skin and hair. A thought struck her while she was underwater. She held her hand up to her face and concentrated. Flames blossomed on her hand like pink magnolia, unaffected by the water.

She laughed in delight, inhaled a nose full of water, and surfaced coughing and spluttering.

Shade was standing in the window.

"Oh. Hey."

Self-consciously she looked down at herself and was relieved to see her breasts were covered in foam.

"Where. Have. You. Been."

Shade's voice was dangerously quiet but Raya didn't immediately recognise the threat.

"I've been practicing my power like you asked. Look."

She let flames ripple along her fingers and up her forearm. Concentrating, she made them turn blue, then back to orange.

"What do you think? I mean, I know it's not brilliant, but it's a start. I think if I..." her voice trailed off as she noticed his eyes had darkened to an indigo tone she hadn't seen before. She let her flames go out. "What's wrong?"

"You have been with the Sylvan. Against my express wishes."

"He was helping me, that's all." Her mouth went dry as she saw anger rolling off him in great black waves. "He realised why I couldn't access my power and helped me overcome it. He's the reason I can make fire now."

His unblinking stare was so intense, she felt an irrational impulse to get up and run. He stalked towards her, stopping briefly as he came to the water's edge. She looked away hurriedly as he unclothed himself, his trousers and tunic melting with a thought. Her heart started hammering as he stepped down into the bath.

"I told you to stay away from him," he growled. "Did I not make myself clear?"

"But I wasn't doing anything wrong." She fought to keep her voice even. She was damned if she'd let him intimidate her. "Tor was being a friend. Which is more than I can say for you."

"I am not your friend. I am supposed to be your betrothed. And it is time you started acting like it." He slid an arm around her waist and dragged her close, so close she could feel his nakedness push against her. "Perhaps you need a lesson. A reminder of the role you are playing."

She struggled against his grip ineffectually.

"What the fuck is wrong with you? Let me go."

"Does *he* hold you like this? Your Sylvan?"

"It's not like that. Tor would never…"

"Of course he would. I have seen the way he looks at you." He slid his hand into the hair at the nape of her neck. "But while our deal is in place, you are mine."

His mouth closed on hers and he kissed her hard, plundering her lips with sensual intensity. He tasted of cinnamon, she thought wildly. She put her hands against his chest, intending to push him away but somehow ended up clinging to him instead.

She had never been kissed like this before. His tongue twined with hers, a languid invasion that left her weak. When he finally released her mouth, she was breathless.

He kissed the hollow under her ear, then trailed his lips with agonising slowness down her neck. His hand slid from her waist to her breast.

"What are you doing?" she whispered.

"Making a point."

Mortified, she realised she was pressing against him. He stroked her nipples, sending bolts of pleasure through her whole body. A slow, heavy pulse began to beat between her legs.

"Shade…"

"Does your woodland boy make you feel like this?"

She couldn't answer. The pleasure he was inflicting made her incapable of thought. She stifled a moan as he lifted her clear of the soapy water. Her legs wrapped round his waist and she arched her back, her eyes closed in ecstasy as he kissed her breasts. He ran his tongue over the dark-rose tips, feeling them tighten.

"Oh, God," she gasped.

She was grinding against him, communicating an unspoken need, and he growled deep in his throat. He was hard, harder than he could remember, and he wanted her. More than he'd wanted anyone in a very long time.

He claimed her mouth again, unable to help himself, revelling in the sweetness of her lips. By the gods, she was intoxicating.

He slid a hand between her legs and found her deliciously wet. His thumb brushed against her most sensitive part, circling it, stroking it, until her hips bucked. He slowed down, delaying her climax, knowing her pleasure would be heightened.

"Tell me," he commanded. "Tell me you want me." He needed to hear it. Strange, as he'd never before doubted whether his partners wanted him. But he needed her to say the words. "Tell me, Raya."

So many sensations, she thought incoherently. So close to exploding. She felt his hardness pushing against her.

But his voice shook some part of her awake.

If she let him do this, she would be just another notch on his belt. Another weak female he'd easily seduced. He didn't care about her. He just needed the power she could bring.

Christ, his touch was so good. She knew she had to stop this. She just didn't know how.

"Tell me you want me," he insisted.

His hardness was nudging at her entrance and she ached for it, ached for the pleasure she knew it would bring. It would be so easy to give into it.

She gathered every last ounce of her resistance and looked right at him.

"I want you to stop," she said hoarsely, even as her treacherous body writhed in pleasure.

"Liar. You cannot deny this feels good."

"Yes. But when it's over, I'll hate you for it." He went very still and she forced herself to continue. "You said it yourself. You're only doing this to make a point. To teach me a lesson. And afterwards, I'll despise you."

He stared into her eyes, evaluating her words. Weighing them. The bleakness in his face terrified her. *I don't mean it*, she wanted to shout. *Please don't stop.* But she knew there'd be a price to pay. After, when he'd taken what he wanted. When the passion had been sated.

Without a word he released his hold on her and pulled away. He climbed from the bath and stalked to the window. He spoke without looking round.

"Tomorrow evening at dinner, I will formally present you to my people as my betrothed. I trust you will act the part."

He stepped off the ledge and dropped from sight, his shadow wings unfurling as he fell.

Raya watched him fly away, her body bereft of his touch. She stayed in the bath until the water turned cold around her.

Twenty Five

Shade hung in the air, his shadows cloaking him in smoky darkness. He was sick to his stomach, furious and disgusted with himself in equal measure. He had been enraged when he discovered Raya had spent the day with the Sylvan but that didn't excuse what he had done.

He had gone too far, let temptation take control, and that was unforgiveable.

He flew to his favourite place. A hill on the other side of Nurhan. A wide grassy plateau at the top of a rocky crag. Impossible to reach unless you could fly.

He came here when he wanted to think. The solitude calmed him. Normally.

Why was he letting her get under his skin? What was it about her that made him act so irrationally?

She was an infuriating mix of contradictions. Tough yet vulnerable. Smart but naïve. And brave, despite the conditions she'd lived in for the past decade. He had never met anyone like her.

And yes, he acknowledged ruefully, he wanted her. By the gods, he hadn't wanted anyone this badly for a long, long time.

He glanced down at his still semi-aroused state. What was that epithet Raya used all the time? The one that summed up his exact mood right now? Ah yes.

Fuck.

He left the plateau and glided back to his room, his shadows trailing behind him like a wake. He would have to apologise for his transgression. He would have to make it right. He would…

He stopped.

Raya was waiting for him. She stood in the middle of his bedchamber, wrapped only in a towel, her hair tumbling wildly down her back.

His throat constricted at the sight of her. He searched her face for any sign of anger or mistrust, and found none.

"What are you doing here?" he asked, his voice hoarse.

"I want you."

"But you said…"

"I changed my mind."

In two strides he was at her side, taking her into his arms as she let the towel drop to the floor. He tangled his hands in her hair as he brought her mouth to his, kissing her with a ferocity which he couldn't control.

In the next moment he pushed her away, eyes blazing.

"Leona."

"Does this form not please you, my Lord? I thought you would enjoy it."

"You thought wrong."

"And yet you seem so pleased to see me." Leona let her gaze drift over Shade's body. "Or should I say, her."

"Take her face off, Leona. It does not suit you."

Leona's lips tightened.

"Is she the reason you don't want to see me anymore?"

"I told you, I have to make the Vulcani believe my betrothal is real."

"The Vulcani don't give a shit whether you're tupping that half-breed. They just want to know if she's really fae."

"Have a care, Leona. An alliance with the Vulcani will help me secure the throne."

"What about *me*?" The si'lat's voice rose to a screech. "What about *our* alliance?"

"I already have your people on my side. Now I need to win over the Vulcani. Here, cover yourself." A shadow snaked out and tossed the towel towards Leona. "You should go. And Leona?"

"What?"

"I do not want to see you wear her face ever again."

With a hiss of rage, the si'lat morphed back into the redhead as she stormed from Shade's chambers. He didn't bother to watch her leave. She was already gone from his mind.

He walked out onto the platform, drawing the night air deep into his lungs. He closed his eyes, remembering the feel of Raya in his arms, her skin warm and damp from the bath, the smell of her hair.

She was only next door. Yet she was an aeon away.

When it's over, I'll hate you for it.

Her words had cut like a knife to his heart.

She wanted you, his inner voice told him. It wasn't all one way.

Was he sure about that? Or was it wishful thinking? Was he any better than that dog, Griggs, who had abused his power over her in the human world?

He roared his shame and frustration, the guttural sound rolling like thunder through the night sky. He had to redeem himself. Somehow, the thought of Raya hating him was an agony he couldn't bear.

It came to him, then. Something he could do to repair Raya's trust in him. It would mean swallowing his pride, but that couldn't be helped.

He knew it would make Raya happy and then, maybe, just maybe, she would forgive him.

Twenty Six

Raya groaned when the knock came at her door. It was almost noon, but she didn't want to get out of bed. She was still mortified at the events of the night before, angry with Shade for making her feel that way, and furious with herself for practically swooning in his arms.

It had been a long time before she got to sleep.

"Go away," she snapped, thinking it was a servant bringing her food.

"It is I." Shade's voice rumbled through the door.

"*Definitely* go away." She pulled the covers over her head.

"Raya, I will stay here until you open the door. All day if necessary."

"You're a fucking jerk, you know that?"

"We need to talk."

"I have nothing to say to you."

"Then I will wait here until you are feeling more communicative."

For fuck's sake. She yanked on a dressing gown and stormed over to the door. Flinging it open, she glared at him.

"What? I'm busy."

"So I see. I wondered if you would care to accompany me to the night-garden."

"Why?"

"I have something to show you."

"I think you showed me everything you needed to last night."

Incredibly, the jinn dropped his eyes.

"Raya, I behaved like an enraged beast. I am not asking forgiveness, for it was unforgiveable. But I do beg your understanding. My temper sometimes gets the better of me."

"You think? I hadn't noticed."

He frowned.

"I am unsure as to whether you are being sincere."

"Take a wild guess."

"I am trying to make amends. Would you get dressed and come with me?"

"Why should I?"

"I know you have no reason to trust me. But if you come with me now, I will try to ensure you never have any reason to fear me again."

Fear him? He thought he'd *frightened* her? Raya cocked her head.

"I don't fear you, Shade. I just don't understand you."

"On that score, halfling, we are evenly matched. Will you accompany me?" He cleared his throat. "Please?"

Raya's mouth fell open. Had she heard right? Please? She never thought that word would come out of his mouth.

"Turn around," she ordered.

"That hardly seems necessary. I have already seen…"

"Turn!" He did as she asked. She hurriedly pulled on a long dress and ran a brush through her hair. "What is it you want to show me?"

"It is a surprise."

He led her out of the castle to the night-garden. They went past the pagoda where they'd sat the other day and into another walled section.

It was a rose-garden. Roses of every colour bloomed from dozens of beds, filling the air with their rich perfume. And in the centre, a brand new rose bush. It stood proudly on its own covered in the most beautiful deep red blooms.

A man was on his hands and knees patting down the soil. She jerked in surprise when she saw it was Tor.

"Is it done, Mr Torven?" Shade asked.

Tor gave them a cheerful smile.

"Morning, Lady Raya. Yes my Lord, it has taken nicely."

"Tor, what are you... what is this?" Raya looked nervously from Tor to Shade. "What's going on?"

"Lord Shadeed asked me to help a cutting take root. Took a few minutes but I think it's bedded in well."

"You grew that whole bush in a few minutes?" She looked at Shade, puzzled. "Why?"

"It is from the bush where your parents' ashes are buried. Caroline and Ross. I found the cemetery. I thought it would be nice for you to have something of them here, with you."

He stopped, awkwardly. Raya's expression was unfathomable. He couldn't tell if she was happy or not.

"You did this for me?"

"I wanted you to feel comfortable. And to apologise. For..." he glanced at Tor. "For my behaviour."

Raya didn't know what to say. She knelt and touched one of the crimson petals.

"It's called Loving Memory. The type of rose, I mean. Red was Caroline's favourite colour." She glanced curiously at the jinn. "It must have taken you a long time to find it."

"Mr Torven did the hard work. He took the cutting and made it grow."

Tor shrugged cheerfully.

"All in a day's work for a Sylvan. Will that be all, my Lord?"

"Actually, may I request one last favour?" Shade looked around the garden. "It is quiet here, and secluded. Raya tells me you have helped her find her power. Would you be kind enough to work with her a little more?"

Raya's brows shot up in astonishment.

"You want Tor to help me practice?"

"If you feel you would benefit."

Raya grabbed his arm and pulled him to one side.

"What about the whole 'keep away from other men' crap?" she hissed.

"I realise if I want you to trust me, then I should also trust you." He unfurled his shadow wings. "The garden is yours. I will see you tonight."

Raya frowned after him as he beat upwards and disappeared behind the castle.

She would never understand him.

Twenty Seven

She knelt down and studied the rose.

"Did you really grow this from a cutting?" she asked.

"Encouraging things to grow is a Sylvan gift. And before you ask, aye, it really is a rose from the human world. Its aura is different."

"Roses have auras too?"

"All living things do. This one is dark red, matching its petals. But it also has touches of other auras. Two, to be precise. I'm guessing they're from the ashes Lord Shadeed mentioned. The rose will have absorbed them from the soil."

Raya stroked a petal.

"So Caroline and Ross are part of it."

"Life is a cycle. Everything becomes a part of something. Nothing ever really disappears."

Raya had a lump in her throat. She felt inexplicably closer to her adopted parents then at any time since the fire. She didn't know if Shade knew what this meant to her, but it was the kindest thing anyone had ever done.

She got to her feet. The least she could do was work on her power.

"We don't have long before the Vulcani get here," she said.

"Aye. Let's see what you can do."

Not a lot, as it turned out. It was definitely getting easier to summon the flames. And this time Raya managed to create a fireball of a more respectable size. A glowing sphere the size of a grapefruit appeared between her palms. Triumphantly, she flicked it at the fountain twenty metres away.

It crawled barely half the distance and fizzled out.

"For fuck's sake. Why is this so difficult?"

She tried again. This time the fiery globe bobbed drunkenly to within a couple of meters of the fountain before disappearing in a splutter of sparks.

Gritting her teeth, she produced another one. It sank to the floor and vanished with a sad *poof*.

Frustrated, Raya threw herself into the grass.

"This is ridiculous. What am I going to do when the Vulcani get here? I may as well light a match and chuck it at them."

"May I make a suggestion?" Tor had been watching critically. "Pardon me for saying, but I don't think you're fireball material."

"But I have to be." Stung, Raya drew herself up. "My mother threw fireballs. I have to do the same if I'm to prove myself."

"No, you don't."

He spoke with such quiet assurance that Raya was brought up short.

"What do you mean?"

"Your mother was a warrior. A fighter. She threw fireballs because it was in her nature. But you, you're not a violent person."

"I can be if I have to."

"But that's the thing. You *don't* have to. You just have to use your power in a way that's true to *your* nature."

Raya shook her head.

"I don't understand."

"Look, Aelah was fierce and aggressive. Her power reflects that. You, you're different. I think you have to quit trying to make fireballs."

"Are you saying I'm weak?"

"No!" He raised his hands immediately. "You're far from weak. But you're not a born fighter like Aelah. You're…" a faint blush stained his cheeks. "You're brave and clever and kind. You have a quiet strength about you. I think you need to manifest your power differently."

"And make what? Flame kittens?"

He shrugged.

"If that's what it takes."

"I'm not making bloody flame kittens. The Vulcani will laugh me out of the castle and Shade will probably explode in embarrassment."

"Make whatever you want. What makes you happy?"

Raya thought about it. The list was short. Not surprising, given she'd spent half her life in therapy. She could count them on the fingers of one hand.

Apple shampoo. Ice cream. Horses. And being here, in the night-garden, when darkness fell.

In her mind's eye she once again saw the glorious glitter of thousands of dazzling lights created by exotic fairy-tale flowers. It had felt like being among the stars.

She wondered if she could recreate them. Only one way to find out. She closed her eyes and took a breath.

Holding the image in her head, she allowed fire to leap from her hands. The thrum of power beneath her skin took shape around her. She moulded it, crafted it, trying to copy the glorious dazzlement she'd seen that night. The energy leapt from her, needing no special coaxing.

She heard Tor gasp but stayed focused, channelling the flames into the direction she wanted them to go. The direction *they* wanted to go. She spread her arms wide as flames rippled down them. She opened her eyes to see what she'd made.

Hundreds of flames dipped and weaved around her. They swirled and spiralled gracefully, burning orange and red and blue and purple. With a thought, she shaped them into flowers, then butterflies. It was easy. Effortless.

Unlike when she'd tried to make a fireball, the flames didn't fight her. And now she understood. Her nature was not to create weapons. It was to create beauty.

"That's incredible. Raya, you're doing it!" Tor grinned in unabashed amazement.

She laughed in delight, catching a flaming butterfly on the tip of her index finger. She made it beat its wings as it balanced there. Wonderingly, Tor reached towards a bright orange flower. He snatched his hand back, wincing.

"By the skies, that's hot. *Really* hot."

Raya span in a circle, and her flames span with her. They spiralled into the sky above, sending birds into a frenzy of alarm. She made them dance, the golden light reflected in her eyes. For a moment, a beautiful, precious moment, she felt like a true fae. A true Vulcani.

One of her flames came too close to a branch and it burst into fire.

"Shit!"

Alarmed, Raya dropped her hands and her lightshow disappeared. All except the tree, which was rapidly being consumed by fire.

"What do we do? Shall we get water?" She looked wildly towards the fountain, knowing they would never be able to carry enough to save the tree.

"Raya." Tor's voice was unexpectedly calm. "You control fire, remember?"

"But I've only just learned how to make it. I can't put it out."

"Yes, you can. Its energy belongs to you. Take it away from the tree."

"But I…"

"Trust me. You can do it."

He sounded so sure. Frowning, not really knowing how to do what he was asking, Raya held her hand towards the branch.

The fire flickered and roared, spitting out heat and sparks. She frowned, trying to get a sense of it. A feel for its energy. Its raw strength.

Fire was such an adaptable element, she thought. It could be so many things.

A source of warmth. A source of beauty. A source of destruction.

But all of it bendable to her will. She felt it now, the shape of the blaze. Almost like an animal, unpredictable and wild. She held it in her mind and beckoned it back to her.

For a moment the flames resisted. The tree was dry, combustible, so easy to burn. But Raya was adamant. *I take you back,* she thought fiercely. *Come back to me.*

And they did. They guttered and waned as she coaxed the energy back into herself. Back to the place where it lived in her muscle and bone.

She felt heat flood through her body, warming her skin like a lover's caress. Thermal currents buffeted her hair, lifting it from her face in heavy rippling waves.

And then everything stopped.

Warily, she lowered her arm. The fire was out. For a moment, she and Tor stood motionless, hearing nothing but the tweeting of birds and the squawk of an outraged peacock.

"You did it."

"I did, didn't I? Oh, but the poor tree." The tree was scorched badly, black welts along its branches. Its leaves had shrivelled in the heat and it looked curiously naked. Raya felt guilt bubble inside her. "I should have been more careful. Will it recover?"

"Aye. It will."

Tor gave her a lopsided smile and placed his hands on the tree trunk. He whispered something too quietly for Raya to hear.

"Tor, what are you…?"

He held up a hand and she subsided. Placing his palms back against the tree, he leaned into it until his forehead rested gently on the bark. Raya watched curiously. For a moment, nothing happened. Then she heard a sound coming from above them, a strange tearing noise. She peered into the branches.

Something was happening to the scorched wood. Charred pieces of bark were being pushed aside as new growth emerged from beneath. The damaged leaves popped off one by one and were replaced by fresh, young foliage which burst into the sunshine. The welts and cracks caused by the fire knitted together, leaving branches whole and healthy again.

Tor stood back from the tree and gave it a little pat.

"There you go, big guy. Good as new."

"That was the single most amazing thing I've ever seen."

The frank admiration in Raya's voice made Tor shuffle his feet, even as his heart swelled with pride.

"It's nothing. A simple trick for a Sylvan."

"You can all do that?"

"To some degree. We're good with living things. But we can't create something where nothing was before. Not like Vulcani or jinn. Not like you."

"Yeah, I created a bloody great inferno. Yay me."

"No, before that. The fire-lights. They were astonishing."

"Enough to convince the Vulcani?"

"Aye. I'm sure of it."

A weight lifted from Raya's heart.

"We should celebrate. Let's go into town."

Tor looked at her strangely.

"Are you not supposed to be getting ready for the dinner tonight?"

"What dinner?"

"The betrothal dinner. Everyone has been invited."

Shit. She'd almost forgotten.

"Oh, um, yes. Of course. The dinner. Hang on. What do you mean, *everyone* has been invited?"

"The head of every household within a span's radius has received an invitation. That's nearly two hundred people."

Raya tried not to let her dismay show.

"Two hundred people? Coming to meet *me*?"

"Aye, of course. You're to be presented as the future First Lady of Nurhan. Everyone in town is talking about it."

"Will you be there?"

"I haven't been invited." He eyed her curiously. "You don't seem very excited."

"I don't like being the centre of attention."

"You'll be fine. And Lord Shadeed will be by your side. He'll look after you."

"I guess." *If he doesn't lose his temper at me for being nervous and tongue-tied.*

Tor studied her closely.

"Is everything all right, Raya? Between you and Lord Shadeed?"

She knew she shouldn't say anything. Tor worked for the Vulcani. Shade had made it clear she was to keep up the charade of their betrothal in front of him.

But she liked Tor. And she didn't have anyone else to talk to. Nevertheless, she chose her words carefully.

"Sometimes I think he only asked me to get engaged to secure the support of the Vulcani," she said quietly.

"I don't believe that's true. Look at what he just did for you. Finding that rose. He cares for you, Raya."

"I think he cares more about getting the throne than me."

"How do you feel about him?"

Good question. Jury's out on that one.

"Look, forget I said anything. And please don't tell Loris what I said." She gazed at Tor imploringly. "It's the one thing Shade asked me not to do."

"I would never betray your confidence."

"You're a good friend."

Tor wasn't so sure. He couldn't deny his heart had lifted a little when she confessed her doubts about Lord Shadeed. The memory of that kiss, that all too brief kiss on his cheek, had somehow got under his skin.

"How about coming to the Melae tomorrow?" He kept his voice casual. "It'll give you a chance to relax."

"I don't know. What would Shade think?"

"He's not going. I asked Pasha. And no-one will know *you're* there either. Everyone will be masked."

An incognito street party. It was perfect. And Tor was right. She *did* need to relax.

"Okay, I'll go. But only if you're going."

"I'm going. And I should warn you, I will insist on a dance."

"I would be honoured. It's the least I can do. I owe you a big thank you for helping me with my power."

He raised an eyebrow.

"Would that be the same kind of thank you as before?"

Raya realised he was flirting but she didn't mind.

"Only one way to find out. Tomorrow?"

"Aye then. Tomorrow."

He started for the exit and Raya called out to him.

"Wait. If everyone's in masks, how will I know it's you?"

"You'll know."

And he was gone.

Raya made her way slowly back to her room, trying not to dread the evening ahead. It was only dinner. She could make it through one dinner.

Now, what did one wear to one's own engagement party?

Twenty Eight

In the end, she didn't have to decide for herself. A dress had been laid out for her on the bed.

It was stunning; a pale gold sheath that skimmed her body in a figure-hugging silhouette. A low cowl neck revealed the merest hint of cleavage. The long skirt appeared demure but a clever slit up one side showed a flash of thigh as she walked.

It was the perfect combination of chaste and seductive, and the champagne silk perfectly complemented her colouring.

She looked at herself critically in the mirror. Her body had filled out since she'd left the hospital. Good food, and plenty of it, had put flesh on her bones and rounded out her hips and breasts. The shadows were gone from under her eyes and her face had lost its gauntness.

She knew she wasn't beautiful. She'd seen enough pictures of models and actresses in magazines to know that. Her lips weren't full enough and her nose wasn't straight enough. But at least she looked more womanly now.

Even her eczema had improved. She rubbed her ears thoughtfully. No dry patches. Her skin shone with health

There was no Leona to help her with her make-up. In fact, she realised she hadn't seen the si'lat for a while. She considered asking Pasha to send someone up, but in the end she contented herself with a coating of mascara to darken her lashes and some rouge on her lips.

Her hair was more of an issue. There was no way she could replicate what Leona had done the other day. So she brushed it through until it was lustrous and glossy, and left it at that.

To be honest, no-one would notice her hair anyway. They'd all be staring at the amazing dress. She wondered if Shade would let her keep some of the clothes when she went home.

Home.

She frowned as the thought occurred to her. Where exactly *was* home? She would never return to the hospital, obviously. But she had nowhere else to go. Maybe... she bit her lip. Maybe if Shade ever found her mother, she could go live with her.

She resolved to ask him about Aelah tonight.

There was a knock at the door. Pasha entered, his customary black robe starched and spotless. Raya had never seen him wear anything different and she wondered if he had a cupboard full of them.

"Lord Shadeed asks that you join him in the Library."

"You have a Library?"

"Of course, my Lady. Please follow me."

He led her down the corridor to a set of large oak doors beautifully inlaid with ornate carvings. The room beyond took her breath away.

Floor to ceiling shelves groaned with books of every size, from large leather-bound tomes to simple cardboard picture books. She ran her fingers over them, delighting in their texture. Some were in languages she recognised, like French and Spanish, others were written in beautiful symbols she had never seen before. There was even a table piled high with novels.

Eagerly, she picked one up.

Ernest Hemingway, the Old Man and the Sea.

She selected another.

Geoffrey Chaucer. Her eyes widened. First edition?

The next book she picked up was a favourite of hers by Maya Angelou. She opened it up and began to read, so absorbed that Shade's voice behind her made her jump.

"I collect the classics from all the major kingdoms. Fae, jinn, and the human world."

Raya put the book down without turning round.

"Why are these books out on the table? Don't they fit in with the rest of your prized collection?"

"I pulled them out for you. I thought you might like to read something in a language you could understand."

He was really making an effort. First the rose, now the books. She finally turned.

For a moment they stared at each other.

He wasn't wearing all-black as usual. His tunic was a rich gold, a perfect match for her dress. It was sleeveless to show off his sculpted arms and the collar was high, dropping to an open vee that revealed his muscled chest. His trousers were of black silk and for once he was wearing boots.

"You look very nice." Raya's tongue seemed to have turned slow and stupid. "Like an Arabian prince."

"They are actual clothes, not my shadow garb."

"They look great."

"They feel itchy."

Raya felt a smile tug at her lips.

"In my world, people say beauty comes at a price. No pain, no gain."

"Who are these people?" he demanded. "They are clearly imbeciles. These clothes would try the patience of a manticore tracking its prey."

"Um, okay. If they're *that* bad, why are you wearing them?"

"Pasha insisted. I did not wish to disappoint him. He left them out for me."

"Me too."

"For you, at least, he made the right decision." His gaze was so appreciative she felt a blush warm her cheeks. "You are exquisite."

She didn't know what to say. She moved back to the book table and picked up a novel instead.

"I love reading. We never had enough books at the hospital, it was mostly old Mills & Boons and regency romances that people donated. I've always wanted to read Hemingway."

"You may come here whenever you want," he said. "When you are in here, you will not be disturbed by anyone. Including me."

It was a strange feeling, knowing he was trying to be nice to her.

"Thank you again, for the rose bush. How on earth did you find it?"

"We have seers in Nush'aldaam. Oracles who know things. I asked one of them. Did you think I simply flew from one cemetery to the next like some Angel of Death until I found what I was looking for? What would your humans have made of that?"

She giggled.

"Probably that the end was nigh."

"Ah. Doomsayers. We have those also. They are a nuisance, are they not?" His lips quirked and she saw he was in a good mood. "Shall we?"

He held his arm out, and together they walked to the main staircase. Raya could hear the hubbub of hundreds of voices below them and she swallowed nervously.

"I'm not sure about this. I don't like being stared at."

"Then you should have worn a different dress."

"Not helping."

"I will tell you a secret. I too loathe these social engagements."

"Seriously?"

"I would rather fight ten jotnars than face a formal dinner and make endless small talk with buffoons and dullards."

"So why are we doing this?"

"Unfortunately, it is protocol. "

"It still sucks."

"Do not fear, Lady Raya of the Vulcani. We will face the ordeal together. I will not leave your side, if you promise not to leave mine."

He gave her a smile then, and it was as if the sun had come out from behind the clouds. His eyes sparkled like sapphires. Unexpectedly, her heart skipped a beat.

"Don't worry. I'll protect you," she told him.

She clutched his arm as they descended into the throng. A band started playing music as they reached the bottom of the staircase and everyone turned to look. Raya's heart started thumping manically as hundreds of eyes rested on her.

Shade squeezed her hand.

"Breathe," he murmured.

The crowd parted to allow the couple to walk through. Raya forced herself to take deep breaths.

"What do I do?" she asked from the corner of her mouth.

"Smile and nod. Repeatedly."

With a rictus grin pasted to her face, Raya proceeded to do just that. Smile and nod, smile and nod, until her jaw muscles ached. Everyone she passed bowed their heads deferentially, but their open curiosity didn't escape her notice.

They were eager to find out who had snared the elusive Lord Shadeed.

"Hm. I should have become betrothed years ago. It seems no-one has any interest in me at all," Shade said drily.

"You're old news, jinn. Humans are all the rage now."

"In that case, perhaps you would like to formally welcome everyone to the castle?" He sounded amused and she shot him a horrified look. His mouth curved into a grin.

She liked the way he smiled, she realised. Quickly she turned away.

"If you make me speak, I'll be sick all over you. How's that for an introduction?"

"It would be a memorable one, certainly."

They reached the banqueting room where several long tables had been set with sparkling crystal and silverware. Shade and Raya were seated at the top table on a raised platform. Dignitaries were placed on either side of them.

The crowd hushed as everyone waited expectantly.

"People of Nurhan, welcome to Castle Elumina. Blessings on you all for joining me on this auspicious occasion marking my betrothal to Lady Raya of the Vulcani. Some of you knew her mother, Lady Aelah who led the clan. It is my expectation that Lady Raya will follow in her footsteps. I bid you welcome her into your hearts, as I have into mine."

Shade took her hand and kissed it. For a moment, the look in his eyes was so warm that the breath caught in her throat.

She knew he was just putting on a show. But she was still flustered as they sat down. At a signal from Pasha, serving staff started moving among the tables with tureens of food and carafes of wine.

Raya's dining companion to the left was a portly gentleman who said he owned a series of salt mines.

"All the salt in this castle, and indeed throughout the land, comes from my mines," he said proudly. Raya agreed it was very fine salt, whilst trying to lean away from his halitosis.

She took a glass of wine, gulping half of it down as he launched into a detailed explanation of salt production. She was relieved when Shade broke off his own conversation with the man to his right.

"His breath could strip paint from a wall," she whispered.

"Hardly worse than what I am enduring. This man seems to have an unnatural amount of knowledge about beans. It is about as interesting as watching the damned things grow."

They grinned at each other, conspirators in a shared ordeal.

"Perhaps we should just get incredibly drunk," she suggested. "It might be more bearable."

"A very fine idea." He held his hand up. "Pasha, more wine."

She relaxed as the evening passed. Various dignitaries came to speak to her, passing on their congratulations or simply introducing themselves to her. One or two mentioned her mother and Raya was gratified to learn she had been well-liked.

Yet nobody mentioned her human heritage, even though Raya could sense there was a lot of curiosity about that.

"No-one's asking about my life before coming here," she muttered to Shade. "They know I'm half human, don't they?"

"I expect so. But it is seen as impolite to point out one's shortcomings. You can be sure they'll be whispering about your human traits."

"Like what?"

"Like your rounded ears."

Raya's hand shot to one ear.

"But *your* ears are normal."

"For a jinn. Yours are entirely abnormal for a fae."

"Oh." She remembered the photo of her mother, with her daintily pointed ears. "I suppose compared to fae ears, mine are quite ugly."

"I like them."

Shade replied offhandedly before turning back to his neighbour, leaving Raya pondering his remark.

He liked her ears even though they were ugly? Or he liked them because he thought they *weren't* ugly?

Fuck. She'd drunk too much wine.

The dinner progressed interminably. The noise levels grew as the wine flowed. The band started playing more upbeat music. Halitosis Man had thankfully turned to his other neighbour to continue his monologue about salt and Raya pushed her dessert plate away, full to bursting.

She was startled when Shade took her hand.

"Dance?"

"Fuck no."

"This is our engagement party. People expect us to dance. And no-one else can dance until we do. So."

She looked at him wide-eyed.

"But I can't dance. I don't know how."

He bent so close she could feel his breath on her skin.

"Do you trust me?"

His voice was like velvet and Raya found herself gazing into his deep blue stare.

"Yes."

"Then let us dance."

He led her to a clear space of floor in front of the band. Raya's neck prickled, conscious that everyone was turning to look.

"Just lean into me," he instructed.

Hesitantly, she put her hands on his shoulders. He was so tall, she had to reach right up. This isn't going to work, she thought cynically. But incredibly, it did.

He pulled her close, one arm around her back, the other at her waist. As one, they moved across the floor, her body melting into his as he controlled the pace and direction. The rhythm of the music seemed to pulse in waves right through her body.

She laid her head against his chest. Maybe it was the wine or maybe it was the shared experience of the past couple of hours, but suddenly she was glad he was there. And perhaps he felt the same, because his hand travelled to the nape of her neck where it rested, his thumb stroking the skin.

"Nearly over, halfling," he murmured. "You have acquitted yourself well."

"Promise me we never have to do this again."

"Not until our wedding day."

Startled, her head shot up and she found him laughing at her.

"Very funny," she grumbled. Other couples had taken to the floor and she spotted Halitosis Man making a beeline towards her.

"I think that guy wants to cut in."

"Should I make way?"

"Not if you want to keep your teeth."

"Then let us make our farewells."

Smoothly, Shade twirled her past the salt merchant and off the dance floor. He led her through the banqueting hall, stopping to speak briefly with Pasha. Then they were climbing the stairs.

"What did you say to Pasha?"

"I told him we could contain ourselves no longer and were retiring to have some passionate alone-time."

Raya spluttered.

"You did *what*?"

Shade roared with laughter, the vibration of his mirth making the lights along the staircase flicker.

"Relax. I told him our obligations were complete. We dined, we talked, we danced. Everyone can now get drunk without the Lord of Nurhan watching them, and we can escape. Thank the skies."

They reached their chambers. In the living area, Shade held up a bottle of amber liquid.

"Nightcap?"

"Sure. A small one."

He poured them both a glass.

"The next big hurdle is the Vulcani test. Do you feel ready?"

"Actually, I do. I'd show you but I'm too drunk and I might burn the castle down."

"Hm. One hopes you have a little more control in the demonstration."

"It'll be fine. Stop angsting. You know, if you keep frowning like that, your face will stay that way. All gothic and brooding."

"You do not like my face?"

She pretended to examine him. His hair was smoothed back, except for one stubborn lock falling over his eyes. Her stomach did a slow flip.

"It's okay." She took a gulp from her glass and coughed as it burned its way down her throat. "Holy hell, what is this?"

"Nectar liqueur. The naiads make it from mountain water. It is excellent, is it not?"

"If I drink this, I will literally fall over." She placed the half finished glass carefully on the table. "Hey, I was thinking earlier about what I'd do when this was all over."

"Oh?"

"Well, I can hardly go back to the hospital. The obvious thing would be for me to stay with my mother. I was wondering if you'd started to look for her yet?"

His face darkened. He tossed back the rest of the liqueur and poured himself another one.

"Are you in such a hurry to leave the castle?"

"I'll have to leave eventually, won't I? Once I convince the Vulcani to side with you, I can get out of your hair. Isn't that what you want? I'm sure you must be missing Leona. Where is Leona, anyway?"

"She has left the castle."

"I'm sorry. But you see? Having me here isn't good for your private life." She was teasing him but his face was granite. She tried again. "I just want to stick to our agreement, Shade. Nothing more, nothing less."

"Fine." He slammed his glass down. Black ripples started emanating around his feet. "I will see what I can do."

"Thanks," she said uncertainly. "There's no rush, you don't have to…"

"I said I would do it." He couldn't look at her. He hadn't realised she was so desperate for the deal to be over. "Just make sure you hold up your end of the bargain."

"Of course." She didn't understand why he was suddenly so distant. Confused, she took a couple of steps towards her bedchamber. "Tomorrow, is it okay if I go to the Melae?"

"What you do is no concern of mine. As long as you impress the Vulcani, that is all I care about."

His tone was ice cold and she felt tears pricking at her eyes.

"Goodnight, Lord Shadeed," she said. "Thank you for the dance."

She shut the door quietly behind her.

Twenty Nine

The day of the Melae dawned fine and clear. Raya could hear the music drifting in through her window and excitement fluttered in her stomach. She'd never been to any kind of festival before and she could hardly wait.

She breakfasted alone. Shade was nowhere to be seen and Pasha told her he was in meetings most of the day.

"Running Nurhan requires administrative duties," he told her. "But I am at your service, my Lady. Is there anything I can get for you?"

"A mask," she said quickly. "For the Melae. Something pretty."

"Of course. I will have it sent up straight away. And I will organise a bodyguard to accompany you."

"A bodyguard? Is that strictly necessary?"

"Everyone knows who you are now, my Lady. It would be safer."

Since the dinner yesterday, Raya's anonymity had evaporated. Everywhere she went, people dropped into curtsies or hurried to open doors for her. It was quite disconcerting.

"But I'll be wearing a mask, Pasha. No-one will recognise me."

"I'm sure Lord Shadeed would want you to..."

"Well, he's not here, and he's not the boss of me. No bodyguard," she said firmly. Pasha nodded unhappily and cleared the table. Raya spent the next hour exploring the Library, curious to see what counted as classic literature for fae and jinn.

The fae books were written in outlandish runes which she had no hope of translating. Strange shapes and symbols which looked like they belonged in a Tolkien novel.

The jinn language appeared a little more familiar though no less incomprehensible; possibly a mix of Arabic and Chinese? She had no idea. For all she knew, it was actually all Swahili.

She found a dark leatherbound volume under the Vetali section and leafed through it. The words on the heavy cream paper were hand-written in some kind of dark red substance. She closed it hastily, hoping like hell it was just ink and nothing else.

Grabbing the Hemmingway from the table, she made her way back to her bedchamber. Pasha had left a long dark blue dress on the bed, and a mask. She held it up to her face.

It was made of green and blue feathers embellished in gold, with peacock feathers rising from the centre. It covered a good portion of her face, and Raya laughed in delight. It was perfect.

Quickly, she got changed and twisted her hair into a knot. She put her soft suede boots on under the dress. If there was any dancing to be done, she wasn't going to be doing it in heels. Then she slipped from the castle, adjusting her mask as she made her way down the road.

She wasn't the only one. She joined a stream of people in masks heading in the same direction, all talking and laughing excitedly. The road was lined with flags and pennants, and the music grew louder as they approached the town.

The Melae had taken over the streets, spilling into every road and alleyway. Stalls and carts were parked haphazardly, selling trinkets and toys. Men were wheeling barrels around and curiously, Raya watched a group of youths approach one with glasses held out. A man opened a tap on the barrel and dark gold liquid gushed out.

Beer, Raya guessed. Or cider. She saw the youths nudge each other as they supped their alcohol, barely old enough for facial hair. Underage drinking wasn't just a human trait, then.

The crowds grew heavier when she entered the main square. People had set up griddles and spits in every doorway. The smell of roasting meat made her mouth water.

Children ran by shouting and giggling, their hands full of candy and pastries. A juggler in a harlequin mask winked at her and threw knives into the air. Gasping, Raya watched as he caught every one.

The town centre was packed with dancers. Bands played on almost every street corner, all belting out their own tunes. It should have been a raucous cacophony but somehow it worked. Men and women twirled together, some in colourfully ornate face coverings, others with just a strip of black painted over their eyes. Most were dressed flamboyantly with feathers, sequins and bold colours. The atmosphere was intoxicating.

An older man with grey hair offered her his hand. His mask was plain white and his eyes sparkled behind it.

"Why not?" she said. He drew her into the sway of revellers. She was twirled and dipped, then pulled into a jig. He was deceptively spry and she laughed, breathless, as she tried to copy his steps.

Raya spent the next hour dancing with one partner after another. Her feet ached and her mouth hurt from smiling but she loved every single minute. It was only as she leaned against a table to catch her breath that she wondered where Tor was.

She scanned the crowds, hoping to catch a glimpse of blond hair or strong arms but there were too many people. And they were all wearing masks.

He'd said she'd recognise him, but she didn't see how. The man in the deer mask was tall enough to be him. The one dressed as a jester had the same broad shoulders.

When she finally recognised him, her face broke into a smile. Of course. He had taken the guise of a wolf.

He gave a little bow in her direction and she pushed her way through the crowd.

"Great wolf mask. But how did you know it was me?"

"The mask hides your face. Not your aura. Dance?"

"Actually, I could use a drink first. Can we try some barrel beer?"

"Barrel beer?" He was amused.

"The stuff on those handcarts."

"That's not beer. It's mead, made from honey."

"So it's healthy, then?"

"Aye. If you don't drink too much. Wait here."

He came back with two glasses of the tawny liquid. Raya took a tentative sip, then a longer one.

"It's lovely. Sort of sweet but it has a kick to it."

"It's quite strong," Tor warned. "Go easy on it."

"You know I've never really drunk alcohol?" Raya looked at her glass thoughtfully. "I'm twenty one years old and I've never been drunk. Never even had a hangover."

"And that's a bad thing?"

"Well, I guess my liver's in good nick at least. Come on, wolf boy. Let's dance."

They inserted themselves into the heaving mass. Raya had to hang onto Tor to avoid losing him in the crowd but he didn't seem to mind. When his hand slipped round her waist it seemed the most natural thing in the world.

"This is the second best thing I've done since I got to Nush'aldaam," she shouted into his ear.

"Only the second? What's the first?"

"Flying with Shade. I love it. Mind you, he did drop me once. On purpose."

"I see," he said drily. "How did the betrothal dinner go?"

"Not as hideous as I thought it would be. It was actually surprisingly fun. Until Shade had a rage-out."

"A rage-out?"

"Lost his temper. He does that a lot."

Tor looked round warily.

"Is he here?"

"No. He's at the castle. Working."

Tor grinned.

"Well, I can't fly you to the stars. But I *can* sweep you off your feet." His arm tightened around her and he whirled her round until she collapsed, giggling, into his arms.

They danced until the evening. Fairy lights came on, strung across the streets and between buildings. People lit candles and lamps, and the party continued.

They watched a series of street performers. One pale young woman in a mask of green foliage held out her arms. All of a sudden, flowers burst through the ground, growing and blooming in a riot of colour all around the feet of an impressed crowd.

"She's a dryad," Tor told her. "Another elemental, like the fire fae. Except she can control earth. They don't leave the forest very often."

A young man created characters of smoke and shadows on a wall and made them act out a slapstick play that had everyone laughing.

"Is he an Ifrit?" Raya asked.

"Yes, but not a powerful one. His shadows have no substance. He has a talent for comedy though."

"Can we get some food? I've always wanted to try street food. Do they have hotdogs?"

"Hot what?"

"Meat inside bread. With onions."

"I think we can do better than that."

Tor disappeared and Raya realised she was hungry. A blonde woman approached her with a plate full of dark berries. She smiled at Raya.

"Try some?"

"What are they?"

"Ambrosia berries. A delicacy in Nurhan. Go ahead."

Raya nibbled on one of the berries. It was large and plump, bursting with juice.

"It tastes like chocolate," she exclaimed. She popped it into her mouth and took another.

"Are you and your young man enjoying the Melae?" asked the woman.

"Oh, he's just a friend. But yes, we're having a great time. And you?"

"I think the night is about to get more entertaining," the woman said. "Will you take one for your friend?"

"Thanks." Raya put a berry in her dress pocket.

"It is my pleasure. Enjoy yourself, Lady Raya."

"Thanks, I… hey, how did you…?"

But the woman had gone. Puzzled, Raya tried to find her in the crowd. She turned as she heard Tor's voice behind her.

"Here, I brought you some raqaq. It's hot, be careful."

He handed her a flatbread heaped high with something sweet and spicy. She took a bite.

"This is delicious." She took another mouthful, trying not to look as though she was stuffing her face.

"It's all locally grown vegetables cooked with herbs and spices. No dogs."

"It's amazing."

"It's one of my favourites."

They munched in silence for a while. He really is good-looking, thought Raya. She finished the raqaq, licking the sauce off her fingers.

"More dancing?" she suggested. He glanced up at the sky.

"Wait just one second. Any minute now…"

Fireworks suddenly lit the sky and Raya gazed upwards in wonder. Starbursts of light cascaded in blues and reds and greens, and each thunderous explosion reverberated pleasantly through her body.

She leaned slightly against Tor, pretending she needed support as she watched the fireworks. When the last blaze of light trailed away in a flash of sulphur, the crowd applauded.

She felt deliciously relaxed as she turned to Tor and looped her hands around his neck.

"I'm having a really good time," she told him. She smiled into his eyes and let herself rest against him. His arms automatically went round her waist. "I think I promised you a thank you, didn't I?"

She stood on tiptoe and pressed her lips to the corner of his. He inhaled at the touch of her mouth so close to his own.

"I think you've had a bit too much mead," he said, a little unsteadily.

"I think you're right." She giggled, then clapped her hand to her pocket. "I almost forgot. I have something for you. It tastes amazing."

She brought out the chocolate-flavoured berry. Tor's reaction was not what she expected. He snatched it from her hand.

"Where did you get this?"

"A woman was handing them out. Why, what's wrong?"

"Have you eaten any? Raya, have you eaten any of these berries?"

Raya gazed at him wide-eyed.

"I ate two. Tor, tell me what's wrong. You're freaking me out."

He dropped the berry to the ground and tore his mask off. She watched, bewildered as he seemed to have an internal debate with himself. Then he grabbed her hand.

"Come with me. We have to go. Now."

"Where? Where are we going?"

"To find Lord Shadeed."

"But *why*? What's wrong with the berries?" A strange feeling was creeping over her body. She clutched Tor's hand, enjoying the sensation of his fingers threaded through hers. "Are they poisonous?"

His voice was grim.

"Not exactly. Now come on. Before it's too late."

Thirty

Tor practically dragged her back to the castle. He refused to answer any of her questions, simply pushed through the crowd as fast as he could.

She supposed she should have been worried by his reaction, but honestly, she was just enjoying the way he used his muscles to shove people aside.

"You're so strong," she commented. "I don't think I've noticed your biceps before. Well, not close up."

He glanced at her, frowning.

"Just hang on a bit longer, Raya. We're nearly there."

Hang on? What on earth was he talking about? She felt great.

"What did you mean, the berries aren't exactly poisonous? What are they?"

"A sort of narcotic. It affects your mood. People normally take it in private."

"Oh, I see." She nodded wisely. "Like cannabis. Well, don't worry. When it comes to drugs, I've had quite a few over the years. Prescribed, obviously. But I'm used to it."

Tor didn't answer. He pulled her up the steps of the castle and grabbed the first person he saw, which turned out to be Pasha.

"Lord Shadeed. Where is he?"

"He's in the meeting room but he won't want to be disturbed."

"It's an emergency. Take us to him."

"Us?" Pasha looked over at Raya and recognition dawned. "Ah, Lady Raya. Of course, the peacock mask. Forgive me. Come this way."

He led them to a room on the first floor, completely ignoring Tor's attempts to make him walk faster. Raya giggled. She stripped off her mask and let it fall to the floor, uncaring. Her body felt deliciously light, as if she was floating in a scented bath.

"How are you doing, my Lady?" Tor asked.

"I need a lie down. My room's on the top floor. Why don't you come with me?"

She stroked a finger down his arm. She knew he was strong enough to lift her. She wondered what it would be like to be pinned against him. The unexpected thought made her warm.

"Let's find Lord Shadeed first," Tor said. Pasha stopped in front of a door.

"Let me just check if he's..."

Tor didn't let him finish. He threw it open, surprising the four or five people inside sitting round a table. Shade stood up, glowering.

"What is the meaning of this?" His face darkened as he saw Tor, still holding Raya's hand.

Tor didn't waver.

"Apologies, Lord Shadeed. But it's a matter of urgency."

Shade strode out, closing the door behind him.

"What do you mean? Raya, are you alright?"

Raya was finding it hard to speak. The sight of Shade storming towards them had done something major to her insides. Heat was rippling up and down her body and her heart was skittering like crazy.

Fuck, maybe she *had* been poisoned.

Tor leaned towards Shade, whispering urgently.

"Someone gave her ambrosia berries. You need to take her somewhere private."

Shade's brows drew down.

"Ambrosia berries? Who?"

"She said a woman gave them to her. My Lord, she's had two. You need to take her *now*."

Shade swore under his breath.

"Pasha, tell the others the meeting is over. And I am not to be disturbed for the rest of the evening." He turned to Tor. "You have my thanks, Mr Torven. A lesser man may have taken advantage of the situation. I was wrong about you."

"Not entirely." Tor met his gaze levelly. "I considered it. But she's already spoken for."

Shade's jaw tightened.

"That would not have been a barrier to someone of fewer morals."

"Maybe not. But I've seen her aura when she's around you and I know who she'd rather be with." He let go of Raya's hand and gave her a small smile. "You'll be all right now, my Lady."

Raya watched him vanish down the stairs.

"Wait! What's going on?"

Her pulse leapt as Shade took her hand.

"Let us go."

"Where are we going?"

"To the bedchamber."

Heat bloomed between her legs. Christ, what the hell was the matter with her?

"I… I feel a bit strange."

A glimmer of a smile ghosted across Shade's lips.

"I am not surprised. *Two* ambrosia berries?"

"But what are they? Are they dangerous? Why won't anyone tell me anything?"

Raya planted her feet, determined to get an answer. With an oath that stripped the paint off the nearest wall, Shade scooped her up.

"They are not dangerous, but they require an antidote of sorts."

Being in his arms was arousing. The heat from his chest warmed her cheek and she had an insane urge to press her lips to it. She wriggled a little, enjoying the way his hands tightened round her.

"You're very handsome," she said dreamily, then clamped her mouth shut in horror. Why the hell did she just say that? Shade didn't answer.

He pushed his way into the bedroom and set her down on her feet, closing the door firmly behind them.

She caught sight of herself in the mirror and stopped, mesmerized by the way she looked. Her lips had plumped up and darkened in colour. Her eyes were smouldering and sultry. And her nipples had hardened, clearly outlined under her dress. They began to ache pleasurably.

"What's happening to me, Shade?" she asked in a low voice.

"Ambrosia berries are an aphrodisiac. A powerful one. They're usually taken by consenting partners as they produce an almost irresistible urge to copulate."

"An *aphrodisiac*?" She looked at him in horror. "I've been roofied?"

"Whoever gave you the berries was evidently hoping you would cause a scandal by fornicating with Mr Torven. Luckily, he is a man of integrity."

"So he brought me to *you*?" Raya digested what that meant. "I'm supposed to have *sex* with you?"

"The only way to neutralise the berries you've consumed is to allow your fluids to mingle with those of a compatible partner. Copulation is not strictly necessary, I assure you."

"No way. Not a chance." Raya shook her head decisively, even as heat flared low in her stomach. "No-one's mingling any fluids."

"Raya." Shade folded his arms, his voice calm. "Either you can stay in this state of arousal for the next few days, which will be uncomfortable and embarrassing, or you can let me help you."

A steady pulse was beating between her legs. She pressed her thighs together, hoping he wouldn't notice.

"Why can't I, you know, take care of it myself?"

"You need physical contact with another to stop the effect."

"Well, that's just fucking convenient, isn't it? Magical Viagra with only one cure. Why the fuck did that bitch give me the berries?"

"We will investigate later. Right now, you must be feeling the effects." His eyes lingered on her nipples, standing proudly. "I give my word I will do no more than is necessary to alleviate your symptoms. May I be permitted to help you?"

The throbbing between her legs was becoming unbearable. Silently, she nodded.

In two paces he was at her side. He took her face in his hands.

"I swear you can trust me," he said gruffly. And he kissed her, slow and deep, the sweetness of it taking her breath away.

Thirty One

The kiss was a trigger. At the first touch of his lips, her inhibitions fell away. She pressed her body to his, rubbing against him, the dress maddeningly harsh against her sensitive nipples.

Impatiently, she broke away to pull the dress from her shoulders. It fell to the floor and she stood before him, almost entirely naked, with just the tiniest wisp of silk protecting her modesty. She basked in his appreciative stare. She had never felt so bold, so confident in her own allure.

Reaching up, she pulled his mouth to hers again, darting her tongue between his lips. A small part of her knew she was acting against character, that she was testing his self-control. But she didn't care. She wanted him.

He cupped a buttock, marvelling at the smoothness of her skin. His other hand curved around her breast and he squeezed gently, her nipple drilling into his palm. She moaned into his mouth as he stroked it, the roughened tip deliciously erect between his fingers.

Eagerly, she arched her back as he trailed his lips down her neck, her collarbone. When his tongue slicked over one dark aureole, she slid her hands into his hair and pulled him closer. He sucked the tip into his mouth, thrashing it lightly until it was diamond hard. The bolts of pleasure he was stoking seemed to shoot straight to her groin.

She rubbed her hips against him, a deliberate invitation. He groaned softly around her breast.

"You are making it very difficult to concentrate."

She reached down and grasped him through his trousers, unprepared for his girth. He was as hard as rock. The feel of him fanned the heat between her legs into an inferno.

"I want you," she whispered. "Inside me. Please."

"I promised I would not."

"I'm releasing you from your promise."

He gently took her hand and removed it, threading his fingers through hers.

"When you make the same request without being under the influence of an aphrodisiac, I will gladly oblige, my beautiful halfling. But for now, let me do my job."

He lifted her onto the bed and laid her down. Her eyes dilated with pleasure as he stroked his hands over her breasts, her waist, the warm curve of her belly. Her hips bucked upwards, desperate for his touch.

He drew off her underwear, making her wait as he drank in the sight of her; skin flushed, eyes half closed, raven hair splayed across the pillow. She is magnificent, he thought.

And then he parted her thighs and tasted her.

The first touch of his tongue sent an exquisite shock through her whole body. She writhed helplessly, unable to stop. She wasn't in control of her reactions anymore. He was.

He licked at her swollen tissues, each stroke creating a delicious tension until she was quivering like a bow. She moaned as he kissed the most sensitive part of her, teasing her with his tongue until she was pressing hard against his mouth.

She had never experienced sensations like this before. She was terrified and elated at the same time. If he didn't stop, she was going to break.

She begged him not to stop.

Her hips rocked frantically as he licked and lapped, driving her closer to the edge. She was nectar to him, her wetness increasing with each pass of his tongue. And when she was poised on the very brink, he took the engorged little nub into his mouth and sucked.

She shattered. Again and again. Shattered into a million pieces. Heat rippled through her, fed by her shuddering ecstasy. Through each glorious wave, he licked at her steadily, pleasuring her until she cried out, unable to stop herself.

And when finally the spasms receded, she was left adrift in a cloud of bliss. Her body felt boneless, weightless, deliciously torpid. She lay tangled among the sheets in a sweet haze and revelled in her newfound knowledge.

So that was an orgasm. She couldn't understand why people weren't having them every single minute of every single day.

She opened her eyes to find Shade watching her. A blush started somewhere round her navel and worked its way up to her face.

"Hi," she said shyly. She wanted to cover herself with a sheet but it seemed pointless.

"Hello." A smile played round his lips. "How do you feel?"

The throbbing between her legs had gone. She didn't feel aroused anymore. Just satiated. And very, very lethargic.

"Amazing. I've never ever felt that way before. I can barely move."

"Then your previous lovers were lacking in finesse," Shade said drily.

"I haven't had any lovers. Locked in a hospital, remember? Very small dating pool."

His expression changed.

"You have never been intimate with a partner?"

The incredulity in his voice made her feel small. She ducked her head.

"Not like that. I mean, I've done some stuff but not… I'm sorry. I hope it wasn't too disappointing for you."

He muttered an oath under his breath. Lifting her chin, he made her look at him.

"Please believe me when I say that what we shared was extremely pleasurable for me too. Your reaction was most… intense." His blue gaze roamed over her flushed face. "And now you must sleep. The narcotic will make you fatigued as it leaves your system."

Tiredness was already creeping over her. She moved closer to him, curling herself against his heat like a cat.

"Stay with me," she murmured.

He ran his hand along her back, soothing her from neck to waist. She fought the drowsiness, wanting to talk to him, to keep their feeling of closeness as long as possible. She wanted to ask if he really thought she was beautiful. But the rhythmic stroking was soporific and before she knew it, her eyes were closing.

Shade tucked a stray curl behind Raya's ear. He could still taste her. It had taken considerable willpower not to renege on his promise to abstain from sex. She would not have objected, not in the grip of her passion. And the thought of sliding into her, joining with her, left him weak.

But somehow, he hadn't wanted to violate her trust. And now, discovering she was unknown to man, he was glad. Her first time should be with someone she cared about.

He realised he was still touching her hair and snatched his hand back with a sinking feeling. No. It was not possible.

He couldn't be falling for her. Not this half-human waif who was counting the days till she could be free of him.

She asked you to stay just now. Only because she was still under the influence of the ambrosia berries. She was tired and emotional and she didn't know what she was saying.

He would be a fool to read anything into it.

The Sylvan said she had feelings for you.

The Sylvan knew nothing. His expertise was animals and plants, not women.

He slid from the bed, his gaze lingering on her a second longer. Then he dove from the open window, suddenly needing to feel the cool night air on his face. He let himself fall, only unfurling his wings at the last possible second.

He couldn't afford to have feelings for her. Not when she had made it so damn clear she wanted to leave the castle. She was here for one reason only; because they had made a deal.

Time to keep his end of it.

Thirty Two

It was still dusk on the other side of the Gate. The kobold had built herself a fire and was sitting close to it, puffing contentedly on her pipe. She raised an eyebrow as Shade alighted, his shadows briefly blocking out the sky.

"Gatekeeper." He nodded courteously, trying to disguise his irritation with her latest headwear, a ridiculously large furry hat with a racoon tail hanging down the back.

"I was expecting to see you sooner, my Lord. Here, take a seat on that log. What's the news on our halfling?"

"She has found her power. It was a little underwhelming at first, but she assures me it has improved." He settled himself on a felled tree trunk and shaped his shadows into a sweater, on the slim chance a human happened by.

"Never mind that. How's the fake betrothal going? Spill."

Shade gritted his teeth.

"It is challenging. In the beginning I found her most aggravating. She did what she wanted and showed no respect for my orders."

"How impertinent of her." Magda rolled her eyes. "I'm sure being given orders is just what every girl wants from a man."

"She agreed to the deal," he said, stung. "And then she started making eyes at some Sylvan peasant."

"Perhaps he's nice to her. Have *you* tried that?"

Shade growled impatiently and a tree fifty yards away dumped its entire load of snow.

"I *am* nice to her. We have reached an... an understanding. An entente cordial."

"How romantic," Magda said drily.

"Romance is not an option."

Magda looked at him sharply. His tone was unusual.

"Why are you here, Lord Shadeed?"

"I wish to uphold my end of the bargain. To find her mother."

"Aelah? I see." The kobold lapsed into silence. Shade smelled the sweet tobacco smoke from her pipe as it drifted into the darkening sky.

"Well?" he prompted. "Can you help me? Do you have any idea where she might be?"

"Why do you think *I* would know?"

"Because you were the last person to see her. And she confided in you. She sent you pictures of herself, did she not? She trusted you."

"She trusted me to keep her secrets."

"The secret is already out. By now, Salaq and his cronies will have heard that Aelah's daughter is in Nush'aldaam. When Raya confirms her powers to the Vulcani in three days time, everyone will know about her."

"Mm." Shade waited but Magda didn't say anything more.

"So?" he prompted. "Do you know where Aelah is? There is no need for her to hide anymore."

"Interesting."

"What is?"

"You. Making an effort for a girl."

Shade glowered.

"I have no idea what you are blathering about, Gatekeeper. I have no interest in Raya in *that* way."

"Really? Does she not have a pulse? That's your normal criteria."

Shade stood abruptly, towering over the kobold who calmly sucked on her pipe.

"Are you going to help me or not, woman?"

"Chill your jets. Sit. Seriously, sit. You're giving me a crick in the neck."

Shade slowly lowered himself to the log again. He waited while she tapped out the spent tobacco in her pipe and refilled it.

"Magda, you try my patience. Do you know where Aelah is?"

The Gatekeeper sighed.

"I know where she is. And I know where Raya's father is too."

"But this is good news." Shade felt a sense of triumph. He would be able to give Raya not one, but both her parents.

The Gatekeeper took a long pull on her pipe. It was time to tell the truth, and she knew the truth would hurt.

"Lord Shadeed," she said quietly. "There's something you should know."

Thirty Three

Shade was gone from her side when she woke up. Raya stretched languidly, still loose-limbed and relaxed from the night before. Her pulse quickened as she remembered what Shade had done to her. His kisses. His tongue.

He'd called it a job, she reminded herself. He hadn't wanted her to embarrass him by acting like a bitch in heat so he'd taken care of her problem. Don't read anything into it.

She rolled from the bed and went to study herself in the mirror. Her lips were a little swollen but other than that, she looked the same as ever. Plain. Unremarkable.

He called you beautiful. And he'd said he'd enjoyed it.

She rejected the quiet little voice trying to persuade her that last night's events were anything more than a duty to him. Shade's only desire was to be emperor. Once the Vulcani were allied to him, he wouldn't need her anymore.

The sooner she completed her task and left, the better.

She bathed and dressed, then went downstairs to get breakfast. She was starving. Pasha served her up some eggs and a thick salty meat that was a ringer for gammon, though she couldn't recall seeing any pigs in Nush'aldaam.

She thought about going to look for Tor but she was too mortified by what had happened with the ambrosia berries. She was pretty sure she'd come on to him.

She wondered who the woman was who'd given her the berries. Had she done it maliciously? Or was it an innocent mistake? She'd probably never know.

Anyway, she had work to do. She went to the night-garden where she could practice uninterrupted.

Her flames now came at the drop of a hat. She could make them erupt from her fingers or the palm of her hand. She could make them ripple up her arms to her shoulders with just a thought. With a bit of focus, she could engulf her face and torso in flames, which tickled.

She'd worried her eyebrows or hair might burn the first time she did it. But she was as impervious to fire as Shade was.

Strange that they had that in common.

She practised making flame birds and butterflies. They fluttered round the night-garden under her control, and she took care this time not to let them get close to anything flammable. The memory of the burning tree was still fresh.

Shade hadn't seen her power yet. Didn't he want to check up on her progress? Surely he didn't want to wait till the Vulcani arrived to see what she could do?

She resolved to show Shade her progress as soon as she saw him. But he didn't return for the next two days. She drifted round the castle, paranoia nibbling at her.

Shade couldn't bear to be near her.

She annoyed him. Disgusted him.

He'd gone to drown his sorrows in Leona's arms.

He couldn't wait to get rid of her.

The thoughts went round and round in her head. She tried to find solace in the Library but she couldn't concentrate on a single book, not even Hemingway.

In the end she swallowed her pride and went to find Tor.

She still hadn't spoken to him since the Melae. Knowing he was fully aware of how aroused she'd been as he dragged her back to the castle made her want to die of embarrassment.

But she couldn't avoid him forever. Anyway, he was a gentleman. He wouldn't mention it if she didn't.

She found him feeding the horses in the stables. He listened patiently as she griped about Shade's absence.

"I know he's not exactly a homebody," she said. "But with the Vulcani arriving tomorrow you'd think he'd be around."

"It means he trusts you."

"He hasn't even seen what I can do. I wanted to show him."

"It sounds like you miss him."

"Miss him? I don't miss him. He's always stamping around and shouting."

"He seemed calm to me on the few occasions I've met him," Tor said mildly. "Even the last one."

Raya felt her cheeks warm.

"Anyway. What about you? Are you all set for the Vulcani delegation?"

"Aye. I've just managed to source the seafood they're so partial to. Even old iron-face Loris will be pleased."

She giggled.

"Let's hope it puts them in a good mood for my display."

"I have no doubt you'll impress them." He paused. "And then what?"

"What do you mean?"

"You told me you thought Shadeed had only made you his betrothed to win the support of the Vulcani. If you succeed, will you continue that alliance? Will you wed him?"

Raya was startled.

"I don't know. I haven't thought that far ahead. But Shade's trying to find my mother so maybe I'll go and stay with her for a while. She's somewhere in the human world, I think."

Tor looked at her, aghast.

"Leave Nush'aldaam? Leave the Vulcani without a leader again?"

"They don't actually need me to take over, do they?" She squirmed under his stare. "I'm not really leader material. Loris seems pretty capable."

"But they *do* need you. They want you to take Aelah's place. The Vulcani are extremely hierarchical, Raya. They expect someone from her bloodline to lead them."

"I'm only half fae," she protested. "I don't know anything about the Vulcani or their ways. How the hell am I supposed to lead them?"

"You won't know until you try," Tor said stiffly. "But I suppose I can't convince you to do something you don't want to do."

"Don't be angry with me, Tor."

"I'm not angry. I'm frustrated. You told me you were locked up in the human world because people thought you weren't right in the head. Well, here you have a chance to make a difference. Be an inspiration. And you're throwing it away."

"I want to find my mother," she shouted. "I don't care about anything else."

"Aye, you keep saying that. But if it were *Shade* asking you to stay, would you give the same answer?"

He looked at her steadily and she found she couldn't hold his stare. She glanced away.

"I don't know what you mean," she mumbled.

"You know exactly what I mean. So what if he asked you to partner him for political reasons? You can't deny you have feelings for him."

"Stop telling me how I feel. Why does it matter to you, anyway?"

Tor smiled bitterly.

"Can't you tell? Or is your head so full of Lord Shadeed that you don't notice any other man around you?"

She was brought up short.

"Tor, I..."

"It's okay. I confess I had an ulterior motive for taking you to the Melae. I thought if you and Lord Shadeed were only together for appearances' sake, perhaps I had a chance. I realise now you don't see me that way."

She hesitated. Was it true? Had her feelings for Shade changed? Or was it simply because he was the first man who'd ever given her sexual pleasure? In which case her emotions couldn't be trusted. It hadn't been real passion on her part. She'd been blinded by lust because of those damned ambrosia berries.

And it certainly didn't mean Shade had any feelings for *her*. Far from it. He hadn't even stuck around after that night.

But here was Tor. Attractive, strong, gentle Tor. He had never let her down and he would never hurt her. Maybe she was meant to be with him and she just didn't know it.

"The truth is, I haven't a clue," she said at last. "I'm not very experienced in... in this kind of thing."

"Well then, let's find out." He gave a lopsided smile. "Kiss me."

"What?"

"You've kissed Lord Shade, haven't you? I imagine you kissed him plenty until the ambrosia berries wore off." She blushed deep red and didn't know what to say. "So kiss me now and see how it compares."

"I couldn't do that!"

"Do you find the idea of kissing me so unpleasant, Lady Raya?"

No, she didn't. She didn't find it unpleasant at all.

He raised a brow as she studied him, hazel eyes twinkling. Broad shouldered and well-muscled. But also capable of sensitivity. His hands especially. His hands could work magic.

She realised she was actually considering it.

"Just one kiss?"

"Aye. And if you feel nothing, then I promise friendship is all I'll ask of you."

It was madness. And yet things would be so much easier if she fell in love with Tor.

Slowly, she closed the gap between them. His smile faded as she wound her arms around his neck. She was close enough to inhale his scent. Fresh cut grass and sunshine. She stood on tiptoe and pressed her mouth to his.

He tasted of wild berries.

He slid one hand around her waist and the other into the hair at the nape of her neck. Her body moulded against his as the kiss deepened, his tongue stroking over her lips and darting into her mouth.

It was a good kiss. Strike that. It was a *great* kiss, in her limited experience. But it wasn't affecting her the way Shade's kiss had.

Tor let her go regretfully.

"Aye, I thought so. Your heart's already taken."

"Stop saying that. I'm not in love with Shade."

"You need to admit the truth to yourself, my Lady. I read auras, remember? And you and Lord Shadeed are a better match than you think."

"You're wrong."

"By the skies, you're stubborn. I'm done arguing. But I would say this." Tor gazed at her seriously. "When the demonstration is over, whatever happens, you should consider staying in Nush'aldaam. This is your home now.

Your mother would want you to take your place with the Vulcani."

She was prevented from answering by a shadow passing overhead. She glanced up. Shade was back.

"I have to go."

Tor didn't say anything as she ran back to the castle.

Thirty Four

Shade poured himself a drink and downed it in one. He rubbed his eyes tiredly. He'd delayed his return to the castle because he wasn't sure what he was going to tell Raya.

Whatever he said, it would hurt her. And worse, she might think she no longer had any reason to stay.

The thought of her leaving made him feel strangely hollow.

The door to the Library slammed open.

"Where've you been?" she demanded. He poured himself another glass of nectar.

"Drink?"

"No. Answer me, Shade. The Vulcani arrive tomorrow. Where did you go?"

He sighed wearily and slumped in the armchair.

"I went to see Magda. About your mother."

Raya's pulse quickened.

"I thought Magda said she didn't know where Aelah was?"

"Her exact words were 'I can't tell you where she is'. She was deliberately being coy. I should have realised earlier but I was too wrapped up in the quest for the throne."

"And?" Excitement bubbled up. She sat in the chair opposite, leaning forward on her elbows. "What did she say?"

Shade held out the bottle.

"Are you sure you will not take a drink?"

"Shade!"

"Fine. But it is not good news." His eyes rested on her, as blue and guileless as the sky. "I am sorry, Raya. Your mother is dead."

Raya felt as if she'd been punched in the gut. For a moment she struggled to catch her breath.

All this time hoping. All this time planning. And her mother was dead.

"My father?" she asked dully.

"He died first. Of an illness. Your mother died later. She could not continue without him."

"When?"

"A few years ago. Magda did not want to tell you when you were already discovering so many new things about yourself."

Raya nodded. She didn't blame the Gatekeeper. She would have been crushed if she'd found out about her mother and then discovered she was dead all in the space of a few minutes.

But it was hard to take in.

She wanted to weep and wail at the unfairness of it all. Losing her adopted parents had been bad enough. Now she had no-one.

She sat in silence. Shade carefully put the bottle down.

"I know it is a shock. But I understand. When I lost Kamran, I thought I would never recover. It is trite to say, but time really does heal all wounds."

"Losing a friend isn't the same as losing your entire family."

"True enough. But Kamran was more than just a friend. He was like a brother to me. Our fathers made us train together. Combat, swordsmanship, archery - he was the only person in Nush'aldaam who could best me. He would have made a wonderful emperor."

His tone was bitter and Raya couldn't help asking.

"How did he die?"

"When Emperor Mazhab became infirm, it was clear that Kamran would soon take the throne. All the rich and powerful began to court him, hoping for favours once he came to power. Aelfric invited him to hunt in the Forbidden Zone in Feyir."

"The Forbidden Zone? Sounds like a computer game."

"It is a very special part of Feyir where the most dangerous game are kept. Hunting there is strictly prohibited except by the express invitation of the elven king. It is tended by the bestials." He saw her confused expression. "The bestials are fae with animal characteristics. Satyrs, centaurs and the like. They are the custodians of the Zone with absolute power to protect it."

He stopped, his expression anguished. He hadn't spoken of this for a long time. Gently, Raya prompted him.

"What happened?"

Shade poured himself another glass of liqueur and knocked it back.

"He never returned. Aelfric claimed they were separated during the hunt. Traces of Kamran's blood were found in the Zone and Aelfric executed a centaur suspected of killing him, but it didn't matter. My friend was gone."

Raya rose from her chair and knelt by Shade's side.

"I'm so sorry."

"I blame myself. Kamran was a good man but he was often reckless. He liked to take chances. I should not have let him go."

"It wasn't your fault."

Shade shrugged bitterly.

"Mazhab managed to hang on for another few decades. But he was grief-stricken and despite the entreaties of his advisors, he did not name his successor. I think he refused to believe his son was really dead."

"And here we are."

"Yes. Here we are." He gave a crooked smile. "So you see, I do understand loss. And that is why I am releasing you from the deal."

There was a pause as she digested his words.

"Sorry?"

"You do not have to perform for the Vulcani tomorrow. It is too much to ask."

"But without the Vulcani, you won't have enough support to take the throne."

"I will find another way." He gazed down at her. "This is not your fight anymore, Raya. Take some time. Decide what you want to do."

She rose to her feet, anger bubbling through her.

"What I want to do is complete the bargain. That bastard Aelfric fucked up both our lives. Kamran deserved better. My mother deserved better. I'm not letting him get the throne, Shade. And I'm not backing out of our deal."

"There is no deal anymore. I am dissolving it."

"Tough. When the Vulcani come tomorrow, I'm performing. With or without your blessing. You know it's the right thing to do."

"And afterwards?"

"Afterwards, I'll get out of your hair. You've upheld your side of the deal. I'll uphold mine. And then we're done."

She turned and walked from the Library, fiercely holding onto her composure until she got back to her room.

Then she curled on the bed clutching the picture of her mother and let the tears flow silently, until she had no more to give.

Thirty Five

The Vulcani arrived the next morning. From her window, Raya saw a procession of gilt-covered carriages approach the castle, pulled by horses bedecked with plumes and finery. Trumpeters announced their arrival and soldiers went to greet them.

Butterflies prickled her insides.

"You've got this," she told herself sternly. But she found it hard to sit still.

She knew the Vulcani would need rest and refreshments before her demonstration. They would be served lunch, a meal planned and overseen by Tor. He assured her that all their favourite foods would be available, so hopefully that would put them in a good mood.

After lunch they would rest once more. And then she would be summoned.

Nervously, she practised her fire show. She seemed to have forgotten everything overnight. Her butterflies moved sluggishly and her birds looked like mutant mosquitoes.

"Shit."

She sat on the edge of her bed and twisted a piece of hair round her finger. Her ears were itchy today. Not for the first time, she wished she had some dermatitis cream with her.

She looked at the photo of her mother again. The fire fae glared back ferociously.

"I bet you weren't scared of anything, were you?"

Fuck. She was going to let herself down. She was going to let Shade down. Why the hell hadn't she accepted his offer to release her from the deal?

She bathed and washed her hair. She reasoned that if she was going to die of humiliation, she may as well smell nice.

Clad in a soft velvet robe, she went to examine her wardrobe. Nothing seemed quite right. She selected and discarded dresses until she'd gone through the entire contents.

"That's it then," she said out loud. "The performance is off. I have nothing to wear."

There was a knock at the door.

Pulling her robe tighter around her, she went to open it. Pasha was standing there with a large box.

"Good afternoon, Lady Raya. Lord Shadeed asked me to deliver this to you. He thought it might be suitable for the demonstration. He says it belonged to your mother."

Carefully, Raya took the box.

"My mother? How did he get it?"

"It is her ceremonial robe from the Vulcani mansion. I believe he asked Loris to bring it."

"The Vulcani have a mansion?"

"Indeed. Though it has, of course, been empty since your mother left Nush'aldaam. I suppose you might have taken residence there, had you not been betrothed to Lord Shadeed."

"Um, yeah, sure. I suppose. Thanks, Pasha."

She closed the door and set the box on the table. Inside was a mass of chiffon in the brightest scarlet she'd ever seen. She drew it out and held it up to herself.

It was a floor length ballgown cut to flatter and show off the female body. It cinched in at the waist and flared into an elegant A-line to the floor. The bodice was slashed to a deep vee front and back, exposing just the right amount of skin. It was dramatic and daring, exactly the type of thing a powerful fire fae would wear.

She stepped into it gingerly, pulling the slim straps onto her shoulders. It fitted like a glove. And when she gazed at herself in the mirror, she saw the epitome of confidence staring back at herself.

It was the perfect armour.

She felt a pang. Shade had gone to all the trouble of finding this for her. In fact, he'd done a lot of things for her.

He'd rescued her from the hospital. Told her the truth about herself. Discovered the fate of her parents. Helped her find a power she never knew she had.

She owed him so much.

"But it's not just gratitude you feel towards him, is it?" she told her reflection. "Tor was right. You have feelings for him."

Yet it didn't matter what she felt. Shade was probably counting the minutes till she was gone.

She could still thank him for the dress though.

She went through into the living room and knocked at his door.

"Come."

She opened it a crack.

"Hi. Um, I didn't know if you'd be here. I know you're busy. I just came to say thanks for the dress."

"Am I permitted to see?"

"Oh. Okay."

She opened the door wider and slipped inside.

Shade had also dressed for the occasion, He was resplendent in a white sleeveless tunic made of raw silk and embroidered in gold, with a thick gold sash around his waist.

Raya swallowed, her mouth suddenly dry.

"Wow. You look amazing."

Shade didn't answer. His eyes were roaming over her, flaring blue with such intensity that heat flooded her cheeks. She tried to laugh it off with an awkward little pirouette.

"What do you think?"

He couldn't speak. She had, he was forced to admit, taken his breath away.

When he eventually found his voice, he was mortified to find he didn't know what to say.

"You look… nice." He cursed himself. By the gods, how asinine was that? He tried again. "Very… nice."

"Um, thanks." She looked down at herself. "I can't believe my mother wore this. It makes me feel really close to her. I can't thank you enough."

"It was nothing. A small gesture. How are you feeling?"

"Scared shitless."

"What is 'shitless'?"

"It means very, very scared."

"You have no need to be. I have every confidence in you."

"Really? Why?"

"Because you are the one who took down a jotnar. This demonstration is a mere formality."

His lip curled in amusement and reluctantly, she smiled back.

"I hope you're right."

"Have you thought about what you'll do afterwards?"

"Not really. Go back to the human world, I guess. Not England, obviously. They're probably still looking for me there. I've always wanted to see Europe, though. Maybe I'll do some travelling."

She kept her tone light, deliberately masking the sleepless night she'd had agonizing over this very question.

Shade's reaction was not what she expected. He turned away abruptly and went to stand by the open window, looking out towards the horizon. He seemed to be wrestling with something. She frowned at his motionless back.

"Shade? What's wrong?"

When he finally answered, his voice was low.

"I want to put an alternative option to you."

"Oh?"

"When the test is over, whatever the outcome, I would like you to stay."

There was a long pause.

"Why?"

"Because I... I have become used to having you here."

"What, like a pet?"

"No, I..." He trailed off. Cautiously, Raya walked towards him.

"Shade, look at me. What are you trying to say?"

Shade turned slowly. He didn't meet her eyes, just clasped his hands behind his back like a schoolboy. She had to strain to hear him.

"I want you to stay because I like you."

"Sorry, what?"

He gritted his teeth.

"I like you."

"You *like* me?"

"I like you a lot."

"You like me a *lot*?"

He glowered.

"Why must you repeat everything I say? I am trying to tell you I like you an inordinate amount. Why is that so difficult to understand?"

"I guess because you look so pissed off by it."

"I am unaccustomed to telling women how I feel." He cleared his throat uncomfortably and tried again. "I am asking if you would consider making the castle your home. With me."

His eyes had darkened to navy and in them, she saw hope.

And something else. It took her a moment to identify it. With a start, she saw it was fear.

Fear that she might say no.

A thousand thoughts crashed through her mind.

He wants me to stay. He likes me. Is liking enough? What about Leona? Leona's not here. But he had feelings for her too, didn't he? Is this what he does? Goes from one woman to the next? What if he changes his mind about me? Could I face that? Maybe it's best if I leave. It would be safer for my heart. But I don't want to leave. I want to be with him. I admit it. I want to be with him. Okay then.

She closed the gap between them and jumped gracefully into his arms. Surprised, he caught her and held her so that her face was level with his.

"I like you too," she told him. And she kissed him.

She felt his mouth curve into a smile beneath hers and then he was kissing her back, claiming her lips for his own, making her senses swirl and lighting a fire beneath her skin.

When he broke off, they were both breathless.

"Just to be clear," he said gruffly, "does this mean you will stay?"

She brushed a lock of his hair from his forehead.

"Yes," she whispered.

With an inarticulate sound he kissed her again, his mouth roaming hers with a possessiveness she found exhilarating.

Her pulse quickened as he trailed his mouth along her jaw to her ear. She tilted her head back so he could explore her throat and he growled his approval.

"Apologies my Lord, my Lady." Pasha's voice broke in nervously, stopping them in their tracks. "The Vulcani are ready for you. Shall I, er, inform them you will be delayed?"

"I dearly wish we could. Tell them we are on our way." Shade's eyes gleamed as he gazed at Raya. "We will continue this later, my beautiful fae. Are you ready?"

He set her down on her feet and she smoothed her dress.

"Definitely," she told him. And it was true. She had never in her entire life felt this strong, this powerful. "Let's get this party started."

He held out his arm.

And they went to face the Vulcani.

Thirty Six

There were more of them in the banqueting hall than she had expected. At least three dozen Vulcani were gathered, resplendent in their finery. They hushed as Raya and Shade entered the room

Raya stopped, feeling the weight of their stares. Her ears were suddenly itching like crazy. Shade squeezed her hand.

"Courage," he murmured.

Loris stepped forward, his amber gaze cool and assessing.

"Are you ready, child?"

"Yes." Her voice was husky.

"You should know the consequences of failing here today. You will be expelled from Nush'aldaam and prohibited from ever returning."

Forced to leave Shade? The blood drained from her face.

"You do not have the power to do that," Shade said sharply.

"On the contrary. If she fails to convince us she is Aelah's daughter we will naturally align with Aelfric. And Aelfric *does* have power over fae, even half-human ones. So be sure you wish to continue, Lord Shadeed. You may lose more than our support."

Black smoke started to curl from Shade's body.

"That is outrageous. You have no right to impose arbitrary conditions after I invited you here in good faith. If Aelah could hear you, Loris, she would be disappointed."

"But Aelah is not here. And until we have a new leader, *I* make the decisions."

Loris wouldn't yield an inch. Shadows boiled off Shade and Raya noticed the Vulcani crowd shift restlessly. She put a hand on Shade's arm.

"It's okay. Really. I'll be fine."

He turned to face her, putting himself between her and Loris.

"But if they aren't persuaded you are Aelah's daughter, they could force you back to the human world. And I... I do not want that."

She put a hand on his face.

"Trust me?"

"More than life itself."

"Then prepare to have your socks blown off."

He glanced at his feet, bare as usual.

"I do not..."

"Figure of speech, smoke boy. It means I've got this."

She spoke with a bravado she wasn't feeling, but she knew she had no choice. She couldn't let Shade start a diplomatic war with the very people whose help he needed.

The woman she recognised as Kaemari appeared.

"Let us see what the girl can do before issuing threats, gentlemen," she said soothingly. "Shall we all be seated?"

She led the older Vulcani to a chair. Glowering, Shade took the seat to the right of him.

The crowd hushed once again. Raya backed up to give herself room. She had a wide space around her; all the tables and chairs had been cleared away, presumably so she didn't accidentally set them on fire.

Nervously, she glanced around the faces watching her. In a far corner, she caught a familiar smile. Tor.

He winked at her, his grin extending ear to ear. A weight lifted off her chest.

Her eyes sought Shade and she found his blue gaze pinned intently on her. Concentrate on Shade, she told herself.

"When I first came to Nush'aldaam," she started, her voice a little shaky, "I was struck by its beauty. First there was the forest where I met the Vulcani and made a dear friend."

She waved her hands and with a roar, the cavernous hall was filled with fiery trees. The Vulcani gasped as they saw every leaf, every branch picked out in lines of orange fire, right down to the texture of the bark.

Raya was careful to control the heat, making sure the power of the flames was contained. When she collapsed the trees, there wasn't a single scorch mark on the ceiling. She glanced at Tor. He knew the fire-forest had been for him. He put his hand over his heart and bowed in her direction.

"Then there was the night-garden, a visual splendour of colour and light."

She moved her hands in a complicated pattern and suddenly the hall was full of flowers. They were a sparkling rainbow of different colours; orange, red, blue, purple, pink. She controlled each element to make it exactly as she wanted.

She floated them among the Vulcani, letting them see her creations up close. Loris inspected a bloom, his face showing no emotion.

Her confidence grew. She added birds and butterflies, making them fly around the room. A rose grew in the centre of the floor and the petals dropped off one by one. Each flame-creation burned at several hundred degrees but none of the spectators would have known it. She frowned in concentration as she cocooned the heat away from the audience.

She chanced a look at Shade and her pulse kicked up a notch. He was watching intently, his expression a mixture of respect and pride. Her heart swelled.

Without thinking she collapsed the flowers and created fireworks. They exploded over her head in a brilliant display, even more spectacular than the Melae. A couple of the Vulcani clapped spontaneously.

"And finally I want to acknowledge the man who brought you all here today. The man you should support as emperor."

There was no sign of any nervousness now. With a flourish, she made her final creation. It wasn't one she'd practiced. She hadn't even known she was going to do it. But it felt right.

Flames rippled up her arms and she clapped her hands together, then threw them wide dramatically. Fire leapt from her fingers. And suddenly a burning figure was flying in the air, larger than life and with a wingspan stretching from wall to wall.

The face and body were unmistakeable. It was Lord Shadeed, picked out in flame. The fiery figure hovered gracefully and beat its burning wings in front of the stunned audience.

With a rush, Raya realised she'd just laid her soul bare for everyone to see. No-one looking at her creation could fail to notice how carefully she'd picked out his likeness. Every muscle, every sinew was exact down to the smallest detail.

His mouth was curved in an enigmatic smile. His nose, his jawline, all were perfect. She even had twin blue coronas burning as his eyes.

It was almost a declaration of love.

Thirty Seven

She brought her hands together abruptly and collapsed the image. Her face was scarlet as she stood in silence. She couldn't bring herself to look at Shade.

Someone started clapping. Startled, she looked into the far corner and saw Tor on his feet. He caught her eye and nodded.

Others followed his lead. And suddenly applause was thundering through the banquet hall.

Loris stood and everyone fell silent.

He stared at Raya, his expression inscrutable. Then slowly, stiffly, he bowed.

The dignitaries around him did the same. One of them, Kaemari, threw her a little congratulatory smile as she did so.

Awkwardly, Raya bowed back.

Shade came to stand next to her.

"I take it you are convinced?" he said to Loris.

"It was an unorthodox display." The Vulcani straightened up. "I was expecting raw energy, perhaps fireballs or projectiles. But the skill and power demonstrated is unequivocal. Only a fae of Aelah's abilities could show such control. You have an extraordinary gift, child."

"And we must not refer to her as a child any longer, Loris." Kaemari chided him gently. "She is Lady Raya of the Vulcani. Our leader. What is your wish, my Lady?"

Raya glanced uncertainly at Shade, but he didn't step in. He waited patiently, as did everyone else. She suddenly understood that he was treating her as an equal. She lifted her chin.

"I wish for the Vulcani clan to pledge allegiance to Lord Shadeed. He belongs on the throne of Nush'aldaam. He deserves to be emperor. We will support his quest."

Loris and Kaemari bowed their heads.

"As you wish, my Lady."

Now, at last, Shade spoke.

"Let us repair to the meeting room to finalise the details. My steward will show you the way."

Pasha materialised from nowhere. Raya wondered if he had teleportation powers, or if it was just a butler trait

The Vulcani were led off. Shade turned to Raya who kept her head down, still too embarrassed by her last creation to look at him. What must he think?

"You were magnificent."

Startled, she glanced shyly at him.

"I told you I'd been practising."

"You practiced all of that?"

"No. The last one was, um, an accident."

"I see," he said drily. "I was a little taken aback to see myself like that. It was… unexpected."

"I'm sorry, I didn't mean to. I know we've only just agreed that you and I… that we…"

She realised she had no idea, actually, what they were to each other. He'd asked her to stay at the castle and he'd said he liked her. That was it.

He put a hand under her chin and made her look at him.

"It made me very happy, Raya," he said softly. She blushed, unable to answer.

Pasha came back into the room.

"The Vulcani are seated and ready, my Lord," he said.

Shade didn't take his eyes off Raya.

"We will talk about this later," he said. "Will you wait for me here?"

"Yes."

"I will be back soon. And then I swear, you will have my undivided attention."

He strode out, followed by Pasha. Raya watched him go in a daze.

"You were amazing." Tor's voice broke into her reverie and she turned, pleased to see him.

"Because of you. I couldn't have done it without you."

"It was my pleasure. And I see you and Lord Shadeed seem to have reached an understanding."

"I like him, Tor. I like him a lot."

"Aye, I think that was pretty clear from the last flame picture you made. Am I allowed to say 'I told you so'?"

Raya punched him playfully on the arm.

"I should have just listened to you. You saw it before we did."

"So does that mean you're staying in Nush'aldaam? Or are you still hoping to find your mother?"

Her heart clenched.

"She's dead."

"Oh, Raya." Tor folded her into his arms and hugged her. "I'm so sorry."

"I didn't really know her. But there are people here who did. I think if I stay in Nush'aldaam, I'll be able to find out a little more about her."

"It's the right decision. And Lord Shadeed will need you for the battle ahead."

She raised her head.

"The battle?"

"Aye. Salaq won't give up the throne without a fight, even if most people want to see Lord Shadeed on it. Speak of the devil."

He let go of Raya hurriedly as Shade strode through the hall. The jinn looked at them suspiciously.

"Am I interrupting?"

"Not at all," said Tor. "I was just congratulating Raya."
Shade narrowed his eyes.
"Yes. It was quite a performance."
Was it her imagination, or was Shade on edge?
"Are you all right? Is there a problem with the Vulcani?"
"No. No problem. Can you come with me? If you can bear to tear yourself away."
"Yes. Of course. Tor, I'll see you later." Tor didn't answer. Probably put out by Shade's rudeness. "Tor?"
"Oh, yes. Later."
Raya followed Shade, trotting slightly to keep up with his long strides.
"Hey, we're not all seven foot tall, you know," she joked.
"Sorry." He slowed down fractionally.
"Where are we going?"
"I want to show you one of my favourite spots. Down by the river."
"What about the Vulcani?"
"Pasha is taking care of them."
"And everything's okay? You have their support?"
"Yes."
"Is it enough? To beat Salaq, I mean?"
"Raya, please stop asking questions."
She closed her mouth, stung. He sighed.
"I am sorry. It has been quite stressful and I just want some time alone with you."

Her heart lifted. He led her towards the back of the castle and down some stairs. There was a door at the bottom, one she'd never seen before. It led into a tunnel.
"Is this a secret entrance?" she teased.
"Yes."
Hm. Clearly not in a talkative mood.

The tunnel was low enough that Shade had to bend to keep from knocking his head. It was dark but there were wooden torches at the entrance. Shade held one out.

"Do the honours?"

She flicked a finger and sent a tiny ball of flame weaving unsteadily towards the flammable end. With a *pop* the torch flared into life.

"Still no good with those fireballs I see," he said.

She didn't reply, surprised by his tone. Not quite sneering, but not far off.

She followed him along the tunnel, stumbling a little on the uneven floor. It was damp and musty. She held her skirt up, hoping it wasn't getting wet, and shivered a little in the cool air. At least it was downhill.

They walked steadily for half an hour, maybe more. Raya lost track. She tried to make conversation but Shade answered in monosyllables and eventually she gave up. She was relieved when daylight appeared ahead of them.

Shade dropped the torch. They emerged into bright sunshine and she saw they'd come out by the riverbank. The castle was quite some distance away and the river was calmer here.

Further up, below the castle, it dropped into a ravine and thundered over huge boulders as it raced towards the sea many miles away. But here, it was a ribbon of serenity. Raya caught a flash of silver as fish darted beneath the crystal surface.

"This is so pretty," she said.

The sky was impossibly blue and the air was fresh, scented by wildflowers. Birds with bright green and yellow wings swooped over the water, catching insects on the fly. It was a beautiful setting.

She wondered why Shade had brought her to such a romantic place. Maybe he wanted to discuss their future.

Her heart skipped a beat. Was that why he seemed a little out of sorts? Was he nervous?

He reached behind a bush and drew out a long, slim bag.

"I want to give you something."

Carefully, he pulled out a single flower. A black rose on a long prickled stem, its petals as soft as velvet. Its scent was heavenly and she immediately wanted to bury her nose in it.

She reached for it eagerly, then paused.

"When did you bring this here?"

"I asked Pasha to arrange it."

Her heart swelled at his thoughtfulness. He held out the flower and she took it carefully, mindful of the thorns. He touched the back of her hand and looked deep into her eyes. His voice was soft.

"I want you to know that I have dreamed of this moment." She smiled at him and thought she'd never been so happy. His hand closed over hers. "Getting rid of you is my heart's desire."

She frowned, sure she'd misheard.

And then she screamed in pain as he crushed her hand around the rose stem, forcing the thorns deep into her palm. Blood streamed from the punctures. She struggled to let go but Shade's grip was inexorable.

"Stop it! It hurts! What are you doing?"

His eyes were pitiless. Almost as icy as the hand that trapped hers.

Abruptly the strength drained from her limbs. She still felt the pain but now she couldn't move. Her arms, legs, her entire body were locked into place. She couldn't even speak.

Not understanding, she stared, terrified, at Shade.

"Just so you know," he drawled. "I hate you. I hate everything about you. And I'm going to enjoy your suffering. Because make no mistake, you whore, you *are* going to suffer."

THIRTY EIGHT

Her mind clouded with shock. She struggled to cry out, to open her hand, but she was paralysed. Even when Shade moved away from her, she couldn't drop the rose.

"Don't bother trying to run. You're holding an imobilis rose. The poison from its thorns will keep you frozen until someone takes it off you."

A single tear rolled down Raya's face. *Why? Why is this happening?*

Shade slapped her. The blow struck her across the cheek and she rocked back on her feet. Amid the jumble of pain and disbelief, a thought rose to the surface of Raya's mind.

His hand was cold. Just as it had been when he touched her earlier. The normal heat that emanated from him was absent.

A second, more disturbing thought occurred to her.

She was entirely at his mercy.

As if reading her mind, Shade slapped her again. Harder. He smiled viciously as her cheek reddened, the imprint of his palm starkly outlined. Her tears were coming thick and fast now, and the salt stung her skin.

"That's enough."

A guttural voice rang out and something moved across Raya's peripheral vision. She strained to see but she couldn't turn her head.

"You're not in charge, Silas," Shade snapped.

"Aelfric will have your guts if you damage her."

"I'm not going to damage her. I'm just having a little fun."

Raya's heart thudded. Aelfric? Was Shade working with Aelfric? She was totally confused. Shade sneered.

"Look at her. Not a clue what's going on."

The shape at the outer edge of Raya's vision moved into view. She tried to make sense of the creature which now stood in front of her.

It had the torso and arms of a man, though its features were thickened and almost neanderthal in appearance. Its brow was low, its nose flattened, and coarse hair grew over its cheeks.

But it wasn't a man, at least not entirely. At the waist, he became a horse. Four hooved legs moved restlessly, the front one almost pawing at the ground.

Centaur. She remembered what Shade had told her. A centaur had killed his best friend. The centaurs were loyal to Aelfric.

The creature came closer and now she could smell him. His odour was rank, the fetid stench of a barnyard animal. He examined her curiously.

"So this is what all the fuss is about?" The centaur snorted and shook his head. "Why does Aelfric want her?"

"Leverage, I think. Who cares? The sooner we get her to Feyir, the better."

Shade's words chilled Raya's blood. Aelfric wanted her. Panicked, she concentrated on her power, trying to make flames burst from her fingers. But it, like the rest of her, was paralysed.

The fucking rose. It was still clutched in her hand, thorns buried deep in her palm. Blood dripped steadily down her forearm and onto the ground.

Shade peered round, frowning.

"Where's Bellemar? I need his help to get her onto your back."

"Can't you use your shadow power?"

"I can manifest his shape. Not his powers, cretin."

Raya looked from one to the other, her eyes the only thing she could control. What the hell was going on? Suddenly she heard a familiar voice and her heart leapt.

"Raya? Are you all right? Raya!"

It was Tor. Relief washed through her. Tor had followed her, he'd found her. He came into her peripheral vision and she strained to turn her head towards him but couldn't. All she could see was the centaur and Shade blocking his way.

"Look who's trying to come to the rescue."

"You're not Lord Shadeed. You don't have the aura of a jinn."

"Clever little Sylvan." Shade sneered. "Shame the Vulcani here doesn't have your smarts."

His features started to swim. Dark hair grew and changed colour. The muscular body shortened, cinching in at the waist and out at the hips until it became more curvaceous. The tunic morphed into a diaphanous dress with a plunging neckline. Leona smiled triumphantly at Raya.

"Recognise me now, halfling? The last time we met, I was blonde. Did you enjoy the ambrosia berries?"

Among all the emotions now tearing through Raya, the uppermost was relief. It hadn't been Shade saying those things.

It was swiftly followed by anger. She glared at Leona and the si'lat laughed.

"Oh, if looks could kill. I was hoping that the berries would make you jump all over your Sylvan in public. It would have made it impossible for Shadeed to keep you around after that. Shame your woodsman here has such high morals. Luckily, I had a plan B."

"Doesn't matter. Your plan has failed. She's coming back to the castle with me." Tor drew a dagger from his belt.

Raya saw it from the corner of her eye and was startled. She'd never seen Tor carry a weapon. "Let me past, bestial."

"You think a tiny little knife like that will do any good?" The centaur snorted and pawed at the ground.

"Kill him, Silas." Leona eyed Tor triumphantly. "While the Vulcani watches."

The centaur started forward and Raya mentally urged Tor to run. But he held his ground. She strained to see what he was doing. It seemed to her his hand was in mid air. The centaur stopped and shook his head irritably. Tor slowly brought his palm down and the bestial sank to his knees.

"Silas, what in the name of the gods are you doing?" Leona shrieked. "Kill him!"

"Don't want to," muttered the centaur sullenly. "Don't take orders from you."

Tor took a step forward and now he was in Raya's line of sight. He glanced over at her and she saw his eyes were a bright emerald. She realised what he'd done. He'd used his Sylvan ability to manipulate the bestial's aura. She hadn't realised he was so powerful.

Tor skirted round the now-docile centaur and came to stand in front of her.

"Let me take that rose from you," he smiled, and reached for her hand. Raya was overwhelmed with relief, eager for him to take the cursed thorns out of her palm.

There was a peculiar noise, almost like an insect whining past them. Tor's expression changed.

What? Raya was puzzled. *What's wrong? Get this fucking rose away from me.*

Then red bloomed on the front of his shirt like a malignant flower. He glanced at it then back to her, his face almost apologetic. Horrified, Raya watched, powerless, as he sank to his knees. He tried to speak but no sound came out.

Tor!

He fell forward. That's when Raya caught a glimpse of the arrow sticking from his back.

THIRTY NINE

Her mind screamed in shock and grief. Tears coursed down her face. Adrenaline flooded through her body and her muscles started to shake. But she still couldn't move.

Tor had fallen below her eyeline. She couldn't look down and she didn't know if he was alive or dead.

A figure walked up to the centaur. Another bestial, she saw through the tears. This one had goat legs and little horns sprouting above furry ears. He was carrying a bow and had a quiver full of arrows slung across his back. He kicked the centaur on his rump.

"Get up, you weak-minded idiot."

"Fralling Sylvans." The centaur heaved himself onto all four legs jerkily. "Always fralling messing with your auras. Where've you been, Bellemar? We were looking for you."

"Saving your hides, that's where I was. Well, hello, there." The satyr turned to Leona and stared openly. "You're as beautiful as King Aelfric described. Is it true you can adopt any form?"

"What did you have in mind?" she purred. He smiled lasciviously.

"A sylph, perhaps? Or maybe a siren. I've always fancied tupping a siren."

"Keep your fantasies to yourself," grumbled Silas. "We've been here too long already. Lift her on and let's go."

The satyr was stronger than he looked. He lifted Raya and dumped her across the centaur's back like a sack of potatoes. Her head dangled down and she saw Tor lying motionless. She tried to see if he was still breathing, but all she could focus on was the blood pooled beneath his body.

Despair filled her heart.

"You can't leave her like that," complained Silas. "She'll fall off and then Aelfric will slaughter us both."

"Fine. You'll have to carry me as well, then."

The satyr vaulted on board. Silas grunted.

"You're heavier than you look, goat."

"Stop whining. And what about you, my fine shapeshifter?" He winked at Leona. "Do you want to scooch in behind me? You can hold on as tight as you like."

"Thank you, but I'll make my own way. It's less conspicuous than travelling with a pair of bestials. You'd better keep off the main route. The jinn will know she's missing soon, if he hasn't figured it out already."

"Very well. Later, then."

The centaur surged forward, his powerful back legs propelling them into a canter. Raya's last sight was of Tor, deathly still, the arrow still embedded in his back.

The next few hours were torture. The constant bouncing motion made her bones ache. Her head pounded against the centaur's flank with each stride and her nostrils filled with its rancid stink.

Bellemar made no effort to support her or keep her from jolting around. He simply did the minimum to stop her sliding from the beast's back. And she couldn't move in the slightest to ease her discomfort. Locked in one position, her muscles were in agony.

She struggled to open her fist which still clutched the rose. Maybe the bumpy ride would work it loose and shake it from her grasp. But the thorns were too deeply embedded. The blood had long since congealed and she could feel the sticky mess all over her arm.

Nausea welled in her stomach and grimly she prayed she wouldn't throw up. She knew she wouldn't be able to open her mouth and would probably choke. The thought terrified her.

She realised she could die, right here on the centaur's back, and no-one would even notice.

Bellemar was whistling a tuneless dirge through his teeth. His hand rested on Raya's back. Occasionally it would stray to her backside and she would feel panic building. It was Griggs all over again. But worse, because she couldn't shove a pen in his eye.

The journey was longer than it had been on the way out, when she had ridden sweet Martha. Or maybe it just seemed longer. Little stones and clods of mud flew up and hit her in the face. Some were sharp and cut her skin. Drops of blood mingled with the dirt on her cheeks.

She wondered if Shade knew she was gone by now. Was he looking for her? Or was he still speaking to the Vulcani council?

And Tor. Poor Tor.

Her head started to throb and black spots crowded her vision. The small patch of ground she was able to see passing beneath the centaur's hooves dimmed and became blurry.

She passed out.

Forty

His enraged roar filled the castle, reverberating through every inch and into every corner. Clouds of stone dust funnelled into the air. If the castle walls hadn't been built to withstand armies, they would have crumbled.

"*Where is she?*"

Smoke boiled off Shade in vast waves, filling the room, pouring from the doors and windows. Pasha lay prostrate, the lowest he could go without physically burrowing into the floor.

"My Lord, we have looked everywhere. She is not in the castle. The last anyone saw of her was when she was speaking with the Sylvan."

"The Sylvan." Shade held onto his rage, conscious that he was very close to losing control. "And has anyone seen Mr Torven?"

Loris shook his head.

"We are missing him too. He cannot be found. Perhaps they are together?"

He asked the question delicately and Shade's face darkened further.

No. It was not possible. He refused to believe Raya would betray him. And regardless of how Tor felt about her, he had shown himself to be morally decent. He forced himself to think rationally through the red mist of his fury.

If they hadn't gone off together, then something had happened to both of them.

"We have to find them. If they are not in the castle, then they must be in the grounds or the town."

"I will send the guards to look," said Pasha, getting to his feet and backing away cautiously.

"We will send our guards too," said Loris. "Lady Raya must be found. And then, Lord Shadeed, we will discuss the castle's security. Or lack of it."

Shade didn't answer. His eyes blazed ice blue and Loris found himself dropping his gaze. With as much bravado as he could muster, he swept out of the banqueting hall followed by the rest of the Vulcani council.

Shade prowled restlessly. For the third time he went up to her room, as if Raya might have been hiding the first two times he searched it. This time he let himself think the unthinkable.

She had run up here playfully to make him look for her. To wait for him to find her. Maybe she had gone into the bathroom, forgetting the bars no longer covered the opening over the drop. Maybe she had stumbled and...

With a groan he shut that train of thought down. It couldn't be true. And it didn't explain Tor's disappearance.

Unless they'd come up here together and he had tried to catch her when she fell, and they had both...

"Enough!"

He roared at himself, sickened by the way his mind kept turning to the worst case scenario. He couldn't afford to think like that. The idea of her being in pain, the chance that she might be dead - these notions were not tolerable.

With a howl of frustration he leapt from the window, forcing himself to confront one possibility of what had happened to Raya.

He let himself fall until he neared the bottom of the gorge, thinking that if he saw a body lying there, if he saw the unthinkable, he would simply let himself keep falling. He wouldn't unfurl his wings.

He saw a body.

Frozen in shock, he hurtled towards it. He didn't believe it at first. The enormity of it was too much. But it was there. A tiny figure lying motionless on the riverbank.

His thoughts turned bleak. *I will join her. And we will be together.*

But then he saw it wasn't Raya. It was the Sylvan. He lay face-down, the cloth of his tunic a mess of scarlet. Something was sticking out of his back and there was a trail of black-red blood behind him, as if he'd dragged himself along the bank.

Shade back-beat the air furiously to keep from crashing into the ground. He landed clumsily, too fast and too hard, and it knocked the breath from him. He dissolved his wings and raced to the Sylvan's side.

"Torven," he said. "Torven, what happened? Where's Raya?"

Incredibly, Tor's eyes fluttered open. He was pale, his breath shallow. He tried to focus but his eyes were bloodshot, the pupils dilated. He muttered something and Shade bent to hear.

"Aelfric. Aelfric's got her."

And a vice closed over his heart.

FORTY ONE

Silas was relieved when they reached the outskirts of Feyir. They were safe here. The Fae Court was deep within the forest and even if the jinn tracked them here, he wouldn't enter. Not without an army. And only a fool would bring an army to face Aelfric on his home turf.

It was another hour before they reached the court. The sun had long since set and the trees loomed over them, dark with shadows. The forest was filled with strange creatures but none dared to approach the centaur and his passengers. They were under Aelfric's protection.

Raya came to as Bellemar hauled her off the centaur's back. He slung her over his shoulder and carried her into the court. From her position Raya could only see the floor. White marble, so white it hurt her eyes. She could hear the goatish hooves clopping on the stone.

They went up some stairs, her head bouncing at every step. At last she was lowered none too gently onto the floor. Now she could see the ceiling. More white marble. The place looked like the inside of a fridge.

"At last we meet. It's been too long."

The voice was pleasant, almost musical, but it set Raya's teeth on edge. As if there was an underlying note of discord which she couldn't quite hear.

"Get the imobilis thorns out of her hand. Let her stand up."

Bellemar squatted next to her and forced her hand open. It had been clutched so tightly for so long that she could feel her finger bones protesting. He grasped the stem and yanked it out, the thorn wounds reopening on her palm. But the flow of blood eased the effects of the toxin and sensation flooded back into her limbs.

She gasped and rolled onto her side, her whole body aching from being in one position for so many hours. She had the impression of a crowd of people watching her, then she curled up into a ball, desperately trying to relieve the tension in her muscles.

"What's wrong with her?" The musical voice sounded querulous.

"She has been frozen in place for hours, sire," Silas said, bowing his head respectfully. "And it was a difficult journey to get here."

"My child, get up. Let me take a look at you."

She didn't know if she could stand, but the voice was difficult to resist. The note of discord had gone - or maybe she'd just imagined it. All she heard now was a lyrical tone of purest silver which tugged at her soul. Painfully, she staggered to her feet and turned to face its owner.

She caught her breath. The room was filled with the most glorious people she'd ever seen in her life.

They were elegant and exquisite in their jewels and finery, the perfect planes of their faces giving them an ethereal allure that filled her heart with yearning. They had a glow about them, an iridescence that made it hard to look away.

And on the throne, the most devastatingly handsome one of all. His ebony hair fell to his shoulders in a perfect wave, framing eyes of deepest violet edged with dark lashes. His pale skin and high cheekbones, indeed his entire bone structure, looked like they had been crafted by the gods themselves.

And when his gaze fixed upon her, she was breathless at the privilege of being the focus of his attention. Her mind was dazed, as if she'd drunk too much wine.

She cocked her head. Just on the very edge of her hearing was the most beautiful sound; the kind of sound a tuning fork might make if tapped against crystal. She didn't think to question where it came from. All she knew was that it calmed her and filled her with wonder.

She gazed at the elven around her and was humbled by their presence. The beautiful folk, Tor had called them. He had not been wrong.

The thought of Tor pained her heart. And with that little stab of anguish, the crystalline haze in her head seemed to retreat a little.

She focused on the throne again, taking in the elegant figure dressed in silk and fur. A golden circlet adorned his head, sitting just above his delicately pointed ears.

So this was Aelfric. He was the most beautiful man she'd ever seen. No wonder her mother had liked him, once.

His perfect brow wrinkled a little.

"Why do you have blood on your face?"

Her hands flew to the cuts on her cheek, mortified at being dishevelled in the king's presence.

"It was while I was travelling. On the horse. The centaur, I mean. I couldn't move… couldn't avoid the stones. I'm so sorry."

"Hush, child. It is not your fault. Bellemar. Did I not ask you to bring her to me unharmed?"

Uneasily, the satyr came forward. As one, the entire elven crowd turned to stare at him.

"I am most sorry, sire. I did not realise."

Raya saw Silas backing away quietly. Any loyalty he may have had to the satyr was evaporating fast. Aelfric's violet gaze locked on Bellemar.

"Tell me, does she look unharmed to you?"

"No, sire. But if I had known, I would have remedied the situation at once, I swear."

"Of course you would. And how could you have known?"

Aelfric's voice was pleasant enough but there was an edge to it that twanged on Raya's nerves. Bellemar obviously felt it too. Droplets of sweat appeared on his forehead.

"I… I should have checked. I see that now."

"Yes. You should have checked. You failed me in a simple task."

Bellemar threw himself to his knees, grovelling at Aelfric's feet.

"I won't fail you again, your majesty. I swear I won't."

"No. You won't. I am sure of that."

Lazily, the king flicked his wrist. Three shards of jet black appeared in the air next to him. They hung with intent, their pointed ends gleaming wickedly. Raya didn't know what they were, but Bellemar seemed to.

He got to his cloven feet and backed away.

"Mercy, sire. I beg of you."

Aelfric's mouth curved into a smile that was both beautiful and terrible.

"You know I do not do mercy, bestial."

He made the smallest gesture, and the jet shards flew at the satyr.

The first struck him in the neck, cutting off his scream. The second struck his chest, flaying skin to bone and driving itself into the heart. And the third embedded itself in the abdomen, twisting and jerking upwards to inflict maximum damage. Blood spurted obscenely and Raya caught a glimpse of glistening intestines before the bestial crumpled to the floor.

The violet gaze flicked towards her.

"Does his death bother you, child?"

Aelfric's query sounded casual but again she felt an undertone. This was a test of some kind, but she wasn't sure what.

The crystal hum in her mind crowded out her thoughts. She looked at the destroyed body and felt nothing. No compassion, no sympathy. Bellemar had killed Tor, she reminded herself. She shrugged.

"He deserved to die."

Aelfric's smile broadened.

"Welcome to my Royal Court. These are my lords and ladies. We are all very pleased to see you."

Soldiers came to remove the corpse on the floor. A pool of blood remained, but Aelfric waved his hand and it vanished.

All around her, the beautiful folk were bowing their heads in her direction. She looked down at her soiled dress and filthy, blood-encrusted hands, and felt ashamed to be among them.

"Your majesty, please let me clean up," she mumbled. "I am not fit to be in your presence."

"All in good time. Let me see you properly."

He stood and approached her, and the crystal jangle in her mind grew louder. It was hypnotic. *He* was hypnotic. He took her face between his long fingers and tilted it this way and that.

"Your ears," he said abruptly.

Shit. Were they covered in eczema? She wanted to die of shame.

"It's a childhood affliction…" she said hurriedly.

"I should say so. It's clumsy magic, but strong to have lasted this long."

She frowned.

"I'm sorry, sire, I don't understand."

"Your ears have been enchanted to appear human. That must have been excruciating at times, as they sought to resume their natural form. Did you not suspect?"

"This *is* their natural form, sire. I'm half-human. I take after my father in the ears department."

He stiffened, anger crossing his face. For a moment, he appeared almost feral. She swallowed, fear stabbing at her guts. Then he smiled patiently.

"Whoever told you that lied to you. You are not half-human. And your ears have been magicked to disguise your true nature."

"I beg your pardon, sire?"

"You are full fae, child."

She tried to make sense of what he'd just said. It wasn't true. It couldn't be true. Magda had said her mother had fallen in love with a human.

"No, that's… that's not possible."

"Do you doubt me?" Spoken sharply. She quailed.

"No it's just… how can that be?"

"Let me show you."

Aelfric placed his hands on either side of her head, covering her ears. The silver haze almost swamped her senses. She gazed at him, wondering how someone so magnificent could be bothered with a nonentity like her.

A burning pain shot through her ears. Gasping, she staggered back but the brief discomfort had already passed. She touched them gently. They'd changed.

The rounded edges had gone. Now they rose into graceful points, a shape that should have seemed alien to her yet somehow felt natural. And for the first time in her life, there was no itching or dryness. No irritation of any kind.

"What did you do?" she asked.

"Restored them. Do you want to see?"

She assumed he would give her a mirror but instead he waved his hand and a figure appeared. It was her, yet not her. Another Raya. A new, improved Raya.

The figure wore a violet dress, the same shade as Aelfric's eyes. Her neck was adorned with priceless jewels. She was taller, fuller in the bust but slimmer at the waist. Her skin was perfect, no cuts or dirt. Her hair curled luxuriously to her waist, the copper strand catching the light. She looked like an elven.

Raya walked round the frozen figure. It didn't move or breathe, and she understood this was merely a three-dimensional image. She leaned in to look at the ears.

They were pointed, just as her mother's had been in the photograph.

She shook her head.

"This can't be true. You're saying someone put a spell on me to make me look human?"

"Kobold magic."

"Magda? Magda changed my ears? But why?"

"Because they were both lying to you. She and your mother. Aelah has been concealing the truth from you your whole life."

"No. She was protecting me. She said… she said you wanted to hurt me because you couldn't forgive her for loving a human."

That feral look again. He caught himself.

"There was no human. Aelah ran because she didn't want me to know about her child. About you. She lied when she said I wanted to harm you. Nothing could be further from the truth."

"None of this makes sense."

"Of course it makes sense. You just have to admit it. Deep down, you know the truth."

It was suddenly hard to breathe. Raya turned to scrutinise her 3-D image again. It wasn't just the ears. Her hair was the same shade as the Fae King's. And she shared other similarities too. Her jaw, the curve of her cheek.

The truth started to scream at her consciousness but she needed to hear it from him.

"Tell me what you're saying," she asked thickly.

"You know what I'm saying. You do not have a human father. *I'm* your father."

Forty Two

She couldn't speak. It couldn't be true. And yet she knew it was.

First she'd believed she was human. Then half-human. Now she wasn't even that. Nothing about her past was true. A slow anger began to burn.

Magda had changed her appearance and Aelah had given her away. Her whole life, a lie.

Another thought struck her. Did Shade know?

No. He would never have asked her to pretend to be his betrothed if he'd known she was Aelfric's daughter. He despised the elven king. And yet...

He tried to end the deal. That day he told you Aelah was dead. He said your father was dead too. Did he know the truth? Is that why he lied?

And the things he'd said about Aelfric. *His mind is twisted. They say his castle is littered with jars containing fairy bones.* The crystal hum expanded in her mind. Lies. All lies.

Shade had deliberately deceived her, just like Aelah had. She was a fool to have trusted him. Aelfric was wonderful. The most charming, charismatic, captivating person she'd ever known.

Her heart welled with pride.

He was her father.

Tor's voice sounded in her head.

Elven are powerful fae. They bend reality around them.

No. Aelfric had opened her eyes. He had restored her fae heritage.

Aelfric's glamours are the strongest and darkest.

No. She knew who she was now.

"What are you thinking, my daughter?"

"That people have been lying to me for a very long time."

"Not me. I would never lie to you."

"Then why did my mother leave you?"

"Aelah was headstrong. For a time, we were inseparable. But then she changed. Became cold and selfish. She wanted to hurt me so she ran away and made sure I would never find you. And I have spent such a long time looking. I had my shaitun scouring for every clue. Following every lead."

"Why did she hate you so much?"

"Your mother was afraid of emotional attachments. That's why she left me. And that's why she gave you away to strangers. You think she wanted to protect you? She never wanted you in the first place."

His words simultaneously hurt her and confirmed everything she'd ever suspected. Her mother had never wanted a baby. She'd abandoned her right after she was born. What kind of mother did that?

But it didn't matter now. All this time she'd been trying to find a woman who wanted nothing to do with her, and instead she'd found a father.

A wonderful, caring father.

"I hope I'm not a disappointment," she said. Aelfric smiled, and his eyes sparkled.

"I'm told your name is Raya?"

"Suraya. At least I… I think it is." Suddenly she wasn't sure of anything any more.

"Suraya." He rolled the word round his mouth as if tasting it. "It isn't an elven name. But it will do for now. Well, Suraya, let us make you look more like a princess." He gestured at the image still standing motionless in front of them. "Do you like the way you look here?"

"Yes, but it's not real. I'm not that tall and my face isn't that pretty."

"Nonsense. It's how other people will see you, if you want."

Raya examined the image again. Aelfric had made her look like a supermodel. How could she refuse that?

"Yes. But how…?"

He waved his hand. The image vanished, but now Raya was wearing the violet dress. Her hands were clean and unblemished, and there were no cuts on her face.

She felt strong and beautiful. Invincible.

The lords and ladies around her applauded and Raya nodded graciously, accepting their admiration.

"Thank you, father." The word felt strange. "Now what?"

"Now you will start learning how to rule a kingdom. Because one day, this will be yours. You are my only heir."

Raya blanched.

"I don't know the first thing about ruling."

"It is about power, child. Power and respect. Make your allies fear you and your enemies fear you more. Don't worry. I'll teach you."

"I can't wait to learn."

He paused and cocked his head to one side.

"Before we start, there is one thing I must know. May I inquire about your feelings for Lord Shadeed?"

The mention of his name jolted her.

Shade. Shade, do you know where I am?

But the crystal clamour in her head made it difficult to think.

"He was forcing me to act the part, that's all. To keep Salaq from the throne."

"And now? Where are your loyalties?"

"To you, of course, father."

He held out his arm and smiled. For the smallest moment it seemed to Raya as if he was baring his teeth. Then the feeling passed and she took his arm. He led her from the throne room.

"Then let us begin."

Forty Three

The next few days were a dream. Were they days? Maybe they were weeks. Or months. Or maybe just a few hours. It was hard to tell at the Fae Court.

She was caught up in a hedonistic swirl. There was dancing and food, and endless glasses of mead wine. Music played wherever she went. Her world was one of laughter and merriment. She was constantly surrounded by her lords and ladies, their sharp eyes and beautiful faces nodding and smiling and hanging on to her every word.

She also had her own personal guards. Two of them, hulking and brutish, barely able to squeeze into their uniforms. She complained to her father that they were ugly and smelled bad.

"They are ogurs, child. One of the strongest fae, just about bright enough to be trained but not renowned for their witty repartee."

"Why do I need bodyguards?"

"For your own protection. You are a princess now. And our family have many enemies."

She made them stand in the corners out of sight. She only wanted to be surrounded by beauty.

Other fair folk came and went from the palace. Sylphs and selkies, piskies and kelpies, nymphs and naiads. All treated her father with deference. None ever met his eyes.

And all the time, even while she slept, that faint crystal jangle in her head. Making it difficult to think. Leaving no room for any doubts.

Aelfric was by her side every waking moment. He spoke to her as an equal and she swelled with pride. Her father trusted her. He wanted the best for her.

"Elven were once seen as dark fae," he explained. "Power-hungry. Not to be trusted. But when my Court was founded here in Feyir, I vowed to make people respect us for what we truly are. Bringers of peace and harmony."

They were walking through the corridors of the palace. The place was vast; white marble hallways that seemed to extend for miles. Sometimes she thought the dimensions couldn't possibly be right and that her perception was off.

"But you support Salaq's quest for the throne, don't you?" she asked. "I thought he was reckless, a bad choice of leader for Nush'aldaam."

Aelfric smiled mockingly.

"And who told you that, daughter?"

"Well... Lord Shadeed."

"The jinn who wishes to steal the throne for himself."

"He said the true heir was Kamran, the son of the previous emperor. But then Kamran died in the Forbidden Zone."

"A terrible accident." Aelfric gestured carelessly. "I allowed him to go on ahead of me to take the best game. I ordered the bestials to protect him but my message wasn't heeded and he was lost to us. Now we must look to the future."

"But how did it happen?" Raya glanced at her father, genuinely curious. "You're all-powerful here, how did your orders get overlooked?"

His violet gaze rested on her for a moment and the haze in her mind kicked up a notch.

"It is rare, but it does happen. Not even I am infallible."

She nodded dutifully.

"Yes, father."

"And now I have a special treat for you, child. Come and look."

He led her into the throne room. The lords and ladies were swarming round something, poking and prodding. They were giggling like children but there was a cruel edge to their laughter. Raya was reminded of hyenas converging on a wounded animal.

"Enough."

Aelfric spoke quietly but everyone immediately stepped aside, bowing their heads low in obeisance.

Raya saw what they had been poking at. It was a gilded cage and inside was a woman. At first it was hard to make out what she looked like. She was filthy. Her clothes were torn and she smelled as if she hadn't bathed for days.

Raya recoiled. Why was such a disgusting creature being allowed to defile the palace?

But then she noticed the red hair.

"Leona?"

The woman in the cage saw her and flew at the bars.

"Help me!"

"Quiet." She fell silent as Aelfric slowly walked around the cage, examining the prisoner. "Suraya, this is the woman who betrayed you. She came to Feyir expecting a reward."

The si'lat's eyes flashed.

"I did as you asked. I don't deserve this."

Raya was impressed by the si'lat's resilience. She refused to drop her gaze and stood straight, despite the dirt and rags.

"I asked you to fetch her unharmed. Silas tells me you struck her on the face. Twice." He turned to Raya. "Is this true, daughter?"

Leona's jaw dropped.

"Daughter?"

"Yes father," Raya answered. She saw fear flash across Leona's face and felt a frisson of satisfaction. "She hit me."

"I... I didn't know, sire. I beg forgiveness." Leona fell to her knees and Raya wanted to cackle in delight. She held it back. Aelfric examined the grovelling woman dispassionately.

"How should we punish her?"

"No, sire, please. After all I have done for you. I acted as your spy. I betrayed Lord Shadeed for you. I persuaded my father to change his allegiance to Salaq. Please. Have mercy."

Leona pleaded desperately, tears tracking through the dirt on her face.

"As I say repeatedly, I do not do mercy. And the allegiance of your people no longer troubles me. I have the Vulcani in my pocket now."

In despair, Leona caught Raya's gaze.

"Raya, I beg you. Lord Shadeed... Shade would not want you to do this."

The name jolted her. For the first time she felt something other than manic glee. It was shame. It pierced the jangle in her head and lodged there, a tiny splinter breaching the haze.

"Daughter, I am waiting. How should we punish this creature?" Aelfric's violet eyes gleamed. "Shall we have fun with her? Perhaps she can be the quarry in a hunt. We have not hunted yet, have we, you and I? This would be a perfect opportunity. What say you?"

"I... um, maybe we should just let her go."

As one, the lords and ladies gasped. Raya felt the weight of their incredulous stares and tried not to squirm.

Weakness. That was a flaw. She could not show weakness. Not in a room full of predators.

She drew herself up and thrust her chin out imperiously.

"You have something to say? To me, Princess Suraya of Feyir, heir to the throne and daughter of the king? You want to question me?" They were silent. "Well?"

One by one they dropped their gazes. All but Aelfric who watched her thoughtfully.

"Explain."

Raya walked round the cage and allowed contempt to play across her face.

"This creature is not worthy of our time or effort. She is nobody. Nothing. She has lost her home and her status. Throw her back into the forest and have done with her."

He put his hand on her shoulder and turned her to face him. The crystal clamour sharpened and suddenly she wanted vengeance against Leona so badly, she could almost taste it.

And yet the tiny splinter of shame in what she was doing, what she was becoming, still hung there.

"This is what you truly want, daughter? To let her go?"

Raya nodded.

"Send her away. I never want to see her vapid face again."

Aelfric's face cleaved into a vicious smile.

"Done."

He walked to the cage and held out his hand.

"My daughter never wants to see your face again. If you agree, I will let you go."

Leona took his hand carefully.

"Thank you. And thank you, Raya. I promise I will never bother you again."

Aelfric yanked hard and her face hit the bars. She gave a cry as he trailed a finger along her cheek.

"Si'lat are so malleable, aren't they? Quite a skill, to be a shapeshifter. To assume any form you choose. But, I wonder, what happens when you assume a form you *don't* want? I imagine that is quite traumatic."

"Sire, please, I promise you won't ever see me again." Leona struggled to free her hand but Aelfric was unrelenting.

"You pride yourself on your allure, don't you? A shifter like you can assume beauty with a mere thought. Let us see what you look like when beauty is no longer an option."

"No, sire, I beg of you…"

Leona's voice rose to a shriek as Aelfric got inside her head. Her features melted and morphed. Horrified and yet fascinated, Raya watched as Leona transformed against her will.

Lines appeared across her skin, etched deep into her cheeks and forehead. Her bones bowed as her muscles shrivelled, forcing her into a stoop. Her taut flesh sagged and wrinkled, her curves now flabby with age. And where once her hair flamed as red as autumn leaves, now it hung in thin grey strands.

The seductive si'lat was gone and instead there was an old crone inside the cage.

Aelfric opened the door.

"Now leave. Before I set the dogs on you."

The elderly creature hobbled out. She cast one agonised look towards Raya with rheumy bloodshot eyes. Then she left the throne room accompanied by the jeers and taunts of the lords and ladies.

"Why did you do that, father?"

"You said you never wanted to see her face again. It was an elegant punishment, daughter, especially for a vain shifter. I applaud you."

"How did you make her change?"

Aelfric shrugged.

"An elven trick. Merely an illusion. But one so powerful, her mind will believe it long after she leaves Feyir. She'll die of old age without ever realising she could have broken the spell, if only she could have seen through the fakery."

"That's quite a power."

He studied her.

"You have your own power, don't you? You've inherited your mother's gift. Show me."

With barely a thought, Raya lifted her hand and called up a flame. It danced in her palm, reflecting in her father's eyes.

"Impressive. A useful power for a ruler to have. I could make a lot of bargains by leveraging a power like that."

"Father?" She closed her fist, extinguishing the flame.

"It strikes me that having a daughter could allow me to extend my territory. If, say, you were to marry Lord Salaq, the fae would finally have a claim to the throne."

"But you're already a king."

"Only to the fae. To rule the whole of Nush'aldaam… now, that would be a prize indeed." He looked her up and down. "Fortunately you are quite attractive, despite not being fully elven. I imagine Lord Salaq would be pleased to have you as his bride."

Bride. I was going to be Shade's bride. At least I think I was.

"I don't think I like the idea of marrying a man I've never met."

"Yet you agreed to play the part of Lord Shadeed's betrothed."

"He offered me a deal. He rescued me in exchange for some play-acting."

"Play-acting. And are you sure that is all it was?"

"Yes, father."

She nodded but inside her turmoil grew. It hadn't been *all* play-acting, had it? When he'd kissed her, that had felt real. Hadn't it?

Why was it so fucking hard to think?

"You look very serious, my daughter. There's no room for serious thought at the Fae Court. Only joy." Aelfric took her hand and led her to a table piled high with food and drink. "Let the band play! Come, my lords and ladies. Let there be frivolity!"

Raya allowed the music to wash over her. It was easier than struggling to remember whatever it was she was trying to remember.

And another day passed. Or week. Or month.

She neither knew nor cared.

Forty Four

"This dispute is tedious."

Raya sat next to her father. He'd had a throne made just for her, a twin to his, crafted from gold and jewels. It was real, he told her. Not an illusion. She was flattered.

Now they were side by side hearing complaints from their subjects. She listlessly picked at her nails while the wizened old man in front of them begged with tears in his eyes.

"Please, your majesties. He's only a boy, he ran away thinking he was playing a game."

"You should have taught him not to go into the Forbidden Zone," said Aelfric in a bored voice. "The centaurs kill any trespassers."

"He didn't know any better. He's a child. I beg of you, let me retrieve him. Or at least warn your centaur guards…"

"How long has he been missing in the Zone?"

"Two hours, sire. If I could just…"

"Then it's too late. Next!"

The old man threw himself onto the ground in front of the thrones.

"I beg of you, sire. You are a father, you know the tragedy of losing a child."

"I lost mine for twenty years, and do you know what? I didn't cry once. Next!"

"Father," Raya said reprovingly. "Surely you were a *little* sad that I wasn't around?"

"I suppose a smidgeon. All right, daughter, what do you propose we do about this man's problem?"

The old man looked up hopefully.

"His son's almost certainly dead," Raya said casually. "Maybe he's due some compensation? I mean, if the boundaries of the Zone aren't clearly marked…"

"Yes, that's a terrific idea. And I'll take it from the centaurs' funding as it's their responsibility. There you go, old man. The princess has solved your problem."

"But my son…" The man was bewildered. "I want to find my son."

Aelfric leaned forward and raised his voice in case the man was deaf.

"Your son's dead. He went into the Forbidden Zone without permission. If the monsters haven't got him, then the centaurs have."

Raya looked at her father with interest.

"Is that true, father? There are monsters in the Forbidden Zone?"

"There are things in there even *I* don't know about."

The old man crumpled again.

"Please, your majesty, please, please…"

Raya rolled her eyes. She didn't want to hear any more of his desperation or fear. She could have ordered the guards to drag him away. And she nearly did. But somewhere at the back of her mind, that worrisome little splinter of guilt was needling her again. She had to make it stop.

"He's getting on my nerves. Hey, Silas."

The centaur was at the back of the room.

"Yes, your majesty?"

"Send word to your mates in the Zone not to kill a small child if they see it. There'll be a reward if they can find him and return him to the village."

Silas flicked his eyes to Aelfric. The king shrugged.

"Do as my daughter says. I don't think I can bear any more wailing."

"I'll do it now, your majesty."

"Thank you, sire, thank you both." The relief on the old man's face was painful to see. Raya hardened her heart.

"You shouldn't have let him wander. Now go away."

The man backed out, bowing the whole way.

"I need more wine." Raya got to her feet. "When can we get back to the fun stuff?"

"What do you suggest?"

"Let's dance."

That sliver of guilt again. It was a whisper, barely registering on her consciousness. But there nonetheless, a constant refrain. *This isn't you. This isn't how you should be acting.*

She danced with her favourite lord, a tall, dark-skinned elven with eyes of midnight blue. There was something about the combination of brown skin, blue eyes that made her wistful. Sometimes, if she squinted, he reminded her of someone. But it wasn't quite right. *He* wasn't quite right.

She frowned, took another gulp of mead, and danced harder.

How could she not enjoy this life? She had no responsibilities beyond offering an opinion occasionally. No-one was relying on her for anything. All she had to do was have fun. Lots and lots of fun.

One day maybe she would have to marry Salaq, but that was just a means to an end. A way of extending her father's territory.

Her feet slowed and stopped again. Dammit, what was wrong with her?

"Are you feeling unwell, your highness?" inquired the elven lord. His sharp eyes scoured her face. "Do you no longer enjoy dancing?"

"I *love* dancing." *I love dancing with Shade.*

The thought popped unbidden into her mind. For just a second, the haze in her mind cleared and her thoughts were as sharp as a blade.

What the fuck am I doing here?

She looked round wildly. The place was full of elven, all of them as beautiful and lethal as sleek hunting dogs. They weren't her companions, she realised in a stab of clarity. They were her guards.

And her father was her keeper.

As if sensing her thoughts, Aelfric turned from his conversation to focus on her.

His illusions, she thought. *So hard to keep my head straight.*

She fought the invasive thrum of the crystalline tone that threatened to swamp her will again. In pure defensive mode, flames lit from her hands. Without thinking, still concentrating on keeping the glamour from engulfing her again, she let them run up her arms and body.

Her torso ignited into blue and orange. Flames licked at her face, their heat comforting and familiar. She hung on to the feeling.

This is who I am, she thought fiercely. Not an elven princess. But the leader of the Vulcani.

The haze receded.

My flames. They're a shield.

Aelfric's face twisted in fury as he realised he could no longer colour her thoughts.

"What are you doing, daughter?"

"Asserting my rights. I'm not your slave anymore, daddy dear."

"Stop this at once. This is your home. We are your family."

"I don't think so. This is all too dysfunctional, even for me. And I've been in therapy for years."

"We could be all-powerful, you and I." Aelfric's eyes gleamed. "We could take the empire for ourselves. Rule as we wanted."

Raya's flames kicked up a notch.

"I don't want to rule," she hissed. "I just want to get the fuck out of here and away from all you weirdos."

"Then you will be sorely disappointed."

At a gesture from Aelfric, the lords and ladies surrounded her. She could feel their collective glamour beating against her fire, testing her defences.

"Not going to work, bitches," she told them. "My power beats yours."

"Maybe for now." Aelfric examined his nails casually. "But there's just one of you. And you can't keep your flames lit forever. You'll need to sleep or rest at some point. And when you do…"

He grinned, and there was nothing charming whatsoever about his smile. His face was as predatory as a ferret scenting blood. How could she ever have thought he was beautiful?

"Dream on, you bastard. I can keep this up all day."

"We shall see, won't we, daughter?"

He was right. As soon as she let her guard slip, it would all be over.

She couldn't even fireball her way out of there. Somehow she didn't think the fae would be terrified by a display of pretty flowers and birds.

Even if by some miracle she got through the crowd of elven, the throne room doors were heavily guarded by bestials and soldiers. Not to mention the ogurs. There was no way out.

It was only a matter of time. And then, she knew, her father would make her pay dearly for rebelling.

Despair rose in her heart.

She sank back down into her throne and let her flames die. The silver jangle crept back into her mind and she didn't fight it.

That's when the world exploded.

Forty Five

The palace doors blew off their hinges as if hit by a tornado. Black smoke poured into the throne room, forcing soldiers to stumble back.

Shade strode in, his eyes twin pools of incandescent fury.

"Aelfric," he snarled. "I've come for my betrothed."

The Fae King leaned forward on his throne, fingers steepled together.

"Lord Shadeed. It is an honour. I don't think I've seen you since that unfortunate incident with Crown Prince Kamran."

Shade's face darkened.

"You think you have got away with his murder. But I know better."

"Have a care, jinn. You're in my territory now. Speaking of which, is this a social call or a full-scale invasion?"

"I do not have my army here, if that is what you mean. I see no reason for senseless deaths. I just want Raya." His gaze fastened on Raya, sitting motionless next to Aelfric. She had not said anything, and he couldn't determine her feelings. "Raya? Are you all right?"

Raya stirred.

"I know you, don't I? You're Shade."

Aelfric watched her carefully.

"Do you remember being with Shadeed, daughter? He kidnapped you. Held you at his castle."

Shade growled.

"That is not what happened."

Raya tilted her head to one side.

"You used me, to make my people ally to your cause."

"Maybe in the beginning. But not now. I came here because I need you. Come home with me, Raya."

Aelfric cackled madly, rubbing his hands together in glee.

"Oh, this is just perfect. The jinn has feelings for my daughter."

"Father, I…" Raya shook her head, trying to clear it. "I need to think."

"Don't let him fool you," Aelfric said sharply. "He's lying to you. He has lied constantly. Ask him why he isn't surprised that I'm your father."

Raya realised it was true. Shade had shown no confusion when Aelfric had referred to her as his daughter.

"You told me my father was dead," she said accusingly. "Did you know it was Aelfric?"

Shade nodded slowly.

"Magda told me. When I went looking for your mother. She said Aelah had sworn her to secrecy."

"So it's true." Her lip curled in contempt. "You've done nothing but lie to me."

"Not about everything." Shade took two strides towards the throne before he was stopped by guards, all pointing their swords at his throat. "Not about my feelings. I miss you."

Raya stared at him. Her face was cold but inside she was in turmoil.

He misses me.

The hypnotic silver tone dimmed.

"That's enough," snapped Aelfric. "Lord Shadeed, you must leave now. My daughter has made it clear she wants nothing to do with you."

"I do not believe she has."

"I'm not offering you a choice. Leave now while you still can."

"I will go when *she* tells me to go," Shade said stubbornly. "Not before."

Black waves started to roll off him, his mood mirrored by his shadow power. Aelfric rose to his feet.

"He's preparing to attack. Guards!"

The soldiers closest to Shade thrust their swords at him. With a roar, he drove a wall of shadows into them, flinging them through the air. They landed on the guards behind, leaving a dozen winded or unconscious.

Two more ran at him. He grabbed them both by their metal breastplates and smashed them into each other, then threw them aside. He started towards the throne again.

"Ogurs," Aelfric screamed. "He's attacking the princess. Protect her."

The hulking figures lumbered towards Shade. Other soldiers hung back, not wanting to get in their way.

The ogurs stopped in front of the jinn and he looked them up and down.

"I do not suppose you would let me pass if I ask nicely?"

The ogurs frowned. Conversation was not in their repertoire. One raised his club, more or less a tree trunk with nails sticking out of it. He smashed it down towards Shade who sidestepped nimbly.

They were slow. That could work to his advantage. But they were strong. Maybe he could take on one, but two was beyond even his strength.

He'd have to separate them.

He manifested his wings, the outer tips knocking over several lords and ladies watching from the side-lines. A thick tentacle of smoke snaked towards one of the ogurs. He dodged another blow from a club and threw himself into the air. His smoke lasso wrapped around the creature and he dragged him off his feet.

He flew up to the marble ceiling. It wasn't as high as he'd have liked but it would have to do. The ogur was grunting and writhing in his grip. By the gods, he was heavy.

Down below, his comrade gazed upwards open-mouthed, his face a mask of bovine confusion. Shade dropped his passenger straight onto him.

The sheer weight of the ogur combined with the drop knocked them both out. They lay splayed on the marble floor, cracks now ruining its pristine surface.

Shade landed lightly and threw a taunting look at the throne.

"Is that all you've got?"

Aelfric rose to his feet, eyes flashing in fury.

"Kill him."

From every corner of the palace, soldiers poured towards the jinn.

Shade manifested shadow swords in each hand and fought grimly, wielding his blades with deadly accuracy. His smoke shifted into solid shields to protect his flank from those behind him. With each soldier he dispatched, he gained a little ground towards the throne.

Raya watched his display of deadly grace and something fluttered in her heart. She leaned forward, her breath coming faster.

Aelfric hadn't expected the jinn to get this far. He was a skilled fighter, of that there was no doubt. But he couldn't win. Not against him.

He rose from his throne and waved his hand. A phalanx of jet shards hung in the air, light glistening from their razor edges. He let them go.

They flew through the soldiers, some hitting those unfortunate enough to be in their way. Shade saw them at the last second. His blades parried two of them, three, four. But the fifth got through.

It buried itself into his abdomen just above his hip. He sucked in his breath, appalled at how much it hurt. He grabbed the edge of it, meaning to pull it out. But it bucked in his hand like a living thing, driving itself deeper.

Blood spurted, making it too slippery to grip.

He battled on, hiding the pain. But watching from the throne, Raya knew he was in agony. How did she know? She just did. She knew *him.*

Her pulse quickened. She glanced at her father standing at the edge of the dais and saw his lips were drawn back from his teeth. He was furious.

Aelfric created new projectiles and hurled them at Shade, cutting down yet more of his own soldiers. But he didn't care. He just wanted the jinn dead.

Raya watched as a second shard hit Shade, this time in the shoulder. The blood was coming thick and fast now. He was nearly at the bottom of the steps leading to the throne dais, but he was weakening.

Her thoughts became anguished, despairing, as he fell to his knees. The crystal hum in her head dimmed fractionally. Beside her, her father crowed in triumph.

"You're done, jinn."

Shade knelt, panting, his blood draining onto the ground. His shadows had become wispy and translucent. All his energy was now concentrated on the blades in his hands, and even they were fading.

A dozen soldiers surrounded him. Silas grabbed his hair and yanked his head back, a dagger to his throat. Raya found herself looking straight into eyes as blue as sapphires. He gave a small smile.

"I suppose if I am to die anywhere, at your feet would be my first choice."

Aelfric looked at the carnage around him. The trail of bodies, the motionless ogurs. All this because of one vengeful jinn? His rage was white hot.

"Slit his worthless throat. I want to see his blood spill."

"No, wait."

Raya rose from the throne and walked down the steps. She bent so her face was level with the jinn.

"Tell me. Did you come here to kill yourself? Because that's the only reason I can think why someone would willingly walk into the Fae Court looking for a fight."

His gaze roamed her face. She looked different. Taller. More elven. Her ears were no longer human. But her eyes... her dark velvet eyes were the same.

"I came for you."

"Why? Because you *need* me? You *miss* me?"

"No. Because I love you."

He lurched forward against the grip of his captors. For the briefest of moments, his lips touched hers.

The shock of it seared her to the bone.

Then he was yanked back, a trickle of blood at his throat where it had pressed against Silas's blade.

"How dare you," screamed Aelfric. "You filthy dog, how dare you defile the princess?"

Shade didn't answer. He kept his eyes locked on Raya. She touched her fingers to her lips, heart thudding against her ribs.

Aelfric was almost unhinged in his fury.

"You won't just die, you son of a whore. You'll die slowly. I'll make it last for days. I'll make you believe your skin is being peeled away inch by inch. I'll make you beg for death. You'll regret ever coming here alone."

His voice dripped with psychotic vitriol. But incredibly, the jinn laughed.

"Alone? Who said I was alone?"

And suddenly a ball of fire came hurtling into the palace. Its speed was shocking as it burned anything and everything in its path.

A soldier slow to move was reduced to ashes in the blink of an eye, not even given the chance to scream.

White hot flames smashed into the dais, engulfing the empty thrones in a roaring inferno. The scorching heat melted them into misshapen lumps within seconds.

The fire flickered out, leaving everyone stunned to silence.

A woman walked in. Copper hair, caramel skin, marmalade eyes. She balanced another fireball in her palm as she faced Aelfric.

"Hello lover," she said. "Miss me?"

FORTY SIX

Raya felt the world tilt around her. That face… it wasn't possible. Yet she recognised it from the countless hours she'd spent staring at a photo.

"You can't be her," she breathed. "You're dead."

The woman cocked her head.

"Escape now. Explanations later." She glanced at Aelfric. "Don't move, you bastard."

The elven hid his shock. He held his hands out to the fire fae and forced a smile.

"Aelah. My *lumen vitae,* light of my life. I knew you'd come back one day."

"Don't call me that. And believe me, I never wanted to set foot in this place again. But there's no way I'm letting my daughter stay trapped with you."

Aelfric's face hardened.

"Don't you mean *our* daughter? Suraya is here of her own free will."

"Yeah, looks like it. The trouble with strong minds is that sooner or later, they break the glamour."

"She doesn't want to break it," spat Aelfric. "I gave her what she wanted. I gave her a family. A place to belong."

"You played on her fears, like you always do, you prick." Aelah glanced at Raya. "He kept me under his spell for months. But I broke free the minute I found out I was pregnant, because of my love for you. Love is a great weapon against mind control."

Love.

Raya looked at Shade. He hadn't moved. He remained on his knees with Silas's knife to his throat. Aelfric's shards were still embedded in his shoulder and abdomen, and he was grey with pain. But his eyes flared blue and she felt her heart leap.

"I think… I think I want to go home now."

"You *are* home, daughter," Aelfric snapped. Raya shook her head, her thoughts becoming clearer with each second.

"Let him go. It's over."

"No. It is not."

Aelfric laid a hand on her shoulder and she heard the tuning fork strike up its chord again.

Shade roared in desperation, trying to clamber to his feet. But he was too weak and the centaur easily held him back.

Aelah created a second fireball, balancing one in each hand. Her eyes glowed dangerously.

"Get away from her, Aelfric. Or I'll fireball the whole fucking place and in case you've forgotten, we three are the only ones here who aren't flammable."

"I think our daughter should speak for herself." Aelfric looked at Raya intently. "I'm the only one who ever told you the truth, Suraya. These two both lied to you. They wanted to contain you, control your life. If you stay with me, you'll have true power."

She met his penetrating gaze and knew he was right. They *had* lied to her.

But they'd done it because they loved her. The thought cut through the hum like a scalpel.

She let her mouth widen into a smile.

"Sorry. The jedi shit isn't working anymore." She looked down at herself and concentrated. The violet dress shimmered and evaporated, morphing back into the torn, muddied red gown she'd been wearing when she was kidnapped. "See?"

The elven king reeled back in shock.

"You dare to defy me? After everything I've done for you? Because of *him*?"

"No. Not just because of him. Because of *me*. Nobody gets to decide for me anymore. *I* decide."

Spittle flew from Aelfric's mouth.

"Fine words, daughter. But if you won't live here, you won't live anywhere."

Suddenly he was behind her, one hand at her throat, the other grasping her wrist and forcing it high between her shoulder blades.

"Raya!"

Aelah drew back her hand to launch a fireball but Aelfric shook his head warningly.

"I'll break her neck before your fire ever reaches me."

The Vulcani dropped her arm, frustrated. Shade's voice cut between them.

"If she dies, it will be a declaration of war between us."

Aelfric sneered.

"I have Salaq and his army on my side. Do you really want to drag the empire into battle? Over one girl?"

"I will not leave without her."

"Then you've signed your own death warrant."

The glamoured spike in Shade's stomach tore itself deeper. He couldn't prevent a groan of pain and Aelfric smiled in satisfaction.

"Wait. Just wait a minute. Do I get a say in this?" Raya twisted her head to look at the elven and he relaxed his hold by a fraction.

"Of course, daughter. If you agree to stay, I will let both of them go. And I promise, you won't feel their loss. I'll make it so you don't remember either of them. And we will rule together for millennia."

"Right. Well, I've thought it over. And the thing is, I don't like it here any more." Without warning, she smashed her forehead into Aelfric's face. He dropped to the floor, stunned. "Headbutts were my specialty in the hospital. I had a lot of time to practice, thanks to you."

Aelfric stared up at her in disbelief, his nose bloodied.

"How dare you strike me. I'm your father!"

"No, you're not. You just contributed some DNA. My father was Ross and he died because of you." She turned to the soldiers surrounding Shade. "Now let him go."

Uncertain, they looked to Aelfric for guidance. He snarled an order.

"Kill him."

As if in slow motion, Raya saw Silas tighten his grip on Shade's hair, tipping his throat back for a clean cut. The light gleamed off his knife. Half a dozen swords and spikes started towards Shade's torso. He strained against his captors, muscles flexing in vain.

She watched all this happen in a fraction of a second, panic and adrenaline flooding her body.

And then a sheet of flame erupted from her. An incandescent wave of heat and fury screaming outwards with the inexorable force of a tsunami. And though she didn't know it, her eyes were glowing orange.

The leading edge of the fire swept through the soldiers like a scythe. Except it was a thousand degrees hotter.

They were incinerated instantly, skin and bone charred to cinders. Silas's knife fell to the floor, the blade a molten mess. The air was heavy with the stench of burning flesh.

The sheet of flame continued on, consuming everything in its path until it hit the far wall and blew it to rubble.

Only the Ifrit and the Vulcani emerged unscathed, and even they felt the burn of its passing.

Forty Seven

Aelfric stared at the destruction. The once immaculate white marble chamber was now grey with smoke and soot. The far wall had flown out, debris flung into the room beyond. His soldiers had all gone, even the ogurs. Instead, the floor was littered with piles of glowing embers. He staggered to his feet.

"*What have you done?*"

Lords and ladies stumbled around, dazed and dishevelled. Only those who had been behind Raya had escaped the blinding wall of fire.

She looked at the devastation and put her hands to her face, distraught.

"I… I didn't mean to. Are they all dead?"

In an instant, Shade was by her side.

"Look at me. Raya, look at me." Hesitantly, she lifted her gaze. "They were going to kill me. You saved my life."

"But I didn't mean to do… to do *that*."

"You had no choice. Aelfric would never have let any of us go."

She swallowed, trying to come to terms with what she'd done.

"I thought I was going to lose you."

"You will never lose me. I love you."

She wanted to say it back, but she was tongue-tied.

"Your wounds. How bad are they?"

"Healing. Your flames dissolved those cursed weapons impaling me."

The deep punctures in his shoulder and stomach were already closing. She touched the scars gently, marvelling at his ability to heal.

"I can't believe you came after me. How long have I been here?"

"Several days. Believe me when I say they were the worst of my life."

Days? It had felt like weeks to her. Months. She lay her hand flat against his chest, feeling his familiar heat beneath her palm. His eyes darkened and suddenly all she could focus on was his mouth.

"Ahem."

They broke apart to see Aelah watching them.

"I suppose I ought to formally introduce myself. I'm your mother."

Raya didn't know what to say.

"I thought you were dead." She turned to Shade accusingly. "You lied."

"Yes. I thought if you knew the truth, it would complicate matters. I see now I was wrong."

"He was trying to protect you," Aelah said.

"I'm not a child that needs to be protected. By either of you."

"You are right," said Shade. "I am truly sorry."

"Look, I know we have a lot to talk about, but can we go?" Aelah gestured at the palace. "We're still in enemy territory here. And I for one do *not* have any happy memories of this fucking place. Pardon my French."

"I still have a lot of questions," Raya said.

"And I will answer every single one as soon as we're out of here."

They started towards the door. They'd barely taken two paces when the ground started shaking. Raya looked about her wildly as huge cracks appeared at her feet. Shade took her hand and they stumbled back, trying to keep their balance.

Suddenly a wall of thorns erupted upwards. It reached to the ceiling, bristling with wicked barbs and completely blocking their way.

"None of you are leaving."

They turned to find Aelfric behind them, his remaining lords and ladies lined up next to him. His face was white with fury. The glamour he usually used on himself was absent. His robes were smudged with dirt and the golden circlet on his brow was askew.

"Give it up, Aelfric." Aelah taunted him. "You've lost. And you deserve it for what you did to me."

"You enjoyed it. You enjoyed *me*."

"Only because you made me think I did, you twisted fuck. You kept me here against my will. The only good thing that came out of it was Raya. And I'm telling you now, the Vulcani will be supporting Shadeed for the throne. There's no way I'm ever letting you get your hands on Nush'aldaam."

"I'm your king!" he screamed. "You obey me!"

"Go to hell."

Mad with rage, Aelfric lifted his hands. A dozen jet shards appeared.

"Then let me show you how it feels to lose something you want so very, very badly."

With a screech, he sent the shards arrowing directly towards Raya.

Shade reacted instinctively, throwing shadows up as a shield. Aelah's reaction was faster and more deadly. Fireballs rocketed from her hands, engulfing first the shards, and then Aelfric himself.

He screamed as his flesh blistered and his bones charred. The crown on his head melted into liquid gold and blended with his ruined features. Raya turned away, the smell of burning meat making her blanch. The screams stopped.

In the silence that followed, a cloud of ash drifted gently to the floor. Nobody said anything.

The remaining elven turned towards them. Lord and ladies, alert and watchful, their beautiful faces intent. Raya braced for attack. Next to her, Aelah readied another fireball and Shade unfurled his shadows.

There was a long moment.

Then as one, the elven bowed. First from the waist, and then down onto one knee, their heads bent in deference.

Only one looked directly at Raya. The lord with the dark skin and blue eyes, the one she'd danced with while under the glamour.

"The king is dead," he said. "Long live the queen."

Forty Eight

"So this rose is linked to Caroline and Ross." Aelah stroked the petals gently and patted down the soil around the plant. "I'm sorry for what happened to them. I chose them because they seemed like good people."

"They were. I was very happy. Until that demon found me."

"He was looking for me. Well, for us. I hoped Aelfric wouldn't realise I was pregnant but I guess he figured it out when I broke the glamour."

"What a bastard. It must have been horrible."

"I was just worried about you. I knew I couldn't stay in Nush'aldaam. So I span a story about falling in love with a human and left. Magda helped me.

"Couldn't you have kept me with you?"

"Darling, I wanted to. I really did. But Aelfric's demons can track anything. They had my scent. I had to keep moving and that's no life for a child. I thought if you looked human, you could fit in. Grow up safe and happy."

Raya picked a blade of grass and began to shred it.

"Why… oh, it doesn't matter."

"Ask me. Ask me anything."

"Why didn't you come for me when I was put in that hospital?" There was a lump in Raya's throat and she tried to swallow it down. "Why did you leave me there?"

"I honestly thought it was the safest place for you." Aelah took Raya's hands, gently stopping her from plucking more grass. "I made a mistake. I'm sorry. Can you forgive me?"

"You're here now, that's what matters. But I need you to know that I still think of Caroline as my mother."

"I understand. And she'd be so proud of you. You're a strong person, Raya. I don't just mean your power, which is extraordinary. But your resilience. Your determination. I'm very much looking forward to getting to know you."

Raya gave a wobbly smile.

"Me too."

"Have you thought about what you're going to do? Now that you're the Fae Queen?"

"I honestly don't know. I have no idea how to rule. And I don't want to live in Feyir. I want to stay here in Nurhan."

"Because of a certain tall, dark, handsome jinn?" Aelah smiled mischievously. "I'd stay here too if I had *that* hunk pining for me."

Raya blushed.

"He's not pining for me."

"Yeah, sure. Have you told him yet?"

"Told him what?"

"That you love him. I mean, he declared his feelings in front of the whole damn Fae Court so presumably he's desperate to know if you reciprocate."

Raya squirmed uncomfortably.

"I haven't told him anything."

"Why the fuck not?"

Aelah's language was worse than hers. At least she knew where she'd inherited it from.

"Look, I haven't had the chance to speak to him yet. And anyway, I don't even know if he meant it. Everything was so chaotic."

"Are you fucking kidding me? When you disappeared, he flew back to Norway and forced Magda to tell him where I was. He tracked me down when no-one else could. He practically shanghaied me to come on a suicidal rescue mission. He said if I didn't, he'd tell every demon in the whole world where I was hiding." Aelah paused. "He was very, very angry. I think I ought to warn you he has a hell of a temper."

"Understatement of the year. Did he roar at you?"

"Loud enough to tear a wall down. I'm pretty sure I've lost the rental deposit."

They both giggled and Raya felt a swell of happiness. Shade had moved heaven and earth to find her. She desperately wanted to talk to him. But she had to make some decisions first.

"What shall I do about Feyir?" she asked. "I can't just abandon it if I'm queen. But I don't want to live there."

"You could appoint a proxy. A regent. They can rule in your name, for a while."

"A regent," Raya said slowly. "Yes. I need a regent to rule for me. What about you?"

"Me?"

"You're already a leader. And technically, the Queen Mother. The fae would accept you."

Aelah shook her head doubtfully.

"I don't know. I've been away for so long, sweetheart. I don't know if I can take up the reins again just like that."

"You could have advisors. What about Loris and Kaemari? And the rest of the Vulcani council? A hell of a lot better than those creepy lords and ladies."

Aelah pondered.

"It would give the Vulcani power over the elven for the first time in centuries. We could make so many changes. Rein in the bestials and their free-for-all in that Forbidden Zone, for one."

Raya sensed her mother weakening.

"And we could bring in new laws. Have an actual legal process instead of expecting people to grovel at the Court."

"And don't forget the most important change of all." Aelah looked at Raya in sudden excitement. "Don't you see? As Queen, you can pledge the allegiance of *all* the fae to Shade. Not just the Vulcani. All of Feyir."

Raya inhaled. The thought hadn't occurred to her.

"Will it be enough to beat Salaq?"

"Maybe. If the Vetali stay out of it. But they usually do."

"Ah." Raya wondered how Tala was getting on and whether she'd managed to track down the vampire with the bounty on his head. "Well, let's hope. So you'll do it? Be my regent?"

Aelah got to her feet and pulled Raya up with her. Then she bowed solemnly.

"It would be my pleasure, your majesty. Now, speaking as your regent, do you need me to show you which herbs prevent pregnancy?"

Raya was startled.

"What?"

"If I'm not mistaken, you might need them very soon."

"No! I mean, I don't… we're not…"

Aelah laughed.

"Yeah, yeah, of course you're not. Now get your butt up to that tower and put the jinn out of his misery."

Forty Nine

Raya stopped to see Tor on the way. The Sylvan was recuperating in the sanitorium, a bright, clean room with nurses bustling around.

Raya was pretty sure the number of nurses had doubled overnight when Tor was brought in.

"How are you feeling today?" she asked.

He grinned at her cheerfully from the bed.

"I feel well enough to leave but they want me to stay in a bit longer for observation." *I bet they do.* "Glad to see you're safe. Shade told me all about it."

"Oh?" Raya raised an eyebrow. "You two are besties now, are you?"

"He saved my life. And he rescued you. Hard not to like him."

"Yeah. He grows on you." She sat on the edge of the bed. "But seriously, you're a hero too. Shade told me you dragged yourself for more than a mile to get back to the castle. You could have died."

"It was nothing. I needed the exercise."

"You tried to stop the kidnapping. You realised it wasn't Shade who came for me after the demonstration, didn't you?"

"The aura wasn't right. But I should have known sooner." The smile dropped from his face. "If I'd put two and two together earlier, I could have prevented the whole thing."

She laid a hand on his arm.

"Stop it. Because of you, Shade knew where I was. He came to get me. And he brought my mother."

"I know. The Vulcani council have been discussing it."

"How do you know?"

"One of the girls in the kitchen told me."

"You're getting visits from the kitchen girls?"

His brow wrinkled.

"I seem to be getting a lot of visitors. I didn't realise so many people cared about me."

"And do these visitors happen to be mostly female?"

"Aye, now you mention it."

Raya rolled her eyes.

"Big surprise."

Tor took her chin and turned her head so he could see her ears.

"Nice. Do you like them?"

"Well, they don't itch anymore." She rubbed the pointed tip self-consciously. "I'm still getting used to them."

"I think they're cute. Do you want to see my scar?"

He pulled his top up and rolled onto his side. A reddish circular mark blemished his otherwise smooth skin. Raya touched a fingertip to it gently.

"No permanent damage?"

"The arrow missed every major organ. Dumb luck."

"It must have hurt like hell."

"Aye. It did. But they've got great healers here." He straightened his shirt. "I hear you're the Fae Queen now. Should I be bowing?"

"Not you. You get special dispensation."

"I'm honoured. So what will you do?"

"My mother will rule for me as regent. She could use help, if you want a job as an advisor?"

He shook his head.

"I want to get back to my simple life. But if you ever need me, I'll be there." He cocked his head. "I guess you've decided to stay here, with Shadeed?"

"I hope so. We have a few things to work out. We haven't really spoken since we got back from Feyir."

"That was yesterday."

"He had stuff to do. And he was giving me and Aelah time to get to know each other." She realised how weak that sounded. "I'm on my way to see him now."

He studied her thoughtfully.

"What's the problem?"

"He told me he loved me. In front of everyone."

"So? You don't feel the same?"

"It's complicated." She tried to explain. "I've spent so long hiding my feelings. In hospital, they encourage you to talk about how you feel all the time. It becomes the only thing you have any control over. So the important stuff, the really deep stuff, you hide. And I don't know if I can break the habit."

Tor looked at her sympathetically.

"You've already changed dramatically from the person you thought you were. If anyone can break a habit they no longer need, it's you." He took her hand and kissed the back of it. "You deserve happiness, Lady Raya of the Vulcani. Now stop dithering and go get it."

Fifty

Shade hovered above the castle. His mind was in turmoil. He had a thousand things to do in the aftermath of what had happened in Feyir, all of them important.

He had to liaise with the leaders of all the different fae clans to convince them this wasn't the start of hostilities. That the battle in the palace was personal, not political. But the fallout was already beginning.

There were rumblings of rebellion among the bestials. Some felt they had been treated as inferior under the elven and now they saw an opportunity to gain independence.

He also had to speak with the si'lat to try to bring them back to his side. He hoped their leader, Leona's father, would be sufficiently outraged by what had happened to his daughter to switch allegiance again.

Leona herself had returned home to her family, the glamour which had been inflicted on her disappearing with Aelfric's death. For that he was grateful. He didn't wish her harm, though he would never truly forgive her betrayal. He knew he was partly responsible for her actions. He hadn't been careful with her feelings.

He still hadn't spoken with the Vetali to warn them of the plot against their Count. By now they would know a contract was out for his head and were under the misconception that Shade was responsible.

All of these things were vital, urgent tasks. And yet he could only think of one thing.

He'd told Raya he loved her. And she hadn't said it back.

His wings beat the air slowly. She was a queen now. She had her own throne, her own calling. And she had her mother back. The deal they'd struck so long ago in the human world was completed.

She did not need him.

He stared unseeing into the distance and wondered what life would be like without her. It took him a little while to notice the butterfly flitting around his head.

He batted it away irritably but it kept coming back, persistently fluttering to and fro in his line of vision.

He squinted. It was made of flame.

Startled, he peered towards the castle. His platform was several hundred yards away but even from here he could see a tiny figure standing at the end of it. Long hair streamed in the wind and a single strand of amber glinted like fire.

Raya.

He flew towards her, suddenly nervous. Desperate to see her but scared of what she might say. Scared of what she might *not* say.

He hung in the air several feet from the platform. She looked beautiful. She was wearing a simple off-white shift dress that made her skin glow.

"I thought you'd be with your mother."

"I wanted to see you."

"Have you come to tell me you are leaving?"

"Why would you think that?"

He spread his arms as if it was obvious.

"You are a queen now. You belong in Feyir."

"Screw that." She laughed and the vice around his heart loosened a little. "Unless you want me to go?"

"No! No, but…" he took a breath. "It would not surprise me. Everything that has happened to you, happened because of me. If I had not brought you here to Nush'aldaam, Aelfric would not have found you."

"I think we both know that's not true. His shaitun found me at the hospital just before you got there."

"But you were lured into a trap because Leona was angry with me."

"And again, you saved me."

"I think on that occasion, you saved me." He smiled faintly. "I have never heard of a Vulcani being able to throw a solid wall of fire before. It was remarkable. And extremely powerful."

"Heat of the moment. Literally."

"Still. I would not blame you for never trusting me again."

Raya cocked her head.

"You think I don't trust you?"

"I don't know what you think. Your mind, as ever, is a mystery to me."

She nodded thoughtfully. Then she turned and let herself fall backwards off the platform. The descent was shockingly fast, the wind snatching her breath away. The cliff face whipped past her and the sound of the gorge below got louder.

And then he was on her, arms tight around her, slowing her velocity. Shade held her close as they ascended, shadows streaming off him in consternation.

"Why in the name of the gods did you do that?"

"Because I knew you'd catch me. I trust you, Shade. I always trust you."

And she kissed him. Her lips explored his, gently at first, then more urgently. He let her take the lead, unsure where this was heading. She darted her tongue into his mouth, surprising him with her boldness.

Her hands were against his chest and she moved them restlessly, stroking his pecs, his ribs, down towards his stomach.

He caught her wrist and pulled his mouth from hers.

"Raya, I need to be clear on this," he said thickly. "What do you want from me?"

"I want you to be my first."

"Your…?"

"I want you to make love to me, Lord Shadeed of Nurhan. You've told me how you feel about me. Now I want to show you how *I* feel."

"Are you sure?"

In answer, she kissed him again. She wound her arms around his neck and wrapped her legs about his waist. They spiralled in the air slowly, just kissing, as his wings beat in time to their hearts.

I could kiss him forever, she thought. He roamed her mouth possessively, his tongue flickering against hers sensuously. He moved from her mouth to her ears, nipping at her lobe before stroking the very tip of his tongue over the delicate points. She inhaled sharply. She hadn't realised how sensitive fae ears were.

"I like these," he murmured. "They are said to be an erogenous zone for elven. Does this feel…?"

"God, yes. Don't stop."

He chuckled into her ear, sending her pulse rocketing.

"I think we need to lie down. I am going to take you somewhere. A special place."

"As long as it's close," she said breathlessly.

She kissed his throat as they flew, her hands roaming the muscles of his back. She wondered what it would be like to feel them flex as he thrust into her. The thought made her hot with longing.

She kept her legs around his waist, enjoying the sensation of his arousal pushing against her. She tried to keep from grinding her hips but the temptation was too much. The friction sent little bolts of pleasure between her thighs.

Her movements were making it hard for him to concentrate. They reached the grassy plateau and he landed clumsily, falling onto his back to take the brunt. She lay on top of him, winded and laughing.

"What kind of landing was that?"

"That's what happens when you distract me, halfling," he growled. He rolled her so she was beneath him and kissed her. He was aware he was almost devouring her in his urgency and forced himself to slow down.

He nuzzled her neck, sucking gently at the flesh above her pulse before trailing to her collar bone. She caught her breath as he pressed his lips to her bare flesh, delighting in the smooth warmth of her skin.

He slipped the straps from her shoulders, glad there were no buttons or ties to slow him down, and pushed the dress to her waist.

He stopped for a moment to take in her beauty. She lay in his arms, shy under his gaze but making no attempt to cover herself up.

He took a breast in his hand and stroked it, watching her eyes dilate in pleasure. When he lowered his mouth to a hard little nipple, she arched against him eagerly. He sucked on the sensitive tip, lashing it with his tongue before moving to the other one.

Each touch seemed to connect directly with the ache between her legs. She held his head, urging him to suck harder.

He slid the dress from her entirely and threw it to one side, catching his breath as he realised she was naked underneath. Naked for him.

He kissed his way down her body, trailing his lips over the smooth curve of her stomach, moving lower towards her hips. She was desperate for him to taste her again, to feel his mouth at the very centre of her. But she stopped him.

"Not yet," she said breathlessly. "I want to see you first."

She pushed him onto his back and straddled him possessively. He made to put his hands on her waist and she pinned them to either side of his head. He acquiesced and lay still as she pressed her lips to his neck.

She breathed in his scent, his warmth. He filled her senses as she kissed her way down his chest. She flicked her tongue against his nipple, curious to know if it affected him the way it affected her. He inhaled sharply and she smiled as she bit down gently.

His hardness was pushing insistently against her but Shade hadn't yet divested himself of his clothing. She moved downwards, running her tongue across his abdominal muscles, feeling them contract beneath her feather touch. He was breathing hard by the time she got to his waistband.

"May I undress?" he asked hoarsely. She realised he was asking permission because he wanted to go at her pace. Her heart swelled.

"Yes," she whispered.

Shadows melted away from his lower half, leaving him naked. Just as he had done, she simply stared for a few moments, drinking him in.

He's beautiful. And huge. That'll never... dear God.

Tentatively, she took him in her hand. She stroked the rigid length of him, becoming more confident when he groaned. Impulsively, she bent to kiss it.

"You do not have to do that," he said, his voice ragged.

"I want to."

She kissed it again, then swirled her tongue around the tip. He gasped, the sensation sending an electric current through his whole body. He touched the back of her head, hardly believing this was happening.

"Is this okay?" she asked.

"It is more than okay."

Encouraged, she closed her mouth around him, taking as much between her lips as she could. She moved sensuously up and down his shaft, enjoying the way he felt, the way he tasted. He clutched at the grass and knew he'd never been so hard.

Abruptly he sat up and lifted her away.

"Did I do something wrong?"

"On the contrary, my beautiful fae. Much more of that and I would lose all control. And I want to make it last."

He lay her down among the clover and kissed her. He would never tire of kissing her, he thought. Her lips were like wine to him. He caressed her breasts again, rolling her nipples between his finger and thumb until she moaned helplessly into his mouth.

He stroked the curve of her waist, her hip. When he slid his hand between her legs, he found her slick with want. The sensitive little nub at her centre was standing proud, fully engorged. He circled it with his thumb and she gasped, grinding her hips hard.

Slowly, not wanting to rush, he slipped a finger inside her. She was tight. He stilled, worried he was hurting her.

"Don't stop," she breathed.

"I do not wish to cause you pain."

"You're not. I promise, you're not."

She kissed him hard and rocked her hips against his hand. He felt her wetness, her heat, and he was reassured. He took his hand away and positioned himself above her. Her eyes were half closed, her face flushed as he slid into her.

There was a momentary resistance. And then he was buried deep in her silken folds and the pleasure nearly undid him. He fought his natural inclination and remained motionless, letting her get used to the feel of him inside her.

"Are you all right?" he murmured, stroking her hair. "Is this…?"

"Shade." She kissed his ear. "I love you. I love you so much."

He thought his heart would burst.

And then she was bucking upwards and he simply couldn't control his body any longer. He drove into her and she wrapped her legs around him, her hands pressing into his back.

It was as if she was made just for him. They fit together perfectly. He was touching her in all the right places, turning her body into liquid gold.

He pulled her upright and sat her in his lap, kissing her breasts as she undulated against him. Every thrust, every stroke pushed her closer to the brink.

Flames began to ripple up and down her body.

His wings unfurled and he pulled them both into the air, she still impaled upon him. Her throes of ecstasy were almost making him lose his mind. He hovered vertically and pushed her backwards, grasping her by the waist as he plunged into her again and again. She arched her back and he savoured the delicious sight of her laid out before him, open and helpless with desire.

Flames were now coursing along the whole length of her body, tickling him with their heat.

Interesting, he thought. *I wonder what will happen when she…?*

He ran his hand over her breasts and down towards the point where her body was fused with his. The little knot of pleasure between her legs was erect and swollen, and she moaned in abandon as he stroked his thumb over it in time to the rhythm of his thrusts.

Waves of bliss crashed through her, sensation piling on sensation, building, building, until they reached a crescendo.

And just when she thought it couldn't possibly feel any better, he changed his angle slightly. And suddenly the tension inside her exploded.

She screamed as she lost control. She wanted to laugh and cry at the same time as she was wrecked and reformed over and over.

Her climax broke the last remnants of his restraint. He buried himself deep inside her and shuddered in release, groaning in ecstasy as he rode every last earth-shattering second of it.

It took several minutes for his heartbeat to return to normal. And a few more to realise she was no longer holding onto him. His eyes flew open, then widened in disbelief.

Wings of fire had erupted from between her shoulder blades, mirroring the shadow ones on his own back.

She was flying.

Fifty One

He touched them cautiously.

"How?"

"It was when I… when I came." She blushed and he adored her for it. "It just happened. I don't know why. It didn't happen the last time you made me… um, you know. After the ambrosia berries."

"Maybe it's because the experience this time was more profound. How are you controlling them?"

"They just sort of do what I need them to. I guess when I don't need them anymore they'll disappear, like yours do."

"They are extraordinary." He eyed the small flames still visible on parts of her body. Most had gone out but a few still lingered. "At least I will know when you are faking."

"It was amazing," she said shyly. "I never thought anything could feel so good."

"On that we are agreed. I have never felt that way before. Unfortunately for you, that means I will never let you out of my sight again."

She rested her head against his chest.

"That suits me."

"And that thing you told me," he said gently. "Were you speaking the truth?"

"Which thing?" she asked innocently.

"When you said…" he cleared his throat. "When you said you loved me."

"Oh, that. Well, I was desperate to get laid so I…" she squealed as he held her down and tickled her mercilessly. "Okay, I give in. I love you. I adore you. I worship you."

"I only require the first from you, halfling. Although I suppose I should not refer to you as a halfling anymore."

She snuggled into his chest again.

"Half Vulcani, half elven. It's still accurate. And I do, you know. Love you."

"As I do you. Love seems so inadequate a word to describe how I feel. I would do anything for you. Even give up my quest to be emperor if you asked it. Help you to rule Feyir instead." He tilted her chin up. "What is your wish, my queen?"

She looked into his blue eyes and knew he was sincere. She shook her head.

"Let's give Salaq a run for his money. You have the fae on your side now. We only have to keep the Vetali from his grasp and we win."

"Then that is what we will do." He dropped kisses into the well of her neck. "In the meantime, I am annulling our betrothal."

"What?" She pulled his head back up. "Why?"

"Because I want to ask you properly this time."

"But, I mean, you know I'm going to say yes."

He shook his head sorrowfully.

"Is there to be no more mystery between us?"

"Very funny. The only mystery is why it's taking you so long to ask."

"Patience. We have all the time in the world."

He kissed her ear, then her shoulder. She took his hand and placed it on her breast. He raised an eyebrow.

"So soon?"

"I know you're old. If you're not up to it…"

He kissed her with a slow, sweet hunger that left her breathless. Her flames reignited.

"Maybe we should take this back down to land," he growled.

"Can we stay here a bit longer? I'm just getting used to flying. It feels right."

They spun in the sky together, bodies entwined, both sets of wings beating in synchronicity.

He would never stop wanting her, he realised ruefully. His days of bedding different women as and when he chose were over.

He caught a nipple between his teeth, biting gently before traversing lower, making her writhe with each stroke of his tongue until her flames were burning as blue as his eyes.

"We can stay here as long as you like," he murmured. "In fact, let us see how high we can go."

If you enjoyed *Kiss of Fire,* please leave a review on Amazon. They're so important for authors.

Now read on for a sneak preview of book two in the Immortal Hearts series, *Kiss of Light.*

Kiss of Light: One

It was her third whisky in less than an hour. Good job she didn't get drunk. The room was dark and dingy, the late afternoon sun fighting a losing battle with the grime over the windows.

The general gloominess was deliberate. This was a hunter bar, a place where mercenaries like her hung out. The pervading air of menace was intended to keep ordinary folk at bay.

Even now, a young couple pushing their way through the door took one look at the denizens within and retreated hastily to find a brightly-lit gastropub.

Tala grinned. Humans. So predictable.

She tucked a stray strand of blonde hair back under her cap and scanned the room for familiar faces. The bar was a good starting point for trackers. Information on the quarry's main haunts would be circulated here, plus any useful tips about recent sightings. Right now, the same details were being shared in similar bars across the world; London, Paris, Moscow, Sydney.

The only advantage of being here in New York was that this was where the target usually hung out. By tomorrow, the city would be crawling with hunters looking for the vampire.

She took another hit of whisky, her mood souring.

Fucking vampires.

She supposed she shouldn't call them that. Technically, they were Vetali. A species from the same supernatural realm she herself hailed from. They were alluring and deadly. Beautiful psychopaths who enjoyed drinking blood rather too much. If they had emotions, they kept them well hidden. They didn't do feelings.

She hadn't met many, but the ones she'd run into had unnerved her. And she didn't scare easy.

Fucking vampires.

"Hey, Blue-Eyes." A large man with a scar over one eye took the stool next to her and motioned to the bartender. "Two more whiskies, Mike."

Tala glanced at him. She knew his dark floor-length coat wasn't just to keep the cold out. It also concealed several blades and a Glock.

"Hey, Blake. You on a job?"

"Same one everyone's on. That's why you're here, isn't it? To scope out the competition?"

"Any use me telling you the job's a scam?"

"I hear you've been touting that around." Blake shrugged. "Doesn't matter. A contract's a contract."

"But it's a lie. The bounty wasn't put up by Lord Shadeed. Someone's trying to frame him."

"Sweetheart, I don't care." He paid the barman and slid one of the whiskies over to her. "Anyway, the hit's for a vampire. I thought you hated vampires, so what's the problem?"

Tala studied the mercenary next to her. He was attractive, with his dark hair and stubbled jaw. He'd earned the scar that bisected his right eyebrow in a knife fight early on in his career. It gave him the rakish air of a pirate.

He was an arrogant son-of-a-bitch, but she didn't hold that against him. He was also one of the few humans who knew about the supernatural underworld. It wasn't a big deal to him. He was a bounty hunter, he'd go after anyone or anything as long as it paid.

She was pretty sure they'd slept together once, after a drunken night in this very bar. She vaguely remembered him trying to kiss her on the mouth, which she never, ever, did. Not with anyone. He'd tried a couple of times and she'd had to punch him to get the message through.

But then she'd woken up next to him with his arm slung over her and their clothes buttoned up all wrong. So she assumed they must have worked it out at some point.

He was the hunter she was closest to, if closeness meant exchanging more than two words. But she didn't trust him one bit.

She took a gulp of whisky, savouring the liquid fire as it ran down her throat.

"Who else is in the running?"

"The usual. A bunch of ex-military. A couple of trolls. And the fae twins over there."

Tala nodded. She'd already seen the red-haired elven in the corner. Seraefa and Kaeron always worked together. And they were good. They'd beaten her to a mark more than once.

She had yet to spot another demon, but that meant nothing. A shaitun could be in the bar with them right now, hiding in another's mind, peering out from their bodies, seeing what they saw, hearing what they heard. And she knew Ravij wouldn't be far away.

She sighed, shaking her head.

"For the price-tag, there's bound to be a load of other freelancers in the mix."

"I wouldn't worry about the amateurs, Blondie. I saw a newbie in here the other day. Fuckwit was carrying a shit-load of garlic. You could smell him a mile off."

Tala snorted. The newbie was going to get himself killed if he believed a member of the onion family was a weapon.

"Blake, look. Offing that vamp could shift the balance of power in Nush'aldaam. Is there any way I could convince you to keep him alive?"

"Sure. If you pay me double."

"You know I can't do that."

He shrugged, downing his whisky in one.

"Then I'm going to take his head, as per the contract."

"You don't even know what he looks like."

"True. What the fuck is up with that? You can't photograph a vamp? That's messed up."

"Something to do with the way they bend light. Don't ask me. They're weird fuckers."

"Good job he's got a distinguishing mark, then."

"It's on his chest, shit-for-brains. What are you going to do? Rip the shirt off every vamp matching the description? Good luck with that."

"You know me, sweetheart. Whatever it takes."

Tala studied him for a moment.

"Have you ever hunted Vetali before, Blake? Ever really gone up against one? You think you know them, but you don't. They're dangerous."

"Don't worry about me, Blondie. I've done my research. Contrary to popular belief, they do have heartbeats and they do breathe. In my book, that means they can be killed." He grinned and slid off his stool. "Try not to get in my way, Blue-Eyes. I kinda like your face. I'd hate to ruin it."

"You're all heart," she said sarcastically. He blew her a kiss.

"Later."

She watched him go, knowing he was off to check out a possible location for the mark. Good luck to him. Normally she'd be doing the same, chasing down one lead after another.

But not this time. Because she knew something he didn't. She had time to finish her drink.

She toyed with the glass, letting her shoulders relax. No-one else seemed to have the tip she did. It had taken several days to find the information but she was pretty sure she could get to the target first. Blake and the elven twins were her most serious competition and right now they were barking up the wrong tree. All she had to do was...

The door behind the bar opened. It led to the cellar and Tala glanced up, expecting to see Mike hauling a barrel. She froze.

Half a dozen vampires strolled out, as if they were taking a walk in the park. She knew they were vampires because she couldn't smell them.

Vampires and ghouls were the only two creatures without a scent, and ghouls were ugly bald fuckers who scuttled around like Gollum looking for cadavers to eat. These weren't ghouls.

They all had hair for a start. She wasn't sure which were the better coiffed, the males or the females. And they definitely weren't scuttling. They took up positions around the room, lounging with an easy grace that reminded her of leopards draped lazily across tree branches. Waiting for unsuspecting prey to pass by below.

She checked to make sure she hadn't been mistaken about the time. Nope. Dusk was still an hour away at least. It was unusual to see vampires awake this early.

She called the barman over. Mike was definitely human. He smelled like he hadn't bathed in a week.

"How did *they* get here?" she asked in a low voice. "It's still light outside."

"Through the tunnels, of course. My bar is very cosmopolitan. Open to everyone."

"Cut the crap. Vamps don't hang out in shit-holes like this. Are they trying to sabotage the contract?"

"Nah. As far as I can tell, they're joining the hunt. I've agreed to let them use the bar as a base. And what do you mean, shit-hole?"

"Are they sticking to the code?"

"Code?"

"No blood from the source."

Mike shrugged as he wiped down the bar.

"I don't know about that. But they've agreed not to feed on my doorstep. So it's not my problem."

Tala glanced at the vampires uneasily. The code was a strict rule laid down by Prince Vassago, the Vetali ruler.

Once it had become known the human world was full of walking meals, many vamps had relocated from Vetali territory. Alarmed that a mass feeding frenzy was about to be unleashed, the Prince had decreed that blood could not be taken from a living person unless permission was expressly given.

Killing a human was a crime punishable by death.

Some Vetali didn't like that. Some Vetali believed Vassago was protecting a less important species at the expense of his own people. And some were angry enough that they wanted to get rid of him as their leader.

It would explain why a load of vamps had shown up at a hunter bar. They were working the same contract she was.

The contract to find Prince Vassago's son and heir, Count Darian Lemar the Third.

Shit fuck bollocks.

She'd given her word to Shadeed that she'd keep Lemar safe. And in a normal hunt, she'd have no problem.

But this was a long way from normal.

She'd never gone up against vampires before. Vetali were stronger and faster than she was. And what's more, they couldn't be possessed. She couldn't control them, like she could almost everyone else in this bar.

It's what made her an excellent tracker. But against a pack of vamps, all bets were off.

Silently, she downed her whisky. She did have one advantage right now, and she intended to use it.

She, unlike them, could travel in daylight.

She sent a quick text. When the answering ping came, she slipped off her stool and headed for the door.

Kiss of Light is now availailable on Amazon.

You can get details on all Lilah's books and get a free short story from the Immortal Hearts universe by visiting her website www.lilahbane.com

BOOKS BY THE AUTHOR

Kiss of Fire (Immortal Hearts 1)
Kiss of Light (Immortal Hearts 2)
Kiss of Steel (Immortal Hearts 3)
Kiss of Ice (Immortal Hearts 4)
Kiss of Magic (Immortal Hearts 5)
Immortal Hearts Complete Series

About The Author

Lilah T. Bane is the daughter of a tough Special Forces soldier and a cookery teacher. She grew up knowing how to deliver a mean right hook and an even meaner cheese soufflé. Now she writes paranormal fantasy full of passion and romance.

She lives in a leafy part of England with a territorial Siamese cat and a very patient boyfriend.

Just to be clear, the tough Special Forces soldier is her mother.

You can visit Lilah's website at www.lilahbane.com for details on her upcoming releases and sign up to her mailing list for a free story.

Printed in Great Britain
by Amazon